PENGUIN BOOKS

THE GIRL
WHO CAME
OUT OF
THE WOODS

Emily Barr worked as a journalist in London but always hankered after a quiet room and a book to write. She went travelling for a year, which gave her an idea for a novel set in the world of backpackers in Asia. This became *Backpack*, a thriller that won the WHSmith New Talent Award. Her first YA thriller, *The One Memory of Flora Banks*, has been published in twenty-seven countries and was shortlisted for the YA Book Prize. Emily's second YA thriller, *The Truth and Lies of Ella Black*, which takes place in the sun-soaked favelas of Rio de Janeiro, was published in 2018. *The Girl Who Came Out of the Woods* is her third YA novel. Emily lives in Cornwall with her partner and their children.

Follow Emily Barr
on Twitter @emily_barr
and Instagram @emilybarr01
#GirlOutOfTheWoods

Books by Emily Barr

THE ONE MEMORY OF FLORA BANKS

THE TRUTH AND LIES OF ELLA BLACK

THE GIRL WHO CAME OUT OF THE WOODS

THE GIRL WHO CAME OUT OF THE WOODS

EMILY BARR

PENGUIN BOOKS

PENGUIN BOOKS

UK | USA | Canada | Ireland | Australia
India | New Zealand | South Africa

Penguin Books is part of the Penguin Random House group of companies
whose addresses can be found at global.penguinrandomhouse.com.

www.penguin.co.uk
www.puffin.co.uk
www.ladybird.co.uk

First published 2019

001

Text copyright © Emily Barr, 2019

The moral right of the author has been asserted

Set in 10.5/15.5 pt Sabon LT Std
Typeset by Jouve (UK), Milton Keynes
Printed and bound in Great Britain by Clays Ltd, Elcograf S.p.A.

A CIP catalogue record for this book is available from the British Library

ISBN: 978-0-241-34522-1

All correspondence to:
Penguin Books
Penguin Random House Children's
80 Strand, London WC2R ORL

Penguin Random House is committed to a
sustainable future for our business, our readers
and our planet. This book is made from Forest
Stewardship Council® certified paper.

For Craig, Gabe, Seb, Charlie, Lottie and Alfie

PART ONE

PART ONE

MAY

I stood behind the door and rattled its handle, even though I knew you needed a key to get in or out and I didn't have one. I had been here for days. The air around me was stale. My hair was tangled. I knew I looked wild. I felt wild. I felt I had lost my mind completely. I had lost all my sense of myself and I didn't know who I was, who I used to be.

The world was still out there. It felt impossible, but it was there. The window high up in the wall was pale with daylight, which meant there were people outside. There were millions of them and they were nearby. Those people might rescue me if they knew I was here, because surely no one was allowed to keep someone locked up like this. People would help me. I just couldn't get to them.

I lifted a fist and banged on the back of the door as hard as I could. It hurt my knuckles but I didn't care. I thumped and kicked at the door, and shouted.

'Let me out!'

My head was aching. I was feeling terrible. I wiped my nose on the back of my hand and tried to focus.

I had paper in here. I had pens.

I was starting to think that I was going to die here. It felt like a place where you could be left to die. Nobody knew I was here and no one out there would be missing me.

I found a pen and decided to start to write down my story, so that one day, when I was discovered, they would know who I was and why I was here. I started to write.

I never meant this to happen, I wrote. *Any of it.*

I stared at the words. It was too difficult. I was not ready to say my truth. I didn't even know what the truth was. I knew that I couldn't try to find it without unravelling. I sucked the pen until ink flooded my mouth, threw it across the room, then found another pen and tried again.

I don't know what I'm doing here, I wrote. It was no use. I needed to write my story but I didn't know where to begin.

In the corner of the room there was a box filled with stuffed animals, and next to it was the white bear. That was my bear. Maybe I would be able to talk things through with the bear.

I picked it up. It was a white teddy with a quizzical face, holding a heart that had the words 'Love You Loads X' embroidered on it. That bear had been with me through everything. I tried to smile at it.

'What are you going to do now, you loser?' said the bear, and it laughed in my face.

I

A baby was born in a forest in India, sixty miles and an entire universe from Mumbai. She was a lively baby who punched the air with her little fists and bellowed when she wanted attention. She roared her arrival to the trees, the birds, the sky. Everyone around her took care of her. They considered her to be a miracle; the moment she was born no one could imagine this place without a child in it.

As she grew up, Artemis tried to understand everything at once. She tackled everything, from learning to walk and learning to read to – later – folding the laundry and collecting the mangoes with passion. She spoke three languages without knowing that was what she was doing. She saw the world in Technicolor and lived with all her senses, and for a long time she was very happy.

Her world was small, though she didn't realize it at first. It was bordered on all sides by thick forest, and, apart from one visitor when she was a baby, new people never arrived. Sometimes new people arrived in her dreams, but they were never there when she woke up.

Artemis grew up with the knowledge that every single person in her world adored her, though there weren't very many of them. Her arrival made her community nine-strong, but one person left to go back to what she called 'the real world', and another arrived and left again, and when those things had happened they were eight. Until she learned to read books Artemis had no idea that it was unusual for a person to have met just nine other people, and to know only seven. At first she felt sorry for the book people living in their chaotic worlds, and then, as she got older, she felt curious.

What would it be *like*, she wondered, out there? She knew it would be bad and corrupt, and she knew that she loved everyone here, so she was happy. Her curiosity was just theoretical.

She loved her mother and father best of all. Arty's mother was the goddess of the clearing – the matriarch – and was now known to everyone as Venus, though once she had been Victoria Jones from a town near Bristol in England, a child from a ruthlessly suburban home. Arty's father, Vishnu, had grown up in Delhi, though he used to say he was 'a citizen of everywhere', with family in India, Afghanistan and Australia, and some other places too, though Arty couldn't always remember what they were called. He was from everywhere, but there was nowhere he wanted to be but here in this clearing with Venus, the love of his life, and Artemis, his daughter, and their friends. Vishnu was a cook. His job was to feed everyone.

She became Arty when she was very small. You can't keep calling a baby Artemis when you could call her Arty instead. Venus called her sweetiepie and darlingheart and babykins and all kinds of other names too, and Vishnu always called her his chikoo. Everyone else called her Arty.

As she grew up, some more babies arrived. Her sister, Luna, was born when Arty was about five, though in the clearing they chose not to count the years in the way the people on the outside did. The adults worried that Arty would be jealous of the new baby, but, in fact, she adored her. Arty and Luna had different parents but they were still sisters.

Luna was a very different child from Arty. She didn't learn to read; she didn't really even learn to talk. She hardly spoke to anyone, and lived behind her eyes in an internal world. But she loved Arty, and the two of them understood each other without words. They shared a treehouse, sleeping on the platform together, and Luna liked to follow Arty wherever she went, and listen silently to every word she said.

The boys came later, in quick succession. First there was Hercules, and then there was Zeus. They had different mothers too, but they were almost twins. They learned to walk, to jump, to shout, to sing (badly). The clearing became much louder once they were there.

The clearing was a happy place, even though no one believed Arty later when she said it had worked, because people always wanted to think that it was impossible for humans to live together in peace and harmony. But it did. It worked because there were rules. It worked because everyone wanted to be there, and it worked because there was no money.

She was largely healthy. When she was about three she fell down from a tree and scraped her arm as she fell, and that scar would be with her forever, but that was the worst thing that happened to her for many years.

The clearing had hills on all sides: the horizons of Arty's world were the tops of the hills, and she never saw what was beyond them. Within her world they grew crops. They kept chickens. They cooked and read and meditated and lived from day to day. Hella, Luna's mother, was the shaman, which meant that she was the only one to cross the hills and go out into the world. She took the herbs they grew and sold them in the outside world, and she brought back anything they needed that they couldn't make for themselves. Although Arty knew it had taken a while to get things working smoothly, she didn't really believe it; as far as she was concerned it had always been like that. That was just how life was.

Life was peaceful and happy, right up until the moment when it went catastrophically wrong.

MAY

The room had turned into hell. I took deep breaths, feeling myself starting to panic again. I was constantly panicking and calming myself, and panicking and calming myself. There were demon bats in the corners of the ceiling, and prowling wolves around the edges. The bear sat on my pillow, and the words on the heart it was holding said 'Hate You Loads'.

I felt sick. I kept being sick into a bucket, however little I ate, and the bucket was about a quarter full of thin acid, disgusting in every way. Sometimes I stared at it and wondered how this could be the stuff that lived inside me, doing the job of normal human digestion.

'Help me,' I said to the bear. 'You're my friend. Please help.'

The bear growled and lunged. Its teeth were sharp and its face had twisted into horror and hate.

'I will not,' it said. 'Because you are evil and you are going to die here.'

I shrank away from it and it ran towards me on its fat little legs. I closed my eyes and screamed, holding my arms up to keep it away, and when I opened them again it was back on the pillow, lying still, pretending.

The bear was right. I had nothing to live for. I couldn't stay here. I couldn't change everything about myself just because they wanted me to be a different kind of person. I didn't know who I was allowed to be now.

I rubbed my scarred arm. I pulled my long fingernails along the scar, trying to make myself feel real pain, but it didn't work. My stomach cramped.

I stood up and felt the ground through my feet. I took some breaths. I breathed in, counting to five, held it for a count of five, and let it out.

That didn't work. It made it worse. I gasped for breath. I kicked the wall. That was better. I kicked it some more. I punched it and yelled for a long time, until I had no voice at all.

Then I curled up on the floor. All the stuffed animals came and stood around me, pointing and laughing. I reached past them and managed to put the television on. It was a tiny little television set but it got a few channels, and I flicked around until I found a children's programme. Then I shifted my position until I was staring at it. I let the pixels calm my brain. The animals sat down to watch it too.

'*Everyone* knows that c-a-t is cat,' I said. I said it out loud, pretending the TV and I were conversing. It replied in its oblique way.

'Cat, cat, cat,' chanted the stuffed animals. One of them was a cat, a black-and-white kitten, and it strutted up and down, enjoying the attention. I watched it and smiled a bit, but I didn't trust these things. They made me smile and then they went for my throat.

2

The day it happened started like any other day, except that at first it was better.

Arty woke early with the sun at the window, and looked up at the wooden ceiling. There was a beetle walking across it upside down. She stretched and remembered that it was Kotta day.

This was the best day of the clearing's year and, even though she was so old now, she still loved it. She looked over at Luna, wondering whether she would be awake too, and excited, but she was fast asleep, her hair all over the pillow. Arty loved to look at Luna while she was asleep. Her face was relaxed and happy in a way it never was when she was awake. As Arty watched, Luna huffed in her sleep and rolled over, wrapping herself tightly in her sheet.

Arty got up from her own mattress and walked quietly to the window. She took the mosquito net off and leaned out, breathing in the forest air. Kotta day was the highlight of Arty's year. Today they would eat lovely food, and no one would do any chores.

The forest was alight with its slanted morning glow, and the birds and insects were yelling about it at the tops of their voices. She stood at the window and drew in a deep breath and hung on to that moment.

Arty stepped back as Chandler appeared right outside the window, baring his teeth at her.

'You're a *stupid idiot*,' she said quietly, and glanced round at Luna, who hadn't stirred. She picked up the broomstick from beside the window and threatened Chandler with it, but he bared his teeth and didn't leave until she jabbed him in the chest. Then he snarled and jumped away, swinging through the treetops.

There had been no monkeys here when she was small. Four of them moved into the area a few years ago, and the humans shared this part of the forest with them because they had to. They were part of nature, and the monkeys were part of nature too. Arty knew she was meant to thank them, so she gritted her teeth and muttered, 'Thank you for sharing our forest, Chandler Bing,' only actually saying it because he had gone away. In fact, the monkeys hung around because they loved to try to steal food, clothes, anything they could manage. Arty hated them, but that wasn't in the spirit of the clearing so she rarely said it out loud.

The people in her books weren't plagued by monkeys. They lived in cities, or in other countries. She had read a lot of books (Hella brought them back whenever there was spare money from the herbs) but she had never read a book about *anyone* being plagued by monkeys.

She pulled on a T-shirt and baggy trousers and went down their ladder to the bottom of the tree. Only Arty and Luna lived up this tree: their names were carved into its trunk.

ARTEMIS & LUNA

At the bottom of the ladder she stepped into the green flip-flops she'd left there last night, and walked out between the trees, following the path to the centre of the clearing.

No one else was here.

Arty walked round the edge of the clearing and focused on her breathing. The smell of early-morning greenery filled her lungs. She sat on the edge of the pit and closed her eyes.

The pit was in the middle of everything, and all the houses were just into the forest, encircling it, built up in the branches wherever there had been a suitable tree. Venus and Vishnu shared a house, and Hella and Diana shared one, and the rest of the adults had one each. The boys shared the lowest of the houses, and they liked to jump down from it, laughing, occasionally hurting themselves but not seriously.

The adults had dug the pit as a celebration when Arty was born, and so she secretly felt it belonged to her. It had two steps down into it, each of which you could sit on, and in the middle was space for a big fire, or a dancing display, or a play, or a demonstration of anything anyone wanted to show you. The pit was where they sat and read and talked and sang. It was packed earth, and Arty took up the brush that someone had left in it yesterday and swept the old ashes into a corner, where they joined a pile of leaves that was ready to be added to the compost.

Tonight was going to be fun. It was going to be (she tried out, in her head, a word from stories) a *party*. No one here called it that; it was always called a feast day or a celebration, but Arty was pretty sure this was what a party was. She sat on the second step, leaning back on the solid earth behind her, and closed her eyes and took a deep breath in. She held it as long as she could, feeling the buzz of the world around her, listening to the sounds of the insects in the forest, the birds singing so loudly that she couldn't believe everyone else was still asleep, a tiny bit of distant monkey chatter. When she couldn't hold it any longer she let it slowly out, feeling the vibrations of the planet as it went. She held on as long as she could before breathing in again.

She did that five times. It made her feel like a part of the forest. She pulled her hair back from her face and tied it round itself and held her face up to the sun. She stood up and did some stretches in the middle of the pit, and then did the I-am-present meditation that Diana always made them do before lessons. She stood in the middle of the pit and said: 'I see the trees. I hear the birds. I smell the early flowers. I touch the earth through my feet. I taste the morning air. I am present in the world. Thank you, universe.'

She walked barefoot to the shack and looked at the three shelves of books, reaching out and stroking the spines of a few of them. Her job was looking after them. Exactly a year ago today, she had been appointed librarian. Keeper of the books. It was a job she adored, though it was very easy. She sorted them quickly now, putting the picture books on the bottom shelf so everyone could reach them, the paperbacks in the middle, the hardbacks and reference books on the top shelf. She arranged them by the colours of their spines. Every day she changed the way they were presented.

Her bear lived down here too. It was the library bear, but it belonged to her. Venus had given it to her when she was very, very small. It was a white teddy, a bit grubby because it was due a wash, and it was holding a red heart with the words 'Love You Loads X' embroidered on it. Arty loved her bear, and used it to watch over the books.

She had everything she needed. Those books were her window on to the world beyond these trees and that was enough. Venus sometimes told her that she should write a book about their life here, and Arty would always say she couldn't, that she wanted to read about other places rather than write about the few things she already knew.

She picked up a book and the bear and went to sit down back in the pit beside the ashes. This book, *The Lorax*, was one of her favourites of the easy ones because it was the book that taught her to read, more than ten years ago when she was very small. She remembered the way the words had clicked into place when she worked out how to decode them, and she remembered that her universe had flashed bright because it had a new thing in it. She didn't need to read the words now, so she just flicked through and looked at the pictures, and the way the sunlight changed the colours, and the fact that the marks on the page could put a story into her head. The poor little Lorax spoke for the trees. Arty stroked its face. The book was battered, because it was loved.

When she was very little Arty used to dream about the Lorax. In her dreams he would step out of the forest and visit her. Arty had loved her Lorax dreams. She used to have them quite often, until they stopped. She wished she could still have them now; she loved the idea of the spirit of the forest coming to the clearing.

'ARTY, IT IS KOTTA DAY!'

The Lorax flew out of her hand and landed in the ashes, as someone hot and determined launched himself on to her back. She jumped down to grab it. It was dusty; she shook it out, then held it carefully and brushed it, getting ashes all over her hand.

'Oh, seriously, Hercules?' she said, and he giggled and danced around. He didn't understand that the books were fragile and precious, because he was so small. Hercules was wearing only a pair of red pants that he said were his lucky pants: Arty knew he saved them for special days. 'You have to be careful with books,' she told him. She lifted up the bear and made it speak to him. 'Be careful with these books as they are very precious,' she said in her bear voice.

'Soz, Arty,' he said. 'Sorry, bear. But it's Kotta day! It's the day of the Dairy Milk!'

She grinned and reached out to ruffle his hair. 'I know it is. My sixteenth Kotta. Your fifth. Pretty cool. Still, though.' She went back into making the bear talk. 'Books are important, Hercules! That's my job and you're making it harder. Is anyone else up?'

'I waked up Zeus. We went to look for you, and Luna was still sleeping. You wasn't there. I don't know about the grown-ups.'

Arty put the bear down. 'Where's Zeus?'

'Getting some cuppa tea.'

'He's boiling water on the fire?'

'Just pretending.'

She pulled her brother on to her lap and read the book to him, brushing ashes off the edges of the pages as she went. Zeus came and joined them, leaning on her, cuddling up. Both of them settled into dozy happiness until Monica appeared in the treetops and hooted and shrieked and threw a seed pod at them.

'Monkey! Monkey! Monkey!' Hercules yelled. 'I am going to be a monkey like you tonight,' he told her, pointing, and threw the seed pod back at her.

Zeus leaped up too, and the boys danced round the pit, making Arty laugh. They jumped up and crouched down, making monkey noises. Their hearts pumped blood around their bodies. They grew imperceptibly, but in a real way, every moment. Their bodies grew a tiny bit bigger. Their smiles were wide. They were filled with joy.

'Why don't you two go and collect the eggs?' said Arty. 'Carefully.' And they ran off. The boys collecting the eggs didn't always go well, but they loved it.

'Here you go,' said Venus, some time later, and she handed Arty a cup of tea. Arty stretched her legs out and took it. It was lovely not to have to do any chores. She was going to play the guitar instead, the way Inari had taught her.

'Thanks,' she said. She loved tea. They made it with whatever was handy, and at the moment it was mint because they always had a lot of mint growing. It was hot and strong. Arty could happily have drunk tea all day long and sometimes she did. All of them did. The stream water boiled gently over the fire for most of the day, and then they just added things to it to make it into any kind of tea.

'You're welcome, sweetiepie.' Venus sat next to her, her hair blowing around in the warm breeze. 'Excited?'

Arty looked into her eyes and smiled. Her mother would always be her favourite person. Venus was everything Arty wanted to be herself. She was feeling lately that she wasn't sure how to get from being about sixteen, as she was now, to a proper adult, without knowing the outside world. She knew she should just do the things that her mother did, but it felt weird, because her mother had come from a family home thousands of miles away, and knew all about aeroplanes and electricity and money, and Arty only knew the clearing. She felt like a child and she wasn't sure how and when that was going to change. She planned to live her whole life here, and she couldn't imagine anything else. The rest of it sounded so scary.

She didn't want to see what was out there at all.

Sometimes she did. Mainly she didn't.

'Very excited,' she said, her voice quiet. She was a little embarrassed by how happy she was. 'I've been up for ages. Has Hella got . . .' She finished the sentence with a smile.

'Of course! It's going to be the best one we've ever had, darling. Twenty years! This needs a big party.'

'So it *is* a party?'

'It definitely is.'

Arty smiled and leaned on her. Venus put an arm round her shoulders and kissed her head.

'We do OK here, don't we?' Venus said, as Hercules and Zeus came back with their hands filled with eggs, and delivered them carefully to the cooking shed, only dropping one as far as Arty could see. 'You're all right?'

'Yes. You know I am.'

Arty looked back at her mother's clear eyes, her pale skin, her freckled face. Venus was wearing a blue vest and a skirt made from a knotted piece of orange cloth.

'You know you can go out with Hella.' They had said this to her a few times lately. 'You can go and see what she does. Look at the world out there. See it for yourself.'

Arty shook her head. 'I don't want to, though,' she said. 'I'm happy here, Mum. I don't want to go out there. I have everything here. Everything I need. This is my home.'

Venus looked at her. Arty could see she was troubled.

'It might be good for you, though,' she said. 'Give you some perspective on what we do here. You could have an adventure and come back. You need to know a bit of the rest of the world.'

'Jesus, Mum! I don't want an adventure!'

Venus sighed. 'All right, crosspatch,' she said. 'But there are lots more books out there. You could go just to see a bookshop.'

Arty didn't reply.

Later, Arty said, 'Tell me about the treehouse.' That was part of the story of the clearing and she loved to hear it. Luna was sitting beside her now, holding Arty's hand.

Venus laughed. 'The treehouse? Oh, all right then.' She sipped her tea. This was their second cup. 'When I was a girl, about your age, Luna, my brother and I used to climb a tree in our parents' back garden. We didn't have a very happy life at home for lots of reasons, and we'd sit up there and pretend like mad. I appointed myself the goddess of our world, and he was everyone else. We made our own rules. We were gods and goddesses. There was no school in our universe, and nobody was allowed to shout or be mean. There were monkeys, in the form of our neighbour's cat Gizmo, though of course we had no idea what a pain real monkeys can be. And I would sit there, with a blanket wrapped round me, and say that I was going to be queen of our world in the trees. I was going to make a space in which everything was always lovely.'

'Always lovely,' said Luna.

'Yes,' Arty said. 'And you did it.'

'We did.'

'What about your brother?' Arty asked this even though she knew. This mysterious brother was her uncle, and she was interested in him.

'Poor Matthew,' said Venus. 'He had a terrible time and he made life hell for everyone around him. He was a heroin addict, like in that book, Arty, but he got through it. I'm proud of him. He was reborn when he came off it all. I hope he's still well.'

'I do too.'

'Addiction isn't a rare thing out there,' said Venus. 'It's horrific. There's a lot of it.'

'I wish Matthew lived here too,' said Arty. 'Like when you were in the treehouse.'

'Yes. It was complicated. Bless him. This has been an experiment, but look at you, Arty.' She took Arty's face between her hands, and then Luna's. 'Look at you both. You wonderful girls.'

They spent the rest of the day getting ready, and singing and dancing. Everyone had their turn. Arty took the guitar and managed to strum and sing 'Everybody Hurts', and they all applauded as if she'd given a magnificent recital. Then she held Luna's hands and they danced around in circles while Inari, who was the proper guitar player, played 'Yellow Submarine'. That was a huge thing for Luna and it made Hella, her mother, cry. The boys put on a gymnastics display. Diana recited Titania's speech about the forgeries of jealousy from *A Midsummer Night's Dream*. Odin and Hercules danced together. Hella performed some martial arts. Everyone did their bit, and everyone else watched and clapped. Sometimes it was boring, but Arty knew that didn't matter so she cheered and applauded and joined in no matter what.

By the evening they were exhilarated. Everyone but Hella was sitting on the second step, waiting. They had all brushed their hair so it gleamed and shone all over their shoulders. Arty's had become a frizzy cloud. The fires were lit, and the mosquitoes were staying away because of the burning potions. The pit was brown, and around it the world was tinged pink by the setting sun. The sun set behind the hill in an instant. It was there, and then it wasn't.

Arty was next to Luna, as she usually was. The two of them were holding hands. In fact, Luna squeezed Arty's hand so tightly that it kind of hurt, but Arty would never have told her that. She never criticized Luna.

'Hella!' shouted Hercules. 'Hella, can you come right now *please.*'

'Shut up, Herc,' said Odin. He was Herc's dad, and Hercules made a face at him, but he did shut up. They all knew they had to be patient.

Venus stood up. She was wearing a long skirt with a football shirt (RONALDO 9, it said on the back). She raised her hands up and everyone watched.

'Hella is about to bring the feast to us,' she said. 'But first I'd like to talk about our twentieth Kotta day. Twenty! This is a special one, all right. Twenty years ago, eight of us arrived here seeking refuge from all the wrong turnings the world out there – and we ourselves – had taken, believing we could do better. Four years after that, Artemis arrived. Only one person found us over the years, and they left voluntarily and kept our secret. One other decided to leave and take her chances in the world outside. Luna, Zeus and Hercules joined us and now we are eleven. We have no violence.'

'No violence,' everyone repeated.

'No crime.'

'No crime,' they all said, though Arty was not really sure what crime would be like in real life.

'No war.'

'No war.' She knew what war was, but couldn't imagine such a thing.

'No pollution.'

'No pollution.'

'We are all gods and goddesses.'

'We are all gods and goddesses.'

'We will never take our health for granted. We will all of us work for the greater good. We will move into the future with happiness and solidarity. Taking the best of the old to make the whole of the new. What happens to one happens to all.'

Venus said variations on these words every year and Arty savoured them. Everyone joined hands around the pit and closed their eyes for long minutes of silent agreement. Then Arty heard Hella – wonderful Hella, the shaman – beginning to sing. They dropped hands. Inari pulled his guitar on to his knees and started to play along with her, and Luna rushed off to help her mother carry the feast. This was also a big moment for Luna.

The Kotta song was called 'Respect'. They sung it every Kotta day, and no other time. It made Arty tingle. She wanted to cry then, because she was so happy. She was with all the people she loved. She belonged, and her world was good.

*

They always ate the food Vishnu made, and it was always vegetable curry. Only once a year, on this full moon, did they get the magic food. And here it was. Arty's mouth watered when she saw that Luna was carrying the tray with twelve bars of Dairy Milk on it. Luna was beaming, delighted with herself, and Arty's heart swelled with love for her sister.

Hella brought out the drink in the big green bottles for the adults, though now, for the first time, Venus prised a metal cap off one and handed the bottle to Arty.

'You're old enough for this now, I'd say,' she said. 'I was certainly knocking them back at your age. Cheers, darling.'

Arty read the label, even though she knew exactly what was written there.

'Kingfisher.' She looked at her mother.

'You're giving her beer?' asked Vishnu.

'She's sixteen,' said Venus. 'And she'll probably hate it.'

'All the same. Do you actually want it, Arty?'

'I don't know.' How could she know, when she didn't know what it was like?

'It's once a year,' Venus said, and Vishnu smiled and said, 'Fair enough. Give it a go.'

Arty hesitated. What she really wanted was the Dairy Milk. It made her head spin and her mouth tingle. It was brown inside purple. It was *chocolate*, but she knew she couldn't have it yet.

She held the bottle tight. Drinking this would be something new. There was almost never a new thing. Something was changing for her.

Everything shimmered. She was excited.

It shimmered again and she was scared.

Venus clinked her bottle on Arty's, like the grown-ups did, and Vishnu reached across and did the same, and then so did Diana and Kali and Odin and Inari and finally Hella. Arty lifted the bottle slowly and let the new thing drip into her mouth.

Then she spat it out and reached for a half-finished cup of tea from earlier to get the taste away. Kingfisher was disgusting, like poisoned water downstream from a dead monkey. It tasted the way she would have imagined something from *out there* to taste, something that had been infected with corruption and badness. She hated it. She hated it more than she could possibly say.

When she managed to speak again, she said: 'That tastes like the *plague*.'

'You think?' Venus laughed at her. The other adults were laughing too. 'You say that now. Everyone hates it at first.'

'It's horrible. Oh my God. You drink it like it's . . . like it's gorgeous. Is it because it tastes like . . . Well, is that what things used to be like? Out there? Does it remind you of the best of the old?'

She thought about books in which people drank beer. They loved beer usually in books. They liked wine too, and if they were feeling shocked they needed brandy.

'Yes,' Venus said. 'That is definitely a taste from out there. When life was out of balance people used alcohol, which is what you don't like in that Kingfisher, to make them happy because they didn't know how to be happy otherwise. It made them forget what their life was like. It made them do different things. Matthew loved it too much before he moved on to worse things, but so did everyone else. I suppose we all had a taste for it then. We were out of balance as much as anyone. We have it now once a year, and that's all. That's OK. It's just fermented hops, or something.'

'Did people drink this *every day*?'

'They did. Lots of people did. I'm sure they still do.'

Arty wrinkled her nose and put the bottle down. 'That's disgusting.'

She looked around at everyone waiting to start the feast. Hella was the only one who was different, because she always wore purple like the Dairy Milk wrapper. Hella was tall and her hair was grey and reached all the way down her back. She had been from Norway once. Hella knew the secrets of the Wasteland, and she was the only one who insisted on calling it 'the Wasteland' all the time. They were supposed to say 'the outside world' because it was less judgemental.

Everyone used to say that Luna would learn all Hella's skills when she was older. When she was born they all said that she would take over being shaman herself one day, but now everyone knew that wouldn't happen. Luna wouldn't do it. Arty knew they wanted her to be the next shaman instead, but no part of her wanted to go out into the corrupt world. She wanted to wait until Hercules was bigger, and give him the job. He would like it. Probably.

The food was arranged in the middle of the pit. There was rice, roti and three different vats of vegetables. Hercules and Zeus were getting into their monkey suits. That part of things didn't really make sense, but it had become a ritual and they loved doing it. The monkeys got very excited when the clearing had a celebration. Arty could hear them in the trees now. Keeping them away from dinner was a consideration every night these days, but keeping them away from Kotta had evolved into its own part of the ceremony.

Inari strummed the songs on his guitar. Odin was singing 'Creep', along with Inari, which Arty liked because it made her shiver and also laugh. Odin really wasn't a creep or a weirdo because the people like that were all on the outside, but the song said he was, and that gave her a strange feeling about things not always being what they seemed. The whole song pulsed in purple and blue in Arty's head, like a bruise, like something that was trying to attract her attention. She wanted to learn that song next.

Vishnu was bringing more rice over from the cooking fire, because even when it was Kotta they still needed sensible food. No one wanted *only* to have Dairy Milk. Vishnu saw Arty watching and raised a hand to wave to her. All the men here were Arty's dad, but Vishnu actually properly was. He was the tallest and thinnest of everyone, and his beard and hair would grow and grow until he looked like a bush, and then he would cut it all off. Arty thought that if she'd been a boy she would have been just like him.

The moon was bright in the sky, the last bits of dusk almost gone by the time the boys were ready. A few years ago Hella had found the monkey suits for sale out in the world beyond the clearing, and Venus had immediately said they would become part of the Kotta ceremony. The two boys had the job of wearing them these days; the monkeys freaked out completely when they saw human monkeys, and they kept away from everything.

'Look at them,' said Venus. 'Adorable.'

The boys danced around the edges of the clearing, making monkey sounds, giggling uncontrollably, periodically shouting, 'Monkeys, monkeys, go away. Thank you for letting us live in your forest, but stay away.'

When everyone was settled Venus stepped back into the middle of the pit.

'Let's eat!' she said, and everybody shouted and clapped and stamped their feet. 'We're here to celebrate. Thank you, Hella, for your boundless skill in bringing us the things we need. Thank you, Vishnu, for cooking. Thank you, Kali, for healing. Thank you, Inari, Odin and Diana, for farming and teaching, and for looking after the home. Thank you, Arty, for looking after the books. Thank you, Luna, for helping Arty and Hella. Thank you, Zeus and Herc, for keeping Chandler and Monica and Phoebe and Joey away from our feast. Thank you, Lorax, for speaking for the trees.' She paused for a second to smile at Arty. 'Thank you, Persephone, for remembering us because I know that wherever you are you will be thinking of us today. Thank you, everyone, for making our world work in peace and harmony. Now dig in.'

Inari started strumming 'I'll Be There for You' and they all reached forward and took a bar of Dairy Milk each.

Arty opened the wrapper slowly. She could feel that it was a bit soft, of course, because of the heat. That didn't matter. She peeled back the purple and savoured every second of it. She touched the chocolate with her finger and licked it off. Her whole mouth came alive and sparkled with pure gold. This was the best thing ever. For the rest of the year mango was her favourite thing, but Dairy Milk was amazing.

They always made a collage from the wrappers. They were purple jewels, not things that could be discarded.

Everyone else was eating slowly too. They all made these last. The boys had to stay on monkey duty until the rest of them had finished, and they kept looking over, but they knew that their chocolate would be waiting when they stopped, and they knew they would get extra for waiting. Arty looked at them, little furry fake-monkeys in the moonlight, and she wanted to run over and give them both a hug. She watched them going into the forest, daring each other to go further into the darkness, taunting the monkeys, laughing and laughing.

She wanted to go with them, to pull them back. But she didn't.

MAY

There were no soft toys any more. There were demons, with wings, flying around the room, and they had the toys' faces. They hated me. They hated me *loads*. Sometimes they flew at me in a cloud and I had to run away and hide in a corner. They hissed and spat and told me I was going to be one of them.

Whenever she came in they all lay down and pretended to be normal. I tried to tell her a couple of times but she just took my hand and pressed it too hard with hers and said, 'You'll feel better soon.'

I could not stay here. Getting out was more urgent than anything had ever been. I tried to find some energy but I seemed to have nothing left. I didn't know how I was meant to do it when I felt like this. I clawed at myself. I tore at my skin and my hair. I kicked the walls. I ran towards the demons and they flew out of my way.

I took my energy and tried to use it properly. Once, long before all of this, I had been sensible. As a young child I had been happy, living in my perfect world in the treetops.

That had all gone now, viciously, but I tried to harness that world, to do the right thing.

We are all gods and goddesses.

I felt myself fill with strength, even though I knew I shouldn't be strong because I hadn't eaten for ages. (I wasn't going to eat her food because I didn't trust her.)

When I felt strong the demons went to the corners of the room and watched me. That was easier.

The door was locked and bolted from the outside. There was a little bathroom with no window, with a loo, a basin and a shower. The loo was smelly, the basin was tiny, and the shower was dribbly. There were books that I didn't want to read, there was the bucket, and there was the television.

It had got dark and then light again six times since I had been here. Possibly more or fewer, but I thought it was six. I had scratched a line on the wall every time I saw the light fading, like a real prisoner, because since I had lost all control over space I knew I had to keep a grip on time. I watched the colour outside the tiny window changing and pictured the world going into darkness, the lights coming on everywhere, and I held on to that. I would see it again. I would.

I had thought they were just leaving me here for a little bit to teach me a lesson. Now, after a week with these demons, I knew what they were doing. They were doing it for their own reasons and they didn't care about me at all.

I started to cry, softly this time. These were tears of sadness, of the loss of my old life. They were tears for an unknown future.

3

Hercules went to bed early but Arty didn't really notice. She saw that Zeus was playing on his own in the late part of the evening, but didn't think anything of it until morning when Hercules was the only one who didn't get up.

'He's ill,' said Venus when Arty asked her. 'He's got a fever. He'll be OK. Can you look after Zeus?'

Arty thought he had been too excited on Kotta night. She imagined that he had made himself ill with dancing and joy and chocolate. However, as the morning turned to afternoon, she began to realize that it was worse than that.

By the end of the day everyone knew that he had a fever and all kinds of pain. Kali was the doctor (she had trained as a doctor in France, which was a place in the outside world), and she looked after him. She didn't let anyone see Hercules apart from Diana, because Diana was his mother.

He was in the sick room. Kali had hung cloths over the window so no one could see in, and she would only let Diana go in to visit him. Venus talked to Kali outside the hut from time to time. Arty heard the tone of their voices (quiet, serious) but Venus wouldn't say anything.

'Kali's looking after him,' she said. 'He should start feeling better soon. Just get on with things and I'll tell you if anything changes. It's just a virus or something. It'll go.'

Arty was doing washing and cleaning that week, so at lunchtime she swept the clearing then piled the clothes together, wrapped them in a sheet and carried them on her head down to the stream. She spent a long time scrubbing them on the flat rock until they were cleaner than they needed to be. Then she went back for the sheets and did them all, even though she had been planning to leave most of them for tomorrow. She thought if she did all the washing, and did it perfectly, she might cause a ripple of goodness in the clearing that could make Hercules get better. The longer she stayed away, the more likely she was, she thought, to come back to happy news.

She sat on the stones by the stream with the afternoon sun on her head. Everything she had washed was lying flat in the sun, weighted down with stones.

She watched a snake whipping past, disappearing between the rocks.

The sun was edging towards the hilltops when she walked back, willing everything to be all right. She walked as slowly as she could, straining her ears for the sounds of normality. She wanted to step into a world in which everything was spangled again, to see Hercules walking around on shaky legs and everyone smiling and making a fuss of him.

Instead she saw Inari crouched down peeling onions. He looked up at her approach and it was clear from his face that there was nothing good.

'Hey, Inari.'

He avoided her eyes.

'Hey, Arty,' he said. Inari was from a village near Tokyo, he said, but had lived in India longer than he had lived in Japan and liked speaking Hindi.

Arty supposed she was from India. She was from the clearing, which was in India, and so she was Indian. She, Inari, Diana and Vishnu often spoke Hindi, but the clearing as a whole did most things in English because it was the language that most people spoke the best.

'Is anything . . .?'

He shrugged and stared at the onion in his hand, turning it over as if it were an alien thing. 'No change. It seems that it's actually pretty serious. I'm sorry. I've heard Herc sounding bad.' He threw the onion down on to the earth, his face contorted. 'I don't understand. You get a fever *from* something. Hercules was well, and then he was ill. Nothing happened. Nobody else is sick. Fever doesn't arrive from nowhere. It doesn't make sense. Maybe it's an autoimmune thing . . .' His voice trailed off.

She crouched beside him and took a knife and an onion. Inari was the most grumpy of the adults. He would just say it straight out when he had a problem, and then you knew what you were dealing with.

'There's loads of food left over from last night,' he said, nodding at the pots. 'Have some. You missed lunch.'

She wasn't hungry but she took some anyway.

Everyone pretended to be busy, but they were all thinking about Hercules. Arty wondered about the unfamiliar word that Inari had spoken. *Autoimmune*. She didn't know it, but when she found a medical dictionary and looked it up she found it gave her lots more questions. An autoimmune disease seemed to be something that happened when your body attacked itself. Inari was saying that Hercules might be making himself ill. She wanted to ask Kali about it, but she also knew this wasn't the time.

She went to find Venus. 'Has he got an autoimmune disease?' she said. 'Has he?'

Venus looked at her for a long time. She reached out and tucked a strand of Arty's hair behind her ear.

'We have no idea,' she said. 'I don't think so. Possibly. Who said that?'

'Inari.'

'Herc's picked up an infection from somewhere. Or reacted to something. We don't know, but we'll get on top of it. I promise.'

Diana was with Hercules all the time, because she was his mother. That meant there was no teacher, which left Zeus with nothing to do. Late in the afternoon, Arty found him sitting outside the sick room, gazing at nothing.

The boys had always been together. She could remember them a few years earlier, Zeus sitting on the ground in the middle of the pit, clapping his hands and laughing, and Hercules crouched beside him, laughing too. As soon as Zeus was mobile they were running around together, climbing the trees, shouting and chasing and getting in everyone's way.

Now Zeus was squatting on his heels, tearing a leaf into pieces. Arty looked at him, then walked over to the sick hut and listened to Hercules weeping. She went back to Zeus.

'Come on,' she said, and she offered him her hand. 'Let's go for a walk.'

He looked at her, and his eyes were filled with all the sadness she had ever seen. She hugged him, and he was stiff in her arms for a long time before he relaxed and moulded his body to the shape of hers.

'Come on, Zeddy,' she said again. He shook his head. 'Come on. Come with me, darling. Let's go and see if we can find a mango. For when he's better. Herc loves mangoes.'

Kali rushed past but barely looked at Arty and Zeus. Arty knew she would work out how to make Hercules better. She absolutely knew it. Because that was what Kali did. They watched Kali pull Hella to one side, heard the low murmur of their voices.

Arty thought of everything she knew about hospitals. Everything she knew told her that a hospital was where Hercules needed to be.

She walked over to them, dragging Zeus behind her.

'Are you going to take him to a hospital?' she said.

Neither of the women answered. They just looked at each other. Kali made a face that Arty thought meant she agreed.

Zeus tugged at her hand. 'Mango,' he said.

They headed off in the direction of the shack. The shack was wooden, varnished and it only had one wall. The rest of it was poles holding up the roof. The library was in there, and the tool collection, and things that were on their way somewhere else, and anything someone couldn't quite be bothered to put away. There were lots of cushions on the floor. In the rainy season they spent a lot of time in there.

Behind it was the farmland, where they grew all the crops, with the stream running through the middle of it and forest all around.

The mangoes grew far away from the house, and that made the orchard an important place for Arty. She loved to sit under those trees with a book when she needed peace. She would read about places and things and try to imagine them. She would close her eyes and fill her head with blue and try to see the sea. She pictured sand, which she imagined as a smooth yellow block like marble, that could be manipulated into castles. She imagined herself on a boat, bobbing up and down on the waves. She looked up to the night sky and pictured herself blasting through space. She travelled everywhere from that mango orchard, without ever having to leave the clearing.

Zeus was so little. Arty knew he was about four, just as she was pretty sure she was sixteen. They lived by the moon, and the only two things that happened every year were Kotta and Diwali, which had got a bit mixed in with the kind of Christmas they understood from books, though they would never have snow like the book people did, and they didn't have that sort of god either. However old he was, Zeus was the smallest person in the clearing. He was too little to understand very much, and yet she knew that both of them understood perfectly that what was happening to Hercules was very bad indeed.

'He'll be OK,' she said, wondering why she was saying that, and she patted his hair.

He gripped her hand tighter. 'Really, really?' he said.

The silence went on too long before she said, 'I hope so.'

They picked a couple of mangoes. Zeus looked at her, assessing the likely response, and then bit into one, pulling its skin back, letting its juice go all over his face. The sun hit them as the clouds parted, and Arty looked at him and for a moment the world was pale and calm. She grabbed another mango and did the same as him. They laughed stupidly even though nothing was funny.

The mangoes were riper than they usually were at Kotta, as if they were a gift from the forest just when Arty and Zeus needed something. They ate a whole one each (that never happened) and then they carried a few more down to the stream because they very much needed to wash faces and hands that were sticky with juice. Arty stood in the water and splashed her face and scrubbed her hands, and then she threw some water at Zeus and he threw some back at her and laughed.

Right then, everything felt all right. Arty felt the water against her skin, the ground beneath her feet, the sun on her face, and she clung on to that.

The laundry she had left out earlier was dry, and she let Zeus carry the mangoes while she packed as much of it as she could into a bundle and put it on her head, back to the shack in the clearing, where, still, nothing had changed except that the sun had gone behind a mountain and it was about to get dark.

'Zeus has mangoes,' she said to Vishnu, who was sitting on the edge of the pit, whittling a twig without concentrating.

'Brill,' said Vishnu. 'Let's put them over here.'

Zeus went with him. Arty found Luna standing on one leg in the shack (always a sign that she was troubled) and took her with her to fetch the rest of the laundry and feed the chickens. Luna said nothing, but she walked close to Arty and smiled a tiny smile when their eyes met. They sat together in the shack, at twilight, and folded the sheets.

Hella had gone to get help in the outside world, and there was nothing to do but wait.

'See,' said Venus, who was standing there. 'She'll fetch what he needs. This needs heavy-duty medication to bring his temperature and pain down, and Hella has gone to get it. She's going to find a doctor and ask for advice. We'll follow that advice, I promise. Everything is under control, Arty.'

'We need to take him to hospital.'

Venus didn't reply.

Arty looked at her. She knew none of the adults wanted to take Hercules anywhere because it would change their way of life forever, and she felt outraged by that. Venus stared back. Sparks flew through the air between them. They argued without speaking a word.

'It's not like there's a hospital nearby,' Venus said after a long time. 'We couldn't just, like, drop into A and E.'

Arty screwed her eyes shut as Hercules yelled, 'But it hurts!'

She wanted to ask where the hospital was in the outside world, and what *drop into A and E* meant, and why they couldn't call an ambulance like people did in books.

Then she realized that she was picturing an ambulance staffed by rabbits, as in *Busy Town Busy People*. A rabbit ambulance would be better than nothing. They also had a book called *Katy* and, while Arty's imaginary ambulances were from Richard Scarry, the inside of a hospital had been created for her by Jacqueline Wilson. Hella had brought the book back a few years ago and Arty had read every word of it many times over. It was about a girl who fell down from a swing and stopped being able to walk. She spent a lot of time in the hospital. This was how they knew about hospitals. This was also how they knew that you had to be careful if you went up high.

The hospital hadn't made Katy better, but she had been all right, even though her legs didn't work. She had stayed alive.

'Go and see if Vishnu needs a hand,' Venus said, clearly trying to make Arty go and talk to her father instead. Arty considered grabbing Hercules and carrying him out of the forest, but she had no idea how long it would take, or where to go, or what to say, and while she was trying to work it out he might die.

The air was static. Vishnu was stoking the fire ready to boil more water, with Zeus sitting right up against him.

'Hey there,' he said as she approached. Vishnu had the most lovely smile. Arty hoped she had one like it. The tiniest mirror hung on the wall of the latrines, and it was hard to tell what she actually looked like. 'How *you* doin'?'

Arty sat down. 'Will Hella be back tonight?' she said. 'Why did she go so late? Why didn't she take Herc with her to hospital?'

Vishnu sighed. 'It's a long way, Arts. He's too sick to be carried that far. She left late because it took them that long to agree to getting help. She'll sleep somewhere on the way to make an early start tomorrow.'

'Well, why don't we get an ambulance?'

He shrugged. 'We don't have a phone? We get an ambulance by sending someone to the nearest village so they can call one. You may have noticed that we've sent someone to the nearest village. Arty, I can see you think we're sitting back and doing nothing, but I promise you that we're really not. I heard you talking to Venus, and for what it's worth I agree. We should take him to hospital. I hope that Hella will bring help when she comes back because this is too much for us.'

Zeus climbed on to Arty's lap and she held him tight. No one said anything for a while, and then Vishnu spoke again.

'And,' he said, glancing at Zeus and then back to Arty, 'look, I'm afraid that Diana's not feeling well either. I don't know what's going on. I'm just the cook right now.' He slapped a mosquito on his arm. 'But we need to keep out of the way of the sick people, because there is something very weird here. *Right* out of their way.'

Arty looked at Zeus. He had closed his eyes.

'Can I have another mango?' he said from inside his eye-cage.

'Course,' said Vishnu. 'Help yourself, mate. Have all the mangoes you want.'

'Is there anything we can do right now?'

'You can pass me that pot.' Vishnu nodded at a big metal cooking pot that was stacked in the shed behind him. Arty fetched it; it was heavy and she had to use both hands to carry it.

'Thanks,' he said. The air was thick with humidity. It was the worst when it was like that. Vishnu ladled food into the pot and set it on the fire.

They sat and stared at it. Nothing happened. They just had to wait. Hercules's cries slid through the forest, touching everything.

MAY

'If you're going to get out,' said the rabbit, 'then you need to make a plan.'

I picked it up and looked into its face. It snarled, but it was the friendliest of all the creatures.

'What can I do, though?' I said, and that brought the others over. The teddy, with its 'Love You Loads X' heart, was the leader. I had loved that bear and now I was terrified of it. Sometimes its heart said 'love' and sometimes it said 'hate'. Today, though, it said 'love'. That spurred me on to start planning.

I started to think of ideas, and went to fetch a pen and a new piece of paper. With the help of the creatures, I started to write.

1. Pretend to be ill so I can be taken to a doctor.
2. Overpower her when she comes in and just leave through the door and deal with whatever else is out there when I find it.
3. Get a message to the outside world by sticking a sign up in the window, or smashing the

window, or somehow making the people out
there notice me.
4. Convince her I'm sorry and I won't do anything
to upset her again.
5. Start a fire.

The ceiling was low. It was low enough for me to hit it
with something if I wanted to, but I was pretty sure I had
tried that for hours (probably days) and nothing had
happened. Everything I did in here, every noise I made,
was contained. It was muffled instantly, and bounced back
at me in a dull way.

I fiddled around with the television controller and ended
up on a channel that seemed to be about nothing but
shopping. I stared at it right up until I felt everything I
thought I knew about humanity and capitalism flying
apart in all directions until there was nothing left. I found
myself at the centre of an apocalyptic wasteland watching
a man and a woman I didn't know trying to convince me
to phone them to buy a necklace I didn't want, and they
were so convincing that if I'd had a phone and a bank
account I would have ordered one just to make it stop.

Help me, I said to them. *Please help me get out of here!*

I stared at them, and I was sure their faces changed
when they understood me. It felt like this was about more
than a necklace; I was sure there was something else going
on but I didn't know how to decode it. Maybe they were
trying to tell me what to do. Perhaps if I wrote down the
words they spoke, the initial letters would give me a

message. I had no idea. I even tried it, but it spelled 'guarawwgioiwty' (give us a ring and we will get it on its way to you), which didn't help.

In a small chink of sanity I saw that my mind had gone.

I couldn't let that happen. I was young. There might be a life ahead of me.

I looked at my list, and decided that I would start at the top and pretend to be ill. As soon as I was in the hands of the NHS I would be out of her control. I knew that I looked terrible, but I was also pretty certain that she didn't care. I would have to find a new kind of ill, a dangerous one that would make her bring in a doctor. It was worth a try.

I knew that there was sometimes a children's programme about doctors and ill people, and so I tore myself away from the necklace and switched to the children's channel so that I could wait for it to come on. I picked up the bear and cuddled it, and it bit my finger.

4

Arty couldn't sleep. She watched Luna, checking she was breathing, touching her forehead occasionally to see whether she had a fever. She did the same to Zeus, who was sleeping in Arty's bed tonight. Both of them seemed healthy.

She stood at the window of the treehouse, leaning out. The moon was lopsided, a few days on from the round moon of Kotta. Everything looked the way it always did. The sounds of the night-time world were the same as they had been all her life. It was very loud when you weren't doing anything else. It had always soothed her. The insects were riotous. Every now and then there was another noise, a human one, and she tried not to think about what that meant.

Arty knew that Luna didn't understand. Zeus did, though. She looked round. He was staring at her with huge dark eyes. She tried to smile, pulling up the corners of her mouth, but it didn't feel like a smile at all, and his face didn't move.

Nothing had happened for hours.

Hella had stayed away all night, like Vishnu had said, but when she came back halfway through the next day she didn't have an ambulance, or a doctor, or anything that could help apart from a bag of tablets.

Everyone ran to meet her. She held up the bag.

'Here,' she said. 'This will sort it out.' Her eyes darted around, checking everyone's reactions, but her mouth was set in a straight line. The sky was heavy with clouds. Arty wanted to cry. Hercules needed a proper doctor from the outside world; she could see that and she knew that her parents could as well. Diana would want that. Only Hella and Inari were against it.

'Did you speak to a doctor?' Venus asked.

'I talked to the pharmacist,' she said. 'Nice man. He was wearing a turban. I've never spoken to him before. He said this would clear it all up. He wasn't worried.'

'Easy for *him* not to be worried,' said Vishnu.

'Oh, shut up.' Hella glared at him. 'You weren't there. I told him how Hercules is feeling and he sold me these. They weren't cheap either.'

Venus actually grabbed her arm. 'What did you tell him? Did you say how sick he is? Did you ask him to fetch a doctor?'

Hella looked her in the eye. 'Of course I didn't ask for a doctor. He took it seriously, and he said to try these. He said he would come back with me himself, but I wasn't having that.'

'He needs proper help. Diana's ill too. We need to bring in the modern world here, Hella. I can't believe he said he would come and you turned him down.'

They stared at each other for a long time. Arty could see the anger passing between them. She went and stood next to Venus and glared at Hella too. Inari went and stood with Hella.

They were split. That had never happened as far as Arty knew. They stood there and argued and argued, but there was nothing they could do except take the pills Hella had bought.

Odin was Herc's dad. He was usually a quiet and kind man, but when he heard that Hella had turned down help he grabbed her by the shoulders and said he was going to kill her. Everyone pulled him off.

Hella said some bad words to all of them.

'Only Inari gets it,' she said. 'Fuck you, all the rest of you.'

She stormed off into the forest and didn't come back. By the end of the day Hercules had died.

Everything had shattered. The world was over.

They all took the pills, but they didn't work. Diana was ill too, and then so was Kali, even though she was the doctor. Diana died. Other people got ill. It happened with a momentum that was terrifying to Arty. Hella came back because she was ill too and she needed to lie down. No one could be bothered to be angry any more because everything was different.

Arty walked over, holding Venus's hand, to look at Hercules and Diana, his mother, lying side by side in the sick room. It was the first time Arty had seen him since Kotta night.

He was so tiny. Arty looked into his little face. He was the second youngest out of all of them, the first boy born in the new world, and he was dead. He had a body, but it would never be any bigger than it was now, and it would never climb trees or jump up and down or chase Zeus through the woods ever again.

He had a body but he didn't have a spirit. Arty looked at his little fingers, and his nose, and all the hairs on his head, and she longed to pull him back from wherever he had gone. It was everything that had once been him, but not him any more. It was impossible to find words for it. When she looked at him everything stopped. The whole world shifted. It would never go back.

Diana had taught Arty everything. She had been a brilliant teacher. It was thanks to Diana that Arty could read and do maths and understand about the water cycle and how engines worked and what had brought the world to its current disastrous state. Arty looked at her still face for a few seconds and then ran out of the hut. A few days ago, Diana and Arty had been reading *Hamlet*. Now Diana had watched her only child die, before dying herself.

Everyone was taking tablets. No one was doing anything. It was hot, and there was a cloud of sickness lying on top of everything.

We might all die. Once Arty had had that thought she couldn't think of anything else. The words were in her head, written everywhere she looked. *We might all die*, it said in the middle of the pit. It was carved into the trees. It was written in tiny letters on every leaf. It was in the birdsong, the splash of the stream, the crackling of the fire.

Kali had gone up to her treehouse to lie in bed. That meant there was no doctor. Hella was trying to pretend she wasn't sick but she was lying in the shack with burning skin and sweaty hair. Luna had shuffled over to her, and was sitting with her, holding her hand, and no one stopped her.

All these things were real. Arty wanted them not to be, but they were real and actually happening. She knew that Kali was going to die. She knew that Hella was going to die. She knew that she might be next.

Arty could make herself go into a kind of trance by telling herself over and over again, *This is really, really, really,* really *real* – until her head filled with infinite pale silver that blanketed everything in the way she imagined snow would do. The repeated words made reality warp and stretch until nothing in the world mattered. She didn't feel that she was actually living. The cosmos was huge, and the world was small. She could see the edges of everything she had ever known and she could see outer space just by looking up.

But the trance couldn't last. She pulled herself back to reality and thought of Venus's words at Kotta, just a few days earlier.

We will never take our health for granted. We will all of us work for the greater good. We will move into the future with happiness and solidarity . . . What happens to one happens to all.

What happens to one happens to all.

She said that every year and Arty had always found it comforting. She had thought it meant that they all did their jobs for the good of everyone, that they helped each other out with anything that needed doing. It was not making her feel good any more, because it seemed to be literally true.

What had happened to Hercules was happening to all. One by one they were getting ill. One by one they would die.

At some point later in the day she found herself curled up on the step to the pit, which Venus was now calling the 'quarantine area', listening to Venus, Vishnu and Inari talking.

'We *have* to.' Venus hit the ground with her fists. Arty could see from her face that she was only just holding herself together. 'Hella didn't do it. She bottled it. We always said that if there was a medical emergency, we'd go. Hella tried not to, but that hasn't worked. We don't have a choice.'

'So we're going to give up?' That was Inari. 'Going back? Back into all that shit. Right where we left it. I'll take my chances here.'

'Don't be a twat,' she said. 'This is life and death. Actual death of a child. Nothing carries on. It's over.'

'Yeah, come on, mate,' said Vishnu. 'Enough.'

Before, there had been a protocol for arguments, which was that you talked it out calmly in front of a neutral person who helped you reach a conclusion, then each person involved made each other a drink or offered them something to eat. Arty wanted to step in and make all this happen but she knew they wouldn't let her. Things were different now.

51

Vishnu was trying to calm things, but neither Venus nor Inari was backing down. Their voices were getting louder and louder. Arty saw Vishnu look over at her and then he scooted over to sit beside her. She pulled herself up to a sitting position.

'They'll work it out,' he said. 'Venus is right. You and I know that. Inari's wrong.'

'Yes.'

Arty and her dad listened as Venus shut Inari down.

'You can do what you want,' she said. 'I'm taking the kids. By all means stay here and die.'

'Oh, fuck you, Victoria,' Inari said. Normally he was grumpy but quiet. Arty had never heard him like this before. His voice got louder and louder as he started to shout. 'We've put everything into this. We renounced that. Gone! All of it. We were meant to live as if we were on a remote island, or a different planet. Are you really going to go crawling back? Oh sorry. We actually want some of your chemicals, in fact. We made our own society but as soon as things went wrong we gave up. Can you cure us please? Screw that.'

'One of our children has *died*. Are you seriously fine with that?'

'I'm not *fine with it*. No. But I'm not moving back there because of it either. Have some integrity.'

'Then you might want to move on somewhere else.'

'Don't slam the door on your way out.'

Venus stared at him. Then she looked away, and from that moment on she acted as if he didn't exist.

'You're coming, aren't you, Vish?' she said. 'And the kids.' She looked around. 'I don't think Odin's going anywhere.'

Odin hadn't moved from the hut. Arty supposed he was sitting with Diana and Hercules's bodies. They should have had a funeral ceremony, but no one could focus on that yet. Later, perhaps, they would do it, when they knew that the dying was over.

'Yeah,' said Arty's dad, squeezing her hand. 'Of course I'm coming. Arty and Zeus and Luna are getting to hospital. Absolutely no way are we losing another kid. That's the thing that matters.'

Losing another kid. The words felt unreal.

Arty looked up at the sky, which was beginning to lose its light. She had read a book about physics, and she knew that space was a strange elastic thing, that it bent and stretched, that time was different up there. She liked that. Feeling insignificant felt like her best way of getting through each minute. She had no idea how the rest of them were able to hold rational conversations when Hercules had died. He had been born here and he had died here. He led an entire life in the clearing.

That thought punctured her defences. Hercules's life was over, and he had spent every moment of it here. She had seen him every day of his life and now she would never see him again.

She struggled to breathe. The fact that Hercules and Diana didn't exist any more blasted through every cell in her body. It was unimaginably huge, yet she felt numb.

They just weren't going to be there. If she called them for lunch, they wouldn't come. If she went to wake them, they wouldn't be in their beds. She wanted to bring them back but she couldn't. Nothing she did would change any of it. For the rest of her life there would be no Hercules. It was too awful. She stared into space and wished for the whole world to end.

Later she lay in the pit, covered with a blanket, and waited. She listened while Venus packed things up. They were going to leave as soon as it was light. They had to keep busy, to try to save the others. Arty focused on the plans, trying to keep her mind on practical things, doing her best to shut out the horror.

Venus went into the shack and sat with Hella, then came out with a list of instructions of places to go in the outside world. She brought Luna out with her, holding her hand.

'We'll go and get help,' she told Luna. 'You come with us. And Zeus and Arty. You can walk with Arty. And we'll send a doctor to your mum, OK?'

Luna didn't respond. She came and lay down with Arty under her blanket, and Arty hugged her as tightly as she could.

In the middle of the night Odin carried Hercules's body into the forest. They heard him yelling at the monkeys, at the snakes and the insects and the whole world, for still existing when his son did not.

He came back and took Diana's body too, dragging her awkwardly between the trees but refusing help. At some point the clouds moved and the moon lit the clearing. Arty could see Zeus lying on his blanket near her, breathing deeply, and asleep at last. She studied the other three. Inari was sitting by himself with an expression that meant no one could approach. Venus and Vishnu were talking quietly, and both of them kept looking round at Arty, and then to the shack, and then back to each other. Luna had gone into the hut, back to her mother.

In Arty's head the outside world was a wild place, a fuzzy one, with bad things happening. It was scary. It was purple and black and dark blue, and it fizzed and crackled. Maybe that was because it had electricity in it and Arty had never seen electricity except in storms, when lightning split the sky. In the clearing they had things with batteries, but Arty knew that real electricity lived in walls, that you plugged things into it, like hairdryers. She couldn't really picture a hairdryer; she had no idea why people used electricity to dry their hair when the sun could do it.

'It's going to be a shock,' Venus said softly to Vishnu. 'For them, and for us. I mean, it's brutal. But we have to. We always knew we would. We've had infinity longer than we ever thought we might. Honestly. Remember at the start? We were aiming to keep our heads down for a year.'

Arty stayed very still. She hadn't known that. They had come for a year, but stayed for twenty.

'You can find Matthew,' Vishnu said.

'If he's still alive.'

Arty lay still, her eyes closed, feeling the hard ground under her and pulling the blanket round her body even though it was too warm. She felt . . . well. She tried to imagine herself ill, with a fever, but she was just not. She didn't feel sick. She was full with the food Vishnu had made her eat even though she hadn't been hungry.

The noises that came from the shack and the sick room were terrible. They were red and orange and harsh. She drifted into a semi-sleep, hearing them in reality and seeing them abstract in her dreams.

When she woke early in the morning she knew someone else was dead. The sun was rising and she got up as quietly as she could. She stood outside the pit and looked down at them.

They were all breathing. Zeus, Venus and Vishnu were alive. Inari had gone, but she walked around and found him asleep behind the shack. Zeus was peaceful, his thumb in his mouth. He had barely spoken since Herc had died.

Arty soon discovered that Hella was dead. She climbed Kali's tree and found that she was too. She also saw that Luna, Venus, Inari and Vishnu were all sick. Odin had stayed in the forest. She looked for him and called for him but he had gone.

Only Arty and Zeus were in the clearing, and well.

Before anyone woke up, she went to the herb field. Hella always took herbs with her when she left. Arty wished she had asked her why, and who she gave them to, and what protection they offered, but now she couldn't. She would never ask Hella anything ever again.

There was a layer of dew on everything. She pushed open the gate and went into the field. All the children were banned from this place because those herbs were what Hella called 'Wasteland things', but there was nobody to stop her now. She started picking them. She liked their leaves. They were pretty, with pointed ends and a dreamy pale green smell. She picked a huge amount of them, and crept back into the house to find Hella's bag. She pushed them in there, and added more and more and more until it was completely full.

Then she walked to the spring and washed her hands and face and wondered why she was still well.

'I'm going,' Arty said to her mother, who was struggling to breathe and dripping with sweat.

She would never have chosen to do this, but everything had changed. Now Arty urgently needed to get out into the world because that was where the doctors were. She was going to do the thing no one else had done, to get real help for everyone who was ill. It was her chance to make this better. Not for Hercules or Diana or Hella or Kali, but for everyone else she knew.

'I'm going to fetch an ambulance,' she said, staring into her mother's face.

'Yes,' Venus said. She could hardly move, though she was trying to be strong. Arty wanted to take her indoors but she couldn't because the two buildings at ground level had bodies and death inside them. Instead she brought blankets out and did the best she could to make Venus, Vishnu, Luna and Inari comfortable, while Zeus shadowed

57

every move she made. She took her 'Love You Loads X' bear and put it next to Venus, who didn't notice.

'Arty?' said Venus.

'Yes?'

'Find a doctor. Tell them everything. All of it. Get them to check you out. Walk that way.' She pointed. Arty knew that because she had watched Hella walk that way for as long as she could remember.

'I'll take Zeus.'

'Yes, you have to. And look. Arty.' She took her hand. Arty squeezed hers, feeling Venus's heart still beating, wanting to hang on to that forever. 'I'm so sorry. I knew you would go one day but I didn't think . . . If . . . Look. If . . . if they can't help, you must find Matthew. He's your uncle. Look for him, or look for Tania. Find the keys and take them. Now. Before you go. *Take my keys and find Matthew or Tania.* They might be in London. I don't know. I hope Matthew's alive. Clean. Be careful of the rest of my family. Don't go into the basement. They'll think you're weird and they don't like weird. Can you bring me a pen and paper?'

Arty listened to the noises of the forest, the sounds that had been there for her whole life. She took all the strength from Venus that she could, and then she went up the ladder to the house her parents shared and looked everywhere for the keys that Venus wanted. Zeus followed her.

Venus and Vishnu's house was the prettiest one on the inside. They were the only two people who had a kind of marriage, as far as Arty could tell. They adored each other. Odin and Diana had sort of been a couple, but they didn't live in the same house, and then Hella and Diana had been in love. Venus and Vishnu were together all the time.

She picked up the book Venus always kept on the table. It was called *Woman on the Edge of Time*, and Arty had watched Venus read it again and again. That wasn't what she was supposed to find, though she put it in her own bag anyway.

She looked everywhere. In the end they were in a box under the bed. The box was almost flat, wooden, with ornate carving on the lid, and inside it there was a notebook and a ring with three keys on it. The notebook was filled with handwriting and pictures, and Arty didn't stop to read it. There were lots of blank pages towards the back, so she took the book and the pen and the keys, and ushered the silent Zeus to go back down the ladder before her.

Venus made the biggest effort, and sat up and took the pen and the notebook. She turned to the back page, tore it out and wrote '*MATTHEW JONES & TANIA ROSWELL*'. She drew a heart and a lot of kisses round the names, then wrote '*please look after my Arty*' in small writing at the bottom of the page. Then she took off her own necklace and handed it to Arty.

'Keys on there,' she said. Arty threaded all three keys on to the chain and put it round her own neck. It felt like a charm. She put Venus's note in her bag.

She couldn't go to London. It was like saying she was going to visit the surface of the sun. She was going to the place at the end of the path to fetch a human doctor, and the doctor would make the ill people better and then Venus would be in charge again. She had no idea what *don't go into the basement*, and the other things, meant. She put them from her mind.

She hugged her mother for the longest time possible. She hugged Vishnu, who muttered lovely things into her hair. She hugged Luna and told her it would all be better soon. She hugged Inari, who was deeply asleep but clearly completely ill, and forgave him for being horrible. She went back to Venus and held her hand.

'Good luck, Arty,' she whispered. 'I love you more than everything in the world, my darling. More than everything.' She handed Arty the cuddly bear, and Arty put it into her bag.

They walked for a few moments, and then Arty turned back. She went to Venus again, and kissed her forehead. Zeus did the same, mimicking every move Arty made.

'I love you more than everything too,' she whispered. 'Hang on. Wait and I will be back. You must hang on. Wait for me.'

They set off again and this time Zeus spoke as they went.

'We thought he'd get better, didn't we, Arty?' he said. 'We thought Hercules would get better.'

'Yes,' she said. 'We did. But now we're going to get help, Zeddy. We're going to do everything we can to make the others get well. We'll fetch a doctor. We'll come back.'

MAY

I tried to sound as ill as I possibly could.

'Argh,' I moaned, clutching my stomach. 'It hurts. It's different from before. It really hurts.'

I was lying on my mattress, curled up, transferring everything I felt to an imaginary pain in my stomach. It was easy to do.

I heard her come in. I felt the blast of different air. I let the tears fall. My face screwed up. I cried and cried and cried. I cried for everything. That was easy to do.

'It hurts.' I said it louder this time. 'It hurts it hurts it hurts and I don't know what to do. It's been hurting all night.'

'Oh, has it indeed?' she said.

'Yes.'

'How convenient.'

'I'm really ill,' I whimpered.

She paused.

'How stupid do you think I am?'

'Not stupid at all. I just feel really ill. It all really hurts.'

I kept my eyes closed as she put a hand on my forehead.

'You're not hot,' she said, 'but I'll get you some paracetamol. Whereabouts in your stomach does it hurt?'

I knew what to say to that. 'Here.' I put my hand where I knew, thanks to *Blue Peter*, that my appendix lived. 'It hurts here. Can't I see a doctor?'

'I don't think that's going to be necessary, do you?'

'Yes,' I said. 'I really do.'

5

Arty hated walking away. She remembered Inari's words and felt that she was betraying everything with each step she took. She stopped often, and decided to take the pure path, to go back to the clearing and wait there. She didn't need to go to the Wasteland. She had been born to a different life.

But she did need to go to the Wasteland, the outside world. She had to go there for help for the people she loved the most. That was the thing that kept her going. She put one foot in front of the other and tried to think of nothing but the path ahead.

She was terrified. After a while she knew they were further from the clearing than either of them had ever been before, walking uphill into the unknown. Although they were hot and sweaty, she and Zeus never let go of one another's hands, except when the narrow path meant they had to.

At one point Arty tried to sing 'Respect' to make him happy, but it sounded stupid. She tailed off quickly, her mouth dry, her body sweaty. 'Everybody Hurts' would have been better, but she didn't think they needed reminding of that fact. The insects bit them because she had forgotten to rub the leaves on their skin. After a while she found the right plant and picked some leaves to rub on their bites.

The path went up and up. Arty knew that it had to cross the hills that were all around, though she had never thought before that the outside world must be uphill and then downhill. Sometimes she or Zeus would slip on the loose stones, but they held tightly to each other and neither of them ever quite fell over. The path twisted between trees, and the leaves unfurled around them, and they strayed into a different dimension altogether. They walked through a world in which time wasn't a thing and death didn't matter. Everyone was made from atoms, and atoms were all around, and as the dappled sun fell on her through the trees she thought that none of it mattered anyway. All the life on Earth would die.

She looked at the insects they passed. The insects didn't care that Arty's family were dead and dying, any more than she cared when she killed a mosquito. There were spiderwebs everywhere, shaped like tunnels that led back into the roots of the trees, and often a big spider sat guarding the entrance, waiting for food. Vishnu had told her that in Australia these spiders were deadly poisonous to people, but here they weren't, so she focused all her energies on being pleased to be here where the spiders, at least, were harmless.

The forest sounds stayed the same as they walked, and that was comforting. They knew the birds, the insects, even the distant monkeys. They walked and walked and walked.

They were high up when they found the thing leaning against a tree. The path was flatter and wider now, and Arty could see strange patterns in the dust, like snake tracks but much bigger. They were connected to the thing, which was made of metal. It had two wheels. In the clearing they had a cart with wheels that they would use to bring in the crops, but this was different.

This was a *bicycle*. There was a picture of one in *Busy Town*. People (and little animals) would ride them to get around. You had to balance. Once you'd learned how to do it you could do it forever. People used it as a simile. 'It's like learning to ride a bike,' they said.

She stopped in front of it, and reached out a shaky hand to touch it. Zeus did the same, copying her movement exactly. The poles of it were smooth and black, and its seat was white, and there was a basket on the front. The two places where you put your feet were attached to a chain that looked dirty with oil.

Arty had never seen anything like this. It might have belonged to Hella. If it did, then why, Arty wondered, had she kept it secret? She could have kept it in the clearing and taught them all to ride it. She touched it and closed her eyes and did calm breathing because this was making her cry and she was absolutely not going to cry.

'Bike?' said Zeus, and Arty was so pleased that he'd spoken that she picked him up and cuddled him.

'It is, isn't it?' she said into his hair. 'I think so. It's a bike. We've found a bike.'

Hella, she said in her head. *Hella, tell me about the bike. Does it belong to us? Can we take it?*

Of course. Hella didn't answer, but Arty heard her voice say it anyway.

Arty thought about everything she knew about a bicycle. You sat on the seat, held on to the handles, and pushed the steps round with your feet. She could even see how that worked: when you pushed the steps you moved the chain, which was connected by some cogs to the wheels, and they moved round.

A bicycle would be useful. She told Zeus to stand to the side for a moment, put the bags into the basket, and got ready to give it a go. She pulled herself on to the seat and pushed the steps with her feet, and set off to see what it felt like.

The bike tipped up and she fell over and landed in a bush that scratched her arms and the side of her face but she didn't care. She knew she must have done it wrong so she tried again, this time ready with her foot to steady herself when it didn't work. She tried again and again but she couldn't balance on it, and that made her take deep shuddering breaths and close her eyes to try to regain control.

After all this she could not allow herself to be destroyed by the fact that she couldn't ride a bicycle. Zeus started to cry, though, and when he did Arty couldn't help it. She let it happen, just for a bit. She had a book where a *rabbit* rode a bike, but she couldn't do it. She held on to him and they cried together, so much that it almost felt good.

Then they pushed the bike to the top of the hill and stood there and looked out.

Everything was new. This was the outside world.

Arty gripped Zeus's hand and he squeezed hers back. When she looked at his face she saw the wonder and fear that she was feeling. The sun was shining, and the land stretched out before them. The slopes were covered in trees. There was more land out there than Arty had ever seen before, and in the distance, at the bottom of the hill and back a bit, there were buildings.

There were roads.

There was life.

There was medicine, and there were doctors.

She sat Zeus up on the bicycle's seat and told him to hold on to the handles as tightly as he could. Arty held them too, and it was awkward with their four hands there, and it was very difficult to keep the bike upright, but eventually she worked out how to push it along the path, taking it very slowly when she had to bump it over roots, or push it round a rock. The sight of the buildings had changed her. She knew, now, where she was going. Arty felt Zeus's forehead, and her own. They both felt normal.

Every step down the path was weird, because Hella had never spoken about what happened out here. They didn't know she went on a bike. They didn't know if they were meant to eat the herbs for protection or use them in some other way, so Arty just left them in the bag and hoped it would be obvious at some point.

The view of the rest of the world vanished as the path got narrow again, the trees closed in, and the branches scratched Arty's legs. They were walking downhill, which was more difficult than you might have thought. Sometimes she had to make Zeus get down so she could pull the bike through undergrowth. There were birds overhead, and she could hear the chattering of monkeys, though they stayed out of sight, which was a shame as, even though the monkeys in the clearing had been so annoying, Arty would have welcomed the sight of them. Monica, Chandler, Phoebe and the others felt like her friends now.

Zeus was leaning on her, drowsy and silent, so as she felt his body breathing in and out she concentrated on the world around her. She tried to make it into a walking meditation. Twigs snapped under her feet. The bike made the plants rustle as it pushed past them. The birds screeched and sang. Arty lived from one second to the next. *I am present*, she said. *I am*.

In the books she had read people were overwhelmed by grief when their families died. Yet Arty didn't feel anything. When she tried to picture Hercules and Kali and Diana and Hella in her head, there was just mist. Her only focus was on the fact that she was putting one foot in front of the other and pushing a bicycle, and that she was in the first bit of the outside world she had ever seen and so far it was like the forest at home.

After a while she propped the bike against a tree, got Zeus down and sat down to drink some water. She closed her eyes and thought that she could have gone to sleep, but she didn't. The sun was beginning to set and they still hadn't reached a building. Arty thought they might have gone the wrong way and wondered whether they could just stay in this forest forever, walking round and round its endless paths. She knew Hella probably used this bike and she must have known how to ride it, but it couldn't have made it that much faster. Could it? Maybe. Arty didn't know. She didn't know anything.

She thought that perhaps they had imagined the buildings, that maybe Hella had just got the things she brought back by magic, or from some kind of cave that Arty didn't know about. She thought that perhaps, in fact, there was no outside world. Maybe there was no one in the world but herself and Zeus. Perhaps the rest of it had been a trick, invented by Venus to make them feel less alone.

She persuaded Zeus to get back on the bike and carried on walking. But then she noticed, with a creeping dread, that the trees were further apart and the light ahead was different. The path was level now, and it was wider because there weren't so many trees. The canopy was thinner. More light was coming in.

She slowed down. Her knees were shaking, and her heart was pounding. She struggled to breathe. She put a hand on Zeus's back to steady herself. He didn't respond.

The forest had been her home for all her life. She had never left it, and now she was walking towards its edge. The thread that bound her to everything she knew was pulled so tight that it was about to snap.

I need a doctor, she whispered.

We need a doctor.

Hello. We need a doctor.

Between the bike and the outside world there was a fence. It was like the one that separated the herbs from the

69

rest of the plants, but much bigger. There was a gate in it, and a big chain that was keeping it closed.

There was a lock on the chain. They were locked in.

Arty had three keys round her neck.

She took a deep breath. She was doing this for her family. She leaned the bike against a tree and swung Zeus down to stand beside her, and she unhooked the thin necklace.

Two of the keys were much bigger than the space in the lock. The third was the right size. She put it in.

It disappeared into the lock. Arty turned it and it pinged open. She fiddled around, her hands shaking so much that it was hard to do, and eventually she took the whole lock off the metal chain and unwound the chain and opened the gate.

She had never seen a lock before, but now she had opened one. She had failed at riding a bike, but she had successfully opened a lock.

She went back for the bike and pushed it with one hand while holding Zeus's hand with the other, and they stepped together out of everything they had ever known, into everything they had never known.

Arty took a step. It was the same so far. She closed the gate behind them and wound the chain back round it, but she didn't close the lock. She needed to be able to go home again, whether or not she had the key. She put her necklace back on and checked it was done up.

She took a deep breath. This was it.

'Are you ready, Zeddy?' she said.

He shook his head. His black hair was full of leaves and twigs from where the branches had hit the top of his head as she pushed him along.

'No,' he said. 'Not ready.'

'Me neither,' said Arty.

MAY

She came back and gave me some tablets, which I swallowed with difficulty. I lay back and pretended to sleep. She left a tray of food but I didn't eat it, which was easy because it was horrible, like her food always was. It was some kind of slimy pasta in a plastic tray, and it had come out of the microwave. I stayed in bed and drifted off to sleep.

When I woke up, it was dark outside. The door was locked. There was no doctor. I wasn't at all sleepy. I just lay there for a long, long time. The toys came and stood round the bed. I thought they were on my side now, though I would never have trusted them. The bear and the rabbit climbed into bed with me and let me hug them for comfort, and that was a new thing.

She came back and stuck something into my ear until it beeped. Then she looked at it, shook her head, and said, 'Oh dear.'

I was pleased about that. *Oh dear* was what I wanted her to think. I had been concentrating so hard on being ill that I almost believed I was now. I did feel terrible. She knew that. She had locked me down here to make me feel bad.

She took my wrist in her hand. Her fingers were cold and poky. She looked at her watch while holding my wrist, and I knew she was taking my pulse. I did everything I could to make it speed up.

'Open your mouth,' she said, so I did, and she pushed my tongue down with a little wooden thing and shone a little torch into my throat. She felt my neck.

Then she jabbed my stomach. She did it suddenly with her other hand and I wasn't expecting it, so it took me a while to realize what she'd done and to react.

'I knew it,' she said. 'You silly child. I love you, but you're not leaving this place until I can trust you. And this shows that I can't trust you at all.'

She looked at me. Her face was disappointed. I felt my heart speeding up. If she came back with a doctor, I was ready. I would tell them everything quickly. I would get out of here. No doctor would let her keep me prisoner. That was why she wasn't going to get one.

'If you're actually ill,' she said, and I got excited again for a moment, 'I'm afraid it would only be with a terrible case of malingering and trickery.'

And she got up and walked out, locking the door and bolting it from the outside.

I cried for ages. The toys stood in a circle round me, looking at each other awkwardly, none of them quite knowing what to say. Then I ate the cold pasta, because I knew I was going to need some energy and even though that food was barely edible it was more edible than anything else in the room.

6

She screamed and screamed and screamed, and Zeus did too. There were lights coming towards them. Arty had never seen anything that bright. It was as if two suns were crashing at them, as if they had taken the path that led into outer space. She clung to Zeus and closed her eyes.

She didn't mean to shout but once she'd started she couldn't stop. It didn't matter, because the noises of the lights were so loud that any sound the humans made was lost.

She took a step back. She dropped the bike and snatched Zeus up into her arms before the thing could take him away. She pressed his body close to hers, feeling his life force and clinging to it as the only certainty she had. They didn't run back into the forest because the gate was closed, but they stood flat against the fence, trying to make themselves so small that they might squeeze through the squares and then reassemble on the other side, in the world they knew.

The fence was the dividing line between worlds. Arty stood pressed to it for a long time.

The lights and the noise passed. It was quiet again, but she could hear sounds far away.

When she spoke her voice hardly came out at all.

'I don't want to,' she said, forcing the words out. 'I don't want to and I wish you didn't have to do it with me, but the thing is we have to. We have to get help.'

His hands were over his ears. She held on to him tightly and left the bike where it was. 'Sorry,' she said again, and she squeezed him because although he couldn't hear her words he would know her touch. Then she stepped out on to the road, and took one hand away from Zeus to wave at the next thing that came past.

It sped by so fast that they both fell over. Arty sat down heavily and Zeus clung on so that his fingers dug into her. The thing made a long noise again, all one note, and didn't slow down at all.

She had never imagined anything going that fast. It burst the boundaries of her mind. It was as if there were a new colour, a new universe, a gateway opening up into a cosmos that had different physics.

They both coughed at the smoke.

Arty took Zeus's face in her hands and made him look at her. She remembered looking down on all this from the top of the hill.

'I think that was a car,' she said. 'And that means cars are not what we thought.'

Cars were brightly coloured. In her head they had chugged along a bit faster than people walked. She had never seen speed before, had never had any concept of it. Arty knew real cars existed and that they weren't like storybook cars; she had a pretty good idea of how their engines worked. She had read an engineering book in lessons with Diana and, although she couldn't really remember the exact details, she was well aware of the fact that they burned fuel and used that to power themselves along. She knew they made pollution and that even when people knew how bad pollution was they just carried on making more and more of it because they couldn't stop themselves once they had started, and because the people who made the petrol wanted to keep getting all the money.

But she had still not expected a car to be like this. These were dragons, breathing out smoke that was making Zeus choke.

'Right, Zed,' she said, taking his hand. She went back for the bike, sat him on it again and started pushing it along the very edge of what she supposed must be the road, with Arty on the road part, and Zeus and the bike on the earth. Her legs trembled as she walked. Everything was strange. It was dangerous.

The road went steeply downhill, and she followed it down because that was where the cars had gone.

Venus had said they needed a shop with a green cross on it, and that when they got there they needed to ask for an emergency doctor. She had said that the people working there would help. She needed to look for the man with the turban and tell him Hella, who had come to see him two days earlier, was dead. Arty needed to do that, and then she and Zeus would go home. And home would be different, and the community would be small and sad, but it would still be home and they would rebuild their world as best they could.

Arty thought about *people*. She tried to imagine new people.

It was nearly dark. She wanted to go home so much that she knew that, even after everything that had happened, she could never live anywhere but the forest. She did not belong in this world.

Cars drove round them, when they came, and they made the same horrible sounds and belched out the same smoke. Zeus cried every time it happened. Arty just kept walking. She made her legs keep going. She thought that she would still be able to walk while she slept and she wondered whether perhaps that was what she was doing, whether this was all a dream. She willed herself to wake up back in her life, in her clearing, with everyone well. She wanted to go back to Kotta morning and do it differently. In some way there would be something she could have done differently that would have stopped Hercules getting ill.

There were no trees on the other side of the road, but lots on the forest side. Arty stayed on this side because she wanted to be as close as she could be to home. There was a sign on the fence a little way along that said DANGER RADIATION, with some symbols underneath it.

After a while someone came past riding a bike, a woman. She was riding it like the rabbit did in the book, the way Arty couldn't, and she was going slowly enough to talk to.

'Hello,' Arty said, and when her voice came out small she said it again but louder. 'Hello!' She actually had to shout it to make her hear. 'Hello!'

She stared at her. This was a woman. A human she hadn't met before.

The woman put a foot down on the road and made it look like an easy thing to do. She turned.

'Hello,' she said back, looking surprised.

Arty stared at her face. She looked at the woman's eyes, at her nose, at her cheekbones. The woman was about the same age as Venus, Arty thought.

I spoke to another person, she said to herself. *I said hello. And she said the same word back.* Everything rose up inside her. She took a deep breath and the words all came out at once. They came out in English, without Arty giving it any thought.

'I need an ambulance please. There are people in the forest, very ill. My mother is very sick. And my father. And Inari and Luna. We need medicine. I need a place with a green cross. They get sick and then they die. We need help. Can you help?'

That was not what she had practised in her head, but it was the way it came out.

The woman's eyes were big and dark brown, and Arty could see that she was a bit confused by what she'd said.

'You need doctor?'

'Yes.'

She pointed, the way they were going. 'You go here.'

Arty's stomach felt as if it were falling, swooping down. She had nothing to hold on to but Zeus and the bike.

'We just keep walking?'

The woman was talking fast, but now Arty didn't understand her words. These words were not English or Hindi. She could see that the woman was asking questions and telling her things, and all she could think was that she had spoken to a new person, and that the pharmacy was that way. When the woman stopped she looked at Arty.

'Not understand,' the woman said in English after a while.

Arty nodded.

The woman smiled, got back on to her bike, nodded to them and rode away.

Zeus was moaning, his voice quiet, but Arty knew he would stay on the seat because he was terrified and he had nowhere to go. She was pushing and walking, and it was nearly dark and she really hated it when cars came past.

She hated it even more when a car came towards them, turned round in the road and stopped next to them. Two men got out. The car said TAXI on the roof. Taxis, then, were real.

'Hey there,' said one of the men. He was wearing a pair of baggy orange trousers and an orange T-shirt, and his hair was cut so short that he was almost bald.

He was not much older than she was. Arty was looking at a man – a boy – who was about her own age. She had never met anyone like that before. She stared at him. He was as exotic to her as a Martian would have been. He made her feel strange. This was the worst of times, but she felt the horizons of the universe moving, further and further and further out, showing her things she would never have dared to seek. Her breath was coming in short bursts and her head was spinning.

The other man had trousers and a T-shirt and his hair was longer, but still short.

'Hey,' said the first one, the young one, the one Arty couldn't stop staring at. 'Are you OK? You speak English, right?'

He was looking back at her. The other man was the one who had been driving the car. *The taxi driver*, she thought, trying out the words. Taxi. Driver.

'Yes,' Arty tried to say, though the word didn't quite work. She nodded her head to make it clear.

'You need to find some medication, is that right? Sarita – she works at the monastery I'm staying at – she said she saw you here and you were agitated and you need a doctor, but that you didn't understand Marathi, and that you spoke to her in English. Are you OK? She asked us to pick you up because she was worried that she couldn't communicate with you well enough to help. We can give you a ride to a pharmacy or we can get you to a doctor. Where are you from?'

Arty didn't know what to say. There were too many questions. She absolutely did not want to get into a car, which she supposed was what *give you a ride* meant. No one had said that they would need to do that. She looked at Zeus, but he seemed to be in a trance. She saw the men looking at him too.

She pointed to the forest to show where they were from.

'We need help,' she said carefully. *I am saying words. A strange boy seems to be understanding them.* 'My mother is sick. And the others. They have a fever and they have pains and then they die. Some of them died.'

Arty closed her eyes as tight as she could. *We are all gods and goddesses. What happens to one happens to all.* Zeus's fingers were digging into her flesh. She tried to take all the strength of all her family. She named them in her head like a mantra. Hercules. Diana. Kali. Hella. She and Zeus had all their strength and Arty had to do this for them. She had to do it for Luna. Venus. Vishnu. Inari. Odin. She had to do it.

She put the bike down by the side of the road and looked at the car door.

'Shit,' said the man. 'Right. Um. I'm Joe. This is Ganesh. He's a taxi driver and we'll take you to the pharmacy gladly. The pharmacist will be able to help, I'm sure.'

'Yes please,' Arty said. She made herself speak as clearly as she could. 'Thank you very much.'

'Please get in,' said the other man. Ganesh.

He held a door open and showed her the back seat of the car with his hand.

Arty looked at Zeus. Zeus looked back. They clung to each other. She nodded. He shook his head.

Arty took a deep breath of the choky Wasteland air and stared at the seat in the car. She just needed to put her bottom on it. She could slide in through the door and sit there and it would make her move faster than anything had ever gone before. She and Zeus would go to wherever the car took them. She didn't have to worry about going the right way. It would take them to the right place.

Arty hoped she and Zeus would be able to tell Luna about this. Luna wouldn't say anything, but she would listen. She would be interested.

She took a half step towards the car.

'It's OK,' said the one called Joe. 'I promise we're just taking you for help. Honestly.'

Arty had no idea whether she could trust him. He was smiling, but that didn't mean he was nice. She had no other options so she took a deep breath.

'OK,' she said, and quickly, before she could change her mind, she pushed Zeus into the back of the car and sat down next to him. The seat felt sticky where she touched it. The smell hurt her nose and she coughed and choked and wondered whether she was going to die now anyway. When Joe closed the door with a huge bang she could hardly breathe because she was stuck in a little place without any air. Zeus was barely behind his eyes at all; he clung to Arty's hand but the rest of him had shut down and gone home. He rocked a little back and forth.

Ganesh had a wheel in front of him and other things to do with his hands and Arty realized that, although she knew about engines a bit, she had no idea how anyone made them go. She watched what he did. A key made the engine start. She fingered the keys round her neck. One had opened the chain. The other two could be anything.

Although she was ready for it to go fast because she had been watching them zooming past, Arty could never have been ready for what it felt like. She closed her eyes and hung on to Zeus with both hands and she was screaming in her head and probably with her mouth too. It went on and on and it was making her sick and she didn't know what to do.

I am a goddess. I am a goddess. I am a goddess.

Arty knew the boy in the front was talking to her, and she couldn't listen because everything was crowding in and there was too much. It was in all her senses. She couldn't open her eyes. She wished she could close her ears too because the noise was impossible. The smell was going to kill her and Zeus. She could taste it all and she had no words for what it was like. She knew the tastes of her home, and she knew what they were. Mango and rice and water and forest air. Not long ago she had tasted beer and thought it was the worst thing in the world. Now she knew that the poison the inside of a car put into your mouth was the worst thing in the world. Cars made people die, and she was in a car. She tried to focus. What was the other sense? Sight, smell, sound, taste and touch. It was touch.

She didn't want to touch anything, but she was still clinging to Zeus, and she could feel his warmth. He was part of her.

She had met three new people.

Everything about this was horrific, but a part of her (it was a small part, but it was there, even at that point) was so proud of what she had done that she thought that when she got back home she would want to talk about this adventure for the rest of her life.

There was a world beyond the clearing, and it was real. People lived in it. And now she was sitting in it.

It had been a grey haze to her before, a scary place of destruction and poison and horror, and she had spent her life hiding from it, sometimes calling it the Wasteland like Hella did. Now things came out of the mist, defined.

She was not the only teenager in the world.

She moved her hand a little and touched Joe's shoulder, in front of her. He reached round and put his hand on top of hers. Arty could feel his pulse. She felt their skin touching. She felt the warmth of the blood in his veins.

When the car stopped and Joe opened the door, she took a deep breath of foulness. She didn't want him to take his hand off hers. Joe helped Arty and Zeus out of the back of the car. She wanted to stay with him, to have him helping her forever.

He looked different from the men in the clearing. He had a different smell, and she could see that he cut his hair much more often and he didn't have a beard. She liked his face.

Arty stared around. This was a road. Those were shops. There were cars that were still, parked beside the road. There were people. Some of them were staring at her and Zeus, but probably not as much as she was staring at them. Everything swirled. She gasped for breath. She touched the car to steady herself. It was smooth and warm beneath her fingers.

Pharmacy, doctor, medicine, help.

The pharmacy had a counter, open to the street, with little cardboard boxes and bottles on it, and Arty realized this was what shops were like. It was on the side of the road and cars were still going past. She tried to shut out everything else behind a curtain of black, and focused only on the shop with the green cross.

'Will we need to pay?' she asked Joe. 'I don't have . . . money.' She looked at him to make sure she'd said it right. When she had met that word in books she had read it as 'moany', and Venus had corrected her, but she still didn't believe it was 'munny'.

Venus hated money. She said it had started out as a convenient way to get things without having to have something to barter directly, but that now it had corrupted everything. She said the love of money was the root of all evil.

'Don't worry about the cash for now,' he said.

'I have these herbs.' Arty passed him Hella's bag. 'I think we use them to pay for things because money is the root of all evil. We barter our herbs. Can I do that? At the pharmacy? Is that . . . right?'

She watched him open the bag.

'Oh shit!' he said. He looked around and closed it again quickly. 'No. Don't worry about the money. I'll take this and I'll pay for your medicine. Don't worry, OK? We'll work it out later. Don't let anyone else see this. Where the hell do you come from?'

He held the bag where the shop man wouldn't see it.

The pharmacist spoke a little bit of English and a lot of Hindi. He had a round face and a turban on his head, just like Hella had said. He smiled a friendly smile at Arty and Zeus.

'Are you a foreigner?' he asked in Hindi.

'I don't know,' she said.

'Where are you from?'

'I'm from here. From the forest. My mother is from England. My father is from India and Afghanistan and Australia and Morocco.' She said those words carefully in English because she didn't know the Hindi words.

He laughed. 'You speak Hinglish! You speak it very well.'

'Thank you.'

'And you are from many places.'

'I'm just from here. Just one place. One. I don't know any other places.'

'And what,' he said in Hindi, 'is the problem?'

Arty took a deep breath. 'Do you remember,' she said, 'a woman who came here with long grey hair? A white woman?'

'White woman?' he said. 'Speaking English? Yes, I remember. She had a little boy who was ill, at her home.'

'Well, the boy died,' said Arty. 'And then so did she. And other people too.'

She said the words and she made them real in the outside world as well as in the clearing. She concentrated hard, and explained, saying what she could in Hindi and the rest in English. She told him all of it. She was aware of Joe next to her not really understanding the Hindi, and Ganesh beside him following all of it.

'Four people are still there,' she said to finish. 'Or five. Sick. Very sick. Please send help. Please send a doctor and an ambulance. Please.'

She said it without melting away or flying into little pieces. She said it while holding tightly to Zeus. It took every bit of all the strength she had taken from her family, and she thanked them in her head.

The man spoke, and Arty saw that his smile had gone.

'This is . . . this is very bad. I think this is very bad indeed. We will send help. I offered help last time but the lady just wanted medications. Please tell us how we reach this place. Now, you sit back in the taxi, please. We'll find a doctor for you too.'

JUNE

I kept pretending to be ill, just in case. Considering that she was keeping me as a secret prisoner away from fresh air and the sun, I thought she really did need to be worried about my health, and I kept coughing and looking pained whenever she came in. At the very least I could see it made her feel bad, and I wanted to work on that, to open the wound, to keep her feeling bad until she remembered that people didn't keep other people imprisoned in basements. Then she could let me go.

'Take us with you when you go,' the toys used to say, and I would promise them one by one that I would.

I would too. They didn't belong down here. I would take them all to a charity shop or something so they could go to smaller children. All but the bear. I was going to keep that bear, because it was important.

I moved on to the next idea, which was to overpower her. On the face of it that should have been easy. She was much older than I was, and I was in my teens and I ought to have been much stronger than her. However, she was turning out to be the strongest person in the world and I knew I couldn't underestimate her.

I should be able to push her over, if I caught her by surprise. Then I would need to get her keys.

The door to this place was actually two doors, one at the top of the stairs and the other at the bottom, so I knew I was going to need both keys. There was no point getting out of the basement if I ended up stuck at the top of the stairs, still locked in.

I could punch her in the face.

That was unthinkable. She was family.

I sat and thought about it. I could punch her in the face. I was going to have to hurt her because she wouldn't give me the keys if I didn't.

I thought of the world out there. I thought of my future.

I had to hurt her.

I had to hurt her so that I could get out of here. I wouldn't kill her. I would just hurt her enough to get the keys. That was all.

7

They were taken in an ambulance to a hospital that was far away. Everyone who came near them wore astronaut suits. They were put in a room together and left alone. Their bodies were side by side in their hospital room while their minds were all over the place.

She knew in a pale second-hand way that there were a lot of things happening. Doctors and other people were panicking about the fever, calling it a plague, asking if they ever ate monkey meat, or got bitten by bats, and things like that. There had been another illness, far away, that came from a bat, and they thought this might be the same thing. Everyone was very worried about it. She told them they never ate any meat, and no one had been bitten by anything, but they kept asking again and again.

Even through her fog of shock and horror Arty could understand that everyone was scared that she and Zeus were going to make more people ill. They flustered around, doing things she couldn't see, but all the time they kept the two of them, and anyone they'd spoken to, away from everyone else in the whole of the world.

All she saw were four white walls and a closed window that was dusty on the outside. There was a fan, which plugged into the wall and worked using the electricity that lived there. When she looked out of the window she saw streets with people walking on them, down below, and she knew that she was higher up than the top of a tree, even though she couldn't remember how she had got here.

She watched cars. She could see that people carried bags with things in them that they had bought from shops. The strangeness of it all melted away quickly, and it became ordinary and horrible.

Arty had still not seen money. She knew about it. It was made from pieces of paper and metal, which went from hand to hand, from person to shop, for years and years and years. It was dirty – it travelled around and around and never got cleaned. It was the most horrible thought to look after a piece of paper that could have been anywhere in this filthy massive world, and to give it to someone else when they had a thing you wanted. Arty could not imagine being happy to swap a bag of mangoes, for example, for a dirty piece of paper.

And it was metaphorically dirty too, as Venus used to say. Money was a shortcut that meant you could get what you needed without having something to barter right then and there, but it had led to people trying to accumulate as much of it as they possibly could, in a way that they couldn't have done if there was still bartering (because then they would just have ended up with a pile of rotting mangoes). She knew that money both did and didn't exist: it existed as tokens people used to pay for things, but it wasn't real. It was a promise. It could all collapse. Venus had talked about it a lot.

Arty didn't see it when a team of people in spacesuits went to the clearing – her clearing, her home, her universe – and discovered no human life. They found the bodies she had seen before she went, plus four more. They found everyone dead. She didn't see any of that, and when they told her about it she shut the meanings out because she couldn't deal with them.

She sat on her bed, with Zeus always next to her, and they stared at the wall. Time passed. Arty felt feelings building and growing inside her, like a seed beneath the soil, getting ready to germinate. She kept them underground. She did not water that seed, didn't put any compost on it, didn't take any notice of it at all, but she knew it was there.

Joe was being kept here too in case he already had the illness in his body, and so was Ganesh and the man from the pharmacy and the lady with the bike. Arty felt bad that Joe and the others had to stay here just because they'd spoken to her. Only Joe came to visit Arty and Zeus. He turned up in their room sometimes, and she spoke to him, but in an absent way. She answered his questions probably, but she didn't really know what she was saying. He talked about the herbs, but she didn't listen. He held her hand, but she didn't care about that any more.

He talked to Zeus too. He showed Zeus how to play games on his phone, and Zeus understood quickly and played them without a word, frowning at the screen. Zeus liked Joe's company; Arty could tell that even though he never spoke. Arty recognized that Joe was being kind to them, that he was the closest thing she had to a friend out here, but she didn't care. She did not want a friend out here and Joe was not her real friend. She wanted her world back. She could see that Joe was ready to answer her questions about the outside world, but she didn't have anything she wanted to ask.

She tried not to listen when they came in and spoke to her. She ate the food when it arrived, even though she didn't want to, and she found a way to begin to tolerate the needle and the liquid that they put into her body, the medicine that was supposed to be taking away the sickness that she didn't have.

She sat back and let it all happen because she couldn't do anything else. After a while she taught Zeus how to read, using the books the hospital people gave her when she begged them (books by Chetan Bhagat and Agatha Christie). She read those books without concentrating. In the clearing she used to get lost completely in her book world, and now she couldn't, even though she knew the books were good. Reality, her nightmarish reality of horror, was always there and however hard she tried she couldn't make it go away. She had her bag, with Venus's note in it, but she couldn't look at it. She knew her bear was in there, but she didn't get it out as this didn't feel like the place for a lovely friendly bear from the clearing.

She thought about dying, because she knew that she couldn't live here in the Wasteland. She knew, although she tried not to look at the fact head on, that both her parents must be dead. She knew that because people kept telling her over and over again and she hated them for that.

She spent hours looking at ways she could die. The window didn't open, but she would be able to get through it if she were able to throw something to smash the glass, and then she could just fling herself down to the dusty concrete in the car park below. She could probably poison herself if she drank all the medicine from their drips. She could stop eating. She could make a blade from something and cut herself with it. She could drown herself by blocking the drain in the shower and letting it fill with enough water. There were lots of things she could do if she tried hard enough.

Zeus was the thing that stopped her. There was nothing to tether her to the world but him, and he was enough. She knew that, although the thoughts comforted her, she would never do it because of him. He was material, real, breathing, and as confused and sad as she was, and she was all he had in the world. She knew that taking herself away from him would be the cruellest act she could ever commit, and she knew that she wouldn't do it. Nor could she take him with her. However much she liked to spend hours imagining the two of them rushing towards their family in the perfect clearing of the afterlife, she knew it was not going happen yet. If she killed him, they would both be dead and that would be the end.

She couldn't do anything but stay in the hospital room, in body, while her mind did whatever it needed to do to survive. So that was what she did. She cuddled up to Zeus and she spoke to him. She got the bear out of her bag at some point, and spoke to it too. The bear seemed to talk back to her more than Zeus did.

In the end it changed. One day the blood that they took out of her with their needle said something different. People started to come in without masks on. There was a flurry of talk about 'arrangements'. About 'successful containment'. A doctor said she must seek immediate medical help any time she had a fever, because this was still a new virus and it might come back.

There were pieces of paper. Sometimes people tried to explain to Arty what had happened but she shut herself away and didn't listen. She refused to hear any of it, until they told her they had found Kali's sister in France, and that she was on her way over to meet them.

JUNE

I went through everything in the room, looking for something to use to overpower her.

'Sorry we're so soft,' said the rabbit, and the rest of them murmured agreement, wishing that they could have helped.

'Can you do that thing where you become demons and fly around the room again?' I asked, but they shook their heads and said they couldn't, that that had just been for me. Lucky me.

I had wanted to punch her but I knew it wouldn't be enough. A punch wasn't going to do it. I needed a weapon. Something sharp. Something that could be serious.

She had, of course, been careful about preparing this place. There was nothing useful in here at all. I could not find a single thing that might help me escape.

'Come on, gang,' I said, and I arranged the toys in a circle. 'I need some help. How can I overpower her so we can get out? Because my bare hands aren't going to cut it, are they?'

The rabbit put its hand up. 'Hit her on the head with one of those books?'

'Yes,' said the bear. 'Then get her keys while she's on the ground.'

'Thank you.' I looked at the books. Some of them were big enough to do something with, but I didn't think it would be possible for me to actually put her out of action with a book. They were stupid books that I hated, so I refused to read them. All of them were by old men talking about their lives and saying what they thought about the world, and I didn't want to read that.

The monkey passed me one of them and I held it in my hands. It was called *Clarkson on Cars* and it was by one of those men. I tried hitting myself on the head with it: the best I could do was to make myself a bit dizzy. The animals giggled.

'I don't think that'll work,' I said. 'Good idea, though. We need something sharp, I think.'

The bear handed me the remote control and I put the television on, hoping it might inspire me. And it did.

8

'You're coming too,' Zeus said. He said it over and over again, and she held tightly to his hand.

'Of course I am,' she said. 'No one's taking you away from me, my darling.'

Zeus looked up at her and smiled. She forced a smile back.

They were walking down a street in the town that had the hospital in it. Walking down a street was a new thing. Arty felt as if she were living inside a book, doing the things book people did. She was wearing a pair of loose black trousers that had appeared from somewhere, and a T-shirt that was the same pink as a flower in the clearing. Zeus was in shorts and a white vest. He was adorable. Arty's heart was full of love for him.

Neither of them could imagine the journey that they had ahead of them. How did you get to France? Arty knew there would be an aeroplane but she couldn't imagine such a thing. They could not picture what might be round the corner when they were walking, let alone what it might be like to travel to a different country, and then to live in France.

Their legs shook and their hearts pounded at each new thing, and that was everything. They clung to each other all the time. The world was scary. In her head Arty wanted to be brave, but it turned out that in reality she wasn't. She was terrified, and sad, and she had no compass. All her certainty had died. She was not the person she used to be, because she had lost her universe. She felt she was walking through the world like a ghost.

The woman ahead of them turned round. 'Nearly there!' she said. Arty walked a little bit slower, but Zeus slowed down even more than that, so that even though she was dawdling she had to pull him along.

The outside smelled of traffic, but when they were indoors it was worse. The hospital had been stifling. The house they were staying in right now belonged to Gita and Vikram, who were nice enough, Arty supposed, and she was working hard on not hating them because none of this was their fault. They were foster carers: their job was to look after children who needed to be looked after. Their house smelled of chemical cleaning stuff and it burned her nose and her throat and she was on the verge of cracking every moment she was there, because she was meant to call it 'home' but it wasn't home.

They had told her to have a shower every day in hospital. Now she knew she needed to have showers using soap, and to wash her hair with both shampoo and conditioner so it would be 'nice and shiny', as Gita had said, fingering a strand of it. 'You're lucky with your hair, Artemis,' she had added.

Arty had looked away. She didn't know why she was meant to want hair that was nice and shiny. She didn't know what was lucky about that. It was just hair. Equally she had no idea why she was meant to care what she looked like, or what other people thought of her.

She and Zeus had to talk separately to some kind of brain doctor every day, but Arty said nothing and she thought Zeus did the same. She knew that the man, who had wiry glasses and a kind face, was trying to make her talk about her feelings, but she didn't have feelings. She knew that seed was putting down roots inside her, but she didn't want to talk about it. She didn't want the man to force her to think about things, and there was no way she was going to tell him about the things she had lost. The idea almost made her laugh. Of course that wasn't going to happen.

She used the time instead to ask him questions about where they were. She was starting to search for a sense of herself now as a single human among billions, rather than one of eleven.

She knew that the nearest city to Lonavala, where she was currently staying, was Mumbai. The doctor had told her not to go there. 'You'll be ready for Mumbai one day,' he said. 'But not yet.' She had that filed away. Mumbai. She imagined a shiny city of skyscrapers and department stores and people moving money around in cars.

Though now, it seemed, they were going to France, and that was thousands of miles away and mainly reached by aeroplane. The good news was that France was near London, and London was where Matthew and Persephone might be, and – very, very slowly, as her brain began to come into focus – Arty was remembering that the last thing her mother had said was that she must find her uncle Matthew and Venus's friend Persephone. Persephone was also called Tania, and she had lived in the clearing until she had argued with Venus and gone away long ago.

Arty wished she knew what had happened. The story she had pieced together was that someone from the outside world had found them in the clearing and had wanted to stay, but that this person hadn't been allowed. And Persephone had thought that wasn't fair, and had left with him or her. And that this might have happened before Arty was born, or else when she was very small. She knew she had it muddled up, though, because no one wanted to explain it properly.

Persephone was a part of her old life. Matthew was her actual uncle. That meant that they were the closest Arty would ever get now to finding her mother. She wondered why Zeus's aunt had come to get them, rather than Arty's uncle.

'We're here!' called the woman, whose name, Arty actually knew, was Pia.

Arty squeezed Zeus's hand and they walked the last few steps to the cafe.

It was strange to walk into a cafe in real life. There were tiles on the floor, and the door and windows were all open, and there was a smell of new food and old food and coffee and tea, and although that smell was strong it was not as horrible as most things. There were eight tables in there, and a white woman was sitting at one of them, looking hot and worried. She stood up and stared and then remembered to smile, and held up a hand and then wiped under her eye with a finger.

Arty and Zeus and Pia walked over to her and, as they walked, Arty saw that Kali's sister, Florence, didn't want Arty. Energy filled every atom of her body. It was like walking through the thick air before a summer storm. Electricity crackled. Arty thought that she must be trailing thunder and lightning behind her. She felt like a warrior.

'Hello,' she said, because the woman hadn't said anything. Arty squeezed Zeus's hand and looked at him.

'Hello,' he whispered to the floor.

Florence looked a bit like Kali. She looked enough like her to be her sister.

Arty had only recently discovered that brothers and sisters, out here, had exactly the same parents. In the clearing all the children had been called brothers and sisters no matter who their parents were, but she could see that that wouldn't work when you had billions of people to sort out.

Florence's light hair was sticking to her forehead, and the air around her was heavy with the dread that was seeping out of her skin.

'Zeus?' she said, and she leaned down and hugged him, then jumped quickly away.

Arty waited for her to look at her, but she didn't. She was only interested in Zeus. He didn't say anything or look at her, so Arty spoke instead.

'He's finding this difficult.' Her own voice trembled even though she was on fire inside.

'*Bien sûr*,' said Florence, and Arty knew that she was speaking French and was pleased that she understood it. Life in the clearing had at least prepared them to speak to people from different countries in different languages. She found she could speak French just by imagining she was speaking to Kali.

'He's OK when he's with me,' she said in French, and Florence shot her a look.

'He will be OK with me too,' she said, 'because I am his blood family.'

Arty tried to let go of Zeus's hand but he wouldn't let her. He was trembling all over.

'Arty must come too,' he said in English, his voice clear. Then he said it in French, and then in Hindi.

'You are clever,' said Florence. 'Speaking these different languages.' She stared into his face. 'You have her eyes,' she said, and she pulled him close to her again and picked him up. He tried to wriggle away, and he wouldn't let go of Arty's hand so she had to twist her arm round to avoid hurting herself.

Pia hesitated, then pulled out a chair at the table and sat down, and after a bit of shuffling they were all sitting round the table. Zeus and Arty still held hands. He looked at Arty, and Arty looked at Florence.

A man put cups of sweet chai down in front of Zeus and Arty. They both loved that drink. Arty hadn't noticed Pia ordering it.

Florence took a deep breath, and started talking. 'Zeus,' she said, 'I know that you are very attached to Arty because you two have been through a terrible, horrible thing. But I am your aunt, and we are your family. I can't take a teenager home with me, but I promise the very best home to you, my nephew. We loved your mother and we missed her every day. We will take care of you so well because you are part of her coming back to us.'

'Arty must come too,' he said.

Arty squeezed his hand. She was desolate inside because she knew that she wasn't going to go to France at all.

'I know it's difficult for you to imagine leaving her behind. Yes, I can see that. But, hey, you're young and you're going to a happy life. Guess what – you're going to love it in France. Because you have two cousins there, my girls, and you'll be a brother to them. So you'll have two new sisters! Coco is four too, about the same as you, and Camille is the baby. Lucky them, getting a new brother!'

'Arty must come too.' He was shaking his head and his eyes were swimming with tears.

'We can phone Arty, and write to her. You can talk to each other on FaceTime. Do you know FaceTime? You'll love that. You'll still have Arty in your life.'

He put his face down on to the wooden table and sobbed, because he could see as well as Arty could that nothing they could say was going to change her mind.

Arty glared at Florence. She didn't care about France or about those little girls. She just knew that anyone who cared about Zeus would be keeping the two of them together.

She tried. She leaned forward and put her face where Florence had to look at her.

'If I could come with you,' she said, 'then I would do everything I could to help. I'm good at doing laundry. I can help Zeus get used to his new life. I can help you with your little girls. I promise to be no trouble at all. I won't be a difficult person. I'll be a useful one. I've already taught Zeus to read since we've been here. You know he's –'

Florence cut her off. 'I'm sorry,' she said. 'But we can't. We have a small house and now we will have three small children. Taking a teenager back from India too – it's just not possible. But you can keep in touch, like I said.' She looked at Zeus, who had climbed on to Arty's lap and wrapped his arms round her. Her T-shirt was soaked with his tears. 'And I don't think this helps. I think he needs to start to be independent of you, Artemis. This isn't healthy.'

Arty stared at her. 'It is healthy,' she said. 'It *is* healthy. That's a horrible thing to say.'

She wanted to stand up and throw all the cups in the cafe on to the floor. She wanted to break every window, to attack the woman in front of her. Pia put a hand on her arm, and she forced herself to give it one last try.

'I could stay with a foster family nearby then,' she said, staring at the table, clinging on to Zeus, fighting to control herself. He was juddering in her arms, holding her so tightly that it hurt. 'Please?' she said to the table. 'Zed needs me.'

'I'm sorry,' said Florence.

Pia stepped in and Arty zoned out of their conversation and muttered what assurances she could into Zeus's hair. It was hard, though. There wasn't much she could say.

When she tuned back in they were talking in English because Pia didn't speak French. Florence was saying, 'My mother is so happy. Delphine went away long ago and we always hoped to see her one day but now we won't. Yet here's her son. Delphine was always so clever.' Arty stroked Zeus's hair and listened to this bit carefully. She wanted to know all about Kali, who, it seemed, had once been Delphine. 'She went to medical school, you know, to become a doctor, and *voilà*. Clever Delphine. She was the clever one *and* she was more pretty – I mean, to a young sister that's not fair, is it? *Ce n'était pas juste*. She was going to, you know, become a doctor, marry a doctor, have doctor babies. She became a doctor, all on track, and then she breaks up with her boyfriend, freaks out and – poof! – off to India. Everyone says, *It's OK, she'll be back. Needs to get it out of her system*. But then we . . . Well, we never heard from her again. We tried to find her but she had gone.' She gazed at Zeus. 'And now we have her baby.'

Arty poured all her strength into trying to pretend to Zeus that it would be OK, but she couldn't imagine how he was going to manage without her. Arty hadn't thought that Florence wouldn't want to take her too. She didn't understand. It hurt. Florence didn't realize that Arty was a part of Kali's family too.

Florence kept talking to fill the silence. 'Really, you'll have your cousins,' she said in French. 'They're going to adore you. Their big cousin . . . I think that Zeus is not quite the right name for our town. Maybe Zachary? I think Zac for school. Then you can still be Zed if you like that.'

Arty wished this woman would go back to France on her own. She even wanted to change his name. Again she wanted to run far away from here, back into the forest, and live with little Zeddy, just the two of them.

She thought she understood why Kali, or Delphine, had run away from home and decided never to see her family again. Her sister was horrible, and the rest of them probably were too.

'You need to be a big boy,' Florence said to him. 'You're a big brother. You'll be a lovely brother to Coco and Camille. We'll get you settled in. Oh God, such a . . . I couldn't believe it when I saw you on the . . . Oh my dear.' She turned to Arty with a tight face. 'Artemis. Thank you for everything you've done for him.'

She looked away quickly. Pia asked Florence whether she'd been to India before (she had, to look for Kali when she vanished, and she clearly hadn't enjoyed anything about it).

Arty examined the fact that she might really have to live out here without Zeus. She would not sit tight any more when he was gone. She would not be pushed around and do as she was told then. She would have lost everything if he went.

And if she lost everything, she would have nothing left to lose.

And if she had nothing to lose, she would go wild.

Neither of them talked about the fact that this was their last dinner together, because it was too big. Arty knew that Zeus was trying not to cry every single second. She was too. She didn't want to tell the foster people how they were feeling, so she tried to pretend everything was all right, while her insides were shrivelled up dead. She did her best to behave the way Gita and Vikram expected them to, and to mind her manners, but it was difficult because she didn't care. She and Zeus wanted to sit on the floor and eat with their fingers, but instead they had to sit at the table and eat in a way that they didn't know or understand at all.

Zeus put down his fork and picked up a chickpea between his fingers. Arty saw Gita frowning and opening her mouth to say something.

'Zeddy,' Arty whispered, feeling as if she were going to die from the pointlessness of it all. She picked up the fork and held it up to him. He jutted out his lower lip and she saw his eyes fill with tears, but he picked his up and tried to balance the perfect little sphere on it. It fell off. He stabbed it, but it shot away off his plate and on to the floor. Arty picked it up and handed it back to him, but Gita intercepted her and put it into the bin.

'Not after it's been on the floor,' she said.

The door banged and Vikram came in from work. He was nice enough. Vikram didn't stare at them as if they were strange animals, at least. He was interested in what they said.

'Hello, children,' he said with a little bow.

'Hello, Vikram,' Arty said, and Zeus gave him a little bow back, looking scared but trying to do the right thing. Gita stood up and fetched him a plate, and he sat down to join in.

'Elbows off the table, Zeus,' he said.

Zeus moved, looking confused, and Arty wanted to tell them all that Zeus had never sat and eaten from a table until very recently indeed, so he was actually doing extremely well. And also that not having a table had not made them savages.

'How has the day been?' Vikram asked.

Arty looked at Zeus. He had the real story, but he wasn't going to say a word, so she took a deep breath and told it for him.

'We met Florence,' she said. 'Kali's sister. Zeddy's aunt. She's going to take him to Mumbai tomorrow and then to France. But she's not taking me.'

Zeus sniffed. He put his head down. Tears fell on to his paneer.

'France will be splendid,' said Vikram, but he looked a bit concerned.

'I have always longed to go to Paris,' said Gita, almost crying herself.

'You'll have to use a fork in France, I think,' Arty managed to say, as Zeus picked up a clump of rice with his fingers again.

'Yes indeed,' said Vikram. 'Table manners will be paramount. The food will be very different. Also, I think the weather will be colder, perhaps even snowing at times.'

They stared at him. Arty hadn't thought about snow being a thing that was real in this world, and she wasn't sure Zeus had any kind of concept of what the word meant, so she said, 'Snow is white, cold stuff that falls from the sky instead of rain, Zeus,' then looked to Vikram and Gita to check that was right.

They both nodded. Zeus looked to the ceiling, as if expecting snow to fall at once.

Gita and Vikram tried to be normal, but when Arty walked into the kitchen with the dirty plates afterwards she heard Gita saying, 'To be honest I'd like to slap the woman. It's cruelty, separating them,' and Vikram agreeing. When Gita noticed her, she walked over and hugged her, and that was the closest Arty came to crying.

'Stay here with us, dear girl,' said Vikram, and everything about him was kind. 'We will take care of you.'

She tried to imagine herself living here and being their foster daughter, as there didn't appear to be any Uncle Matthew turning up for her. She supposed Venus had never said he would come and collect her. She was meant to go and find him, but how could she? She would have to go to school now, and she knew Vikram and Gita would help her to work it all out. It might turn out all right.

Then when she was eighteen, which seemed to be the age you needed to be to do things on your own, she would get herself to France and battle through the snow to find her little brother, and he could come and live with her forever. The two of them would go together to London and Matthew and Persephone. She considered it.

As they lay in bed that night, cuddled up together, she put her face into his hair and tried to say the right things.

'You might have to stay in France for a little bit,' she whispered. 'But then I'll come and find you. I promise I will. I'll go to Mumbai where it's a huge city, and I'll go to France and find you, and you and me will go to London to find Matthew and Persephone. And they will help us to know what to do.'

'Persephone,' he said.

'Yes. She's one of us. She's from our home. Matthew's my uncle so he might not understand, like your aunt, but Persephone will help us.'

They talked late into the night. Arty whispered to him about the clearing, about their family. She told him they would always have each other. They talked about each of their family members in turn, because Arty knew that by the time they came to do it again Zeus might have forgotten. He was so small. They talked about Luna, their quiet sister. She was the baby born after Arty, and Arty told him how exciting it had been when Hella's baby finally arrived. They talked about Hercules, who had been so close to Zeddy that they were practically twins. She told him about his own birth, how Kali had been in labour for three days, sometimes walking around the clearing yelling her power to the skies, and sometimes shut in the hut with Hella and Venus sitting with her, but that then finally a baby boy had cried and the clearing had a huge celebration.

They went through their parents, and all the other grown-ups.

Zeus said: 'I want Kali.'

It was the first time he had said that. Arty held him tight and they never wanted to let go of each other.

He fell asleep. Arty didn't. She lay awake all night and watched it getting light outside the window. She had said goodbye to everyone she had ever known, and now she was going to say goodbye to Zeus too.

The next morning she helped Zeus into the car, knowing they had lost. She hated Florence for taking him away. Arty knew that she could have lived with a foster family in France, if Florence had helped to set that up.

'Kali was my family too,' she said in a quiet voice in French, as Florence stepped towards her with a fake smile on her face. 'Zeus is all I have left.'

'I'm sorry,' said Florence.

Zeus and Arty were staring at each other. They had already hugged and said goodbye. She had promised to get in touch with FaceTime and the other things Florence had said. She had promised him the whole world.

Florence got into the back seat, blocking Arty's view of Zeus, and said thank you to Pia for helping them. The car started up and Arty watched Florence talking to Zeus, and Zeus leaning as far away from her as he could. As the car drove away she knew she had failed him. This was wrong.

And now she had nobody.

JUNE

I pulled the back off the remote control, and snapped it, and then I had a point that would hurt if it stuck into a soft part of your body. I sat and stared at the television, poking myself with the sharp bit and trying to work out how I could use it.

Eyes were soft. I didn't want to poke this into someone's eye, and particularly not hers (we were related, after all). But if I was going to get out of here I had to do it, and I couldn't think of anywhere where it would work, apart from her eye. This was my problem.

It was small. I kept it up my sleeve. The toys all approved. They were changing again before my eyes. The bear, the rabbit and the monkey were becoming softer, like cartoon animals from the television. And there were other things. There were cartoon bluebirds singing in the corner of the room, and squirrels that climbed up the walls. I knew they were all trying to get me to be strong and brave, so that I could attack the woman and get out.

The bear sidled up to me and spoke out of the corner of its mouth. 'I love you loads,' it said, 'but you're a bit smelly, you know?'

I went to have a shower. The bear was right. If I was going to get out I needed to look presentable, and not to smell, because I would need to run away and blend in. It was scary, and I would only get one chance, and I had to do it right. It was for the greater good.

The water in the shower wasn't very warm, and it came out in a dribble, but I stood under it for ages. The water raining on top of me made me think about standing outside in the rain, and I closed my eyes and imagined myself out of here.

I dried myself with the towel and got dressed quickly. My hair was wet and it made my shoulders wet too. I was a bit cold and the room had a nasty musty kind of smell.

I was desperate to see the sun. I put on a long-sleeved top and pushed the weapon up my sleeve. I psyched myself up and up and up.

'You can do it!' said the animals, and the birds flew around the ceiling, and the edges of the room became grass. Flowers bloomed in the wallpaper, even though the walls had been painted white before. The whole room was coming together to help me.

'I'm not going to kill her,' I told the rabbit.

It looked a bit disappointed. 'You're going to hurt her, though,' it said, and I agreed that I was. I was going to get out, and that was fair and right. I was doing the right thing to free myself.

By the time she came in I was ready to do it. All my friends were hiding behind the box, tense and excited, waiting.

She was holding a tray. I watched as she went through her usual routine. She unlocked the door, turned round and picked up the tray she had left on the other side. When she was through the door she put the tray down again, and locked us in. She brought the tray over and put it down on the floor beside me. It had a sandwich and a bag of crisps and a banana on it. I liked bananas. I didn't like crisps. They were too nothingy and they made me feel ill inside. I wasn't planning to eat these ones anyway.

'Good afternoon,' she said.

I looked at her and forced a smile. 'Hello,' I said as I stood up.

I heard the animals gasping and chattering.

'Someone smells better,' she said, and I could see that she was pleased. She thought she had tamed that part of me. 'Your hair looks nice like that. Clean.'

'I had a shower,' I said.

'Yes. Clearly. Don't think you're getting a hairdryer.'

'I don't want a hairdryer.'

I was breathing heavily, steeling myself. I waited. I let her tell me about things I didn't care about, about what her friends were up to today. I let her talk. I didn't really listen. I could hear the bear saying, 'Do it! Do it now!' and the rabbit saying, 'Not yet. Wait a minute!'

'It's just you and me,' she said suddenly. 'Doing this. No one else is interested. One day you'll realize this is all for your own good.' Her eyes were glinting with madness.

'I will not,' I said. There wasn't much more to it than that.

When she turned to leave I got up too. I walked behind her to the door, knowing that the toys were following me. She stopped to get her keys off her belt and turned to look at me.

'What are you doing there?' she said. 'Looming.' She flinched away from me.

I didn't answer. This was the moment. I held the weapon in my hand, and I thought of everything in the world outside, and I thought about how she had no right at all to be keeping me prisoner, and I pushed it into her face.

9

Arty started running, desperate to follow the car. But it was faster than she was. Of course it was; that was how cars worked. When she stopped running, Pia was there behind her. She put both hands on Arty's shoulders.

'They will look after him,' she said.

Arty liked Pia's smell because it was like flowers. She liked Pia, who was quite young and tall and wore nice clothes. But Arty knew that, right now, Pia was wrong. She knew that the only thing she could do was to get herself to France and to rescue her brother and look after him forever.

Pia was kind but she couldn't see that Arty was on fire. Florence had taken the last thing she cared about and now there was nothing left. This was not her world, because she had no world. She was a spirit here. Nothing bad could happen because the worst things had happened already, every single one of them. She felt a surge of power. She would keep it inside for now. But, when she needed to, she would let it out and she would power through the world like a hurricane, like the monsoon rain, like the ocean.

'At least it's done,' Pia said. 'He will be OK, you know. He will.' She didn't seem to see at all that Arty was different. She did not see that she was a girl who had come out of the woods to power through the world.

'Can I go for a walk on my own?' Arty said. 'I'll come back here later.'

'No, Artemis. Sorry. Actually there's someone who wants to see you, and I think it would do you good today. Distract you.'

'Who wants to see me?'

'You'll see.'

They went back to the same cafe. Arty was hoping against hope that the friend who wanted to see her was, somehow, Zeus, or Venus miraculously saved from the plague, or perhaps her uncle Matthew. She thought it might even have been Persephone, but it wasn't. She tried not to look disappointed as she walked through the smells of tea and coffee and food and sat down at a different table, where Joe was waiting. The boy from the taxi.

He stood up and kissed her on the cheek. That was odd. She shrank away a bit. In fact, though, she was pleased to see him. He had been at her side through that time in hospital. No one else would ever know what that time had been like.

'Artemis,' he said. He was wearing a yellow T-shirt and a pair of blue shorts and flip-flops. His hair was still really short. She thought he must cut it all the time to keep it like that. 'How are you doing?'

She sat at the table. Pia sat at the next one, close enough to keep a proper eye on them, but not part of their conversation.

She knew it wasn't his fault but she glared at him anyway. 'Bad,' she said. 'They took Zeus. They took him away.'

'I know,' he said. 'I can't believe you've been separated. I'm so sorry.'

'I'm going to get him back.'

'Good. You do that.'

'I don't know how to get to France. Or anything. But I'll find him. I shouldn't have let them go. I saw him, Joe. As they drove off she talked to him and he did this.' She leaned to the side as far as she could without falling off her chair. 'He needs me. I hate her.'

Joe sighed. 'Yes. I know. For what it's worth I hate her too.'

They talked for a bit, and it was good to get it all out. Arty asked Joe about himself because that was better than talking about the fact that Zeus had gone, and she discovered that Joe, like herself, was from lots of places. He was Nepalese but had grown up in Germany and spoke Nepali, German and English fluently. That made her ask lots more questions, and he answered them all patiently.

Pia was nice but she was always trying to contain Arty. With Joe it was different. He felt like a . . . She tried the word out in her head. He felt like a *friend*. Not family, but friend. That was a new thing. He drank a Kingfisher, and she had a Coke, which she loved very much. She forgot that Pia was there, forgot for a moment that Zeus had gone.

'How old are you?' she asked, after a while, staring at the Kingfisher.

'Nineteen.'

'And you like Kingfisher?' She was struggling with that, blocking out the memories.

'I do. It's nice when it's cold. Refreshing.'

'I hate it.'

'I can imagine.'

She stared at its label and didn't hear lots of the things he said to her. Kingfisher meant Kotta. Kingfisher was the last thing that had happened in the clearing. Kingfisher sent her head into a whirlwind and she had to work hard to keep herself from spinning out of control. And here Joe was, drinking it as if it were a normal thing.

After a while Pia's phone played a tune and she looked at it.

'Excuse me,' she said. 'I have to go to take this. I won't be long.'

They both watched her walking out of the cafe. As soon as she was through the door, Joe changed. His dark eyes glinted and he leaned forward. Joe's smell was more like clearing people than outside people.

'Right,' he said. 'Thank God she's gone. I was going to ask her to give us a minute but I thought she probably wouldn't have dared to leave you unchaperoned. Arty, I have to give you something. You remember the grass you had, when we first met? You were going to try to use it to pay for medicines.'

'Of course I do. It's not *grass*. It's herbs.'

'Mmm. Well, I took it away from you and hid it. You won't remember because you were too shell-shocked, but when I realized we were being taken to hospital, and that they would definitely take control of all our stuff, I hid it in the bushes behind the pharmacy. When I went back for it, it was still there. So I've managed to sell it for you. It's quality stuff. Look, take this envelope. It's money. Hide it from everyone, for God's sake. Whatever happens, you can't tell them where you got it.'

She took the envelope, dazed.

'Money,' she said.

'Yes,' said Joe. 'Lots of it. It won't get you to France, but it'll help you along the way. You haven't got a bag, have you? Really, don't let Pia see it.'

Arty tucked the envelope into the waistband of her trousers and pulled her T-shirt down over it. It was perfectly hidden.

'Thank you,' she said.

It felt odd having money. Actual dirty money that had travelled around the world without ever being cleaned. She could feel the envelope against her skin, could feel the money inside it. She wasn't going to let it make her evil.

She had never had an envelope before either, but that seemed less momentous.

'You're welcome,' Joe said. 'I hope you manage to get to Zeus. Look, why don't we take another selfie? I'll send it to you when you get an email address.'

He had to stop and explain what a selfie was, and he told her that they'd taken some while they were in hospital. She vaguely remembered. She remembered discovering that a phone in the outside world was not at all the thing she'd thought it was. It was a camera and all kinds of other things, and not a thing that you used to ring people with unless you absolutely had to.

He did things with his phone and then he showed it to her. There was a photograph of Arty and Zeus smiling out of the phone. She moved, but the Arty on the screen didn't move, and anyway she knew that Zeus wasn't next to her now. This was them in the hospital.

She stared at the photos of herself and Zeus for ages.

'Can I have these pictures?' she said. 'Can I have all the pictures of Zeddy?'

'Of course. When you've got an email address, then message me and I'll send them right over.'

Then she and Joe leaned their heads together, and he held the phone out with his arm straight, and took pictures of them. Pia came back at that point and smiled at them.

'Let me get one of you two together,' she said, and she stood a little way back from the table, and got them to pick up their drinks and clink the bottles together, and she took pictures of them in the cafe.

'Can we meet again?' Arty asked Joe when Pia said they had to leave. She liked being with Joe. He was the only person who treated her as just another person. She really wanted to see him again.

He did a kind of smile that didn't look happy. 'The thing is,' he said, 'that I'm off to Mumbai tomorrow. I'm going to a retreat. It's a Buddhist thing, a silent meditation. Just outside Mumbai. So I'll be out of action for ten days or so. You can email, but I won't get it for a while. I'll reply as soon as I'm done.'

'You're a Buddhist?'

'We talked about this in the hospital. Yes, I am.'

'Buddhism isn't a religion in the same way that the others are.' She remembered that Diana used to talk about this. 'It's a philosophy. A way of life. Is that right?'

'Yes, that sort of thing. It clears the mind. Keeps you grounded.'

Arty touched the envelope of money through her clothes. 'Can I come to the Buddhist thing with you?'

Pia stepped in. 'Not until you're older. You can read about Buddhism, but you can't go on a retreat. Now we need to go. Joe, thank you for this. It's been very good for her.'

'I didn't want to go away without saying goodbye,' he said with a wink at Arty. She stepped forward to kiss his cheek the way he had done but they ended up in a huge hug instead. She felt his heart beating the way she used to feel Zeus's.

The bedroom was bare without Zeus in it. The bear was on her pillow, and Arty was annoyed because she realized she should have given it to Zeus to remind him every day that she loved him. She put the envelope under the pillow and started to think. She helped Gita with the laundry, still thinking. She enjoyed the work. She liked taking dirty things and making them clean, taking crumpled things and making them tidy. It made her think of the story of

Rumpelstiltskin – taking a pile of straw and spinning it into gold.

She had to think of a plan. Joe had changed her options. He had opened the world up. She had counted the dirty notes again and again, and she knew that Joe had given her twenty thousand rupees and, although Arty wasn't sure, she thought that was a lot of money. It certainly sounded like a lot.

Later, she had dinner with Gita and Vikram, and did her best to keep her elbows off the table, to use a fork, and not to talk with her mouth full, because she knew those things mattered. She looked at Zeus's empty chair often.

'You've never eaten meat at all, Arty?' Vikram said, taking a fork full of biryani.

'Oh, God, no,' she said, and she shuddered. 'I can't imagine.' That people actually ate dead animals when they didn't need to was a horrible thing.

'I don't like the idea either,' said Gita. 'I have never eaten it either, like you. Vikram did in his youth. Many people do. You are lucky to be placed in a vegetarian household.'

'Yes.' Arty agreed with her, even though she disagreed. Nothing felt *lucky*. She changed the subject, looking at Zeus's chair. 'So Zeus is in Mumbai tonight,' she said, biting her lip. 'What's it like there? I can't even imagine what a city is like. Can you tell me about Mumbai so I can imagine him?' She hoped what she was really doing wasn't too obvious. She did not want to imagine Zeus in Mumbai at all. She wanted to imagine him with her in the clearing.

'Oh, a big, big city,' said Vikram. 'Young Zeus will be in a comfortable hotel, no doubt. Air-conditioned. Ideally sound-proofed. The city of Mumbai is not for me. Bad air, too many people. Super noisy. It is certainly not for you, Artemis. Nor for Zeus, though he's just passing through, so that will be fine. But there's much to see for the tourist. Many shops. Oh, and he will see the sea, no doubt.'

'The sea? Mumbai is by the *seaside*?'

Gita smiled. 'Yes. It's by the seaside. Very famous. The Gateway of India is there, on the coast where the British monarchy first landed.'

'Are there lots of hotels to stay in?'

Vikram jabbed his fork into the air for emphasis.

'Oh, many, many hotels. Hotels for all budgets. For sure, his aunt will have booked one and no doubt a good one.'

Arty didn't know whether to ask this, but she knew she needed to know it now, so she took a deep breath and said, 'I don't really understand about money. I've never had any. Where I grew up . . . well, it was seen as the thing that corrupted people. Money makes it possible to have more things than you need. If you were growing crops and bartering them, then hanging on to lots of crops wouldn't work because they would go rotten in the end. And then when there was money, as a token of the thing you'd made or grown to sell, then people started wanting to have lots of money, to feel secure. And then by having lots of money that means that other people will have less. It's like storing all the food for yourself and never sharing, but with pieces of paper instead of food.'

Vikram nodded slowly. 'Interesting. Carry on.'

'And now I'm here. So, even though I hate the idea of it, I think I need to understand how it works. How much money is a hotel? How much is food? How much is an aeroplane to France? A train trip to Mumbai? How much do you need to work to get that much money? Would Florence have had that much money just lying around?'

Arty saw them looking at each other. They smiled. She thought from that smile that they loved each other a lot.

'Right,' said Vikram. 'This is complicated, but you're right that you need to get the hang of it and I am impressed with your thirst for understanding. I can see your distaste, but everything you're eating was purchased with money. The house you're living in. No one can manage without it. Even in your previous life there would have been money involved. You just didn't see it.

'So. Average wage in India is very low by world standards. Difficult for most people to fly to France. Food can be very inexpensive, or it can be as much as a flight on an aeroplane if you go to the fine-dining restaurants, though the likes of you, and indeed us, will be unlikely to do so. Wages vary vastly depending on the sector. The economy is about supply and demand. If supply is plentiful compared with demand, prices are low. If demand exceeds supply, prices are high because people will pay more if a thing is rare . . .'

Arty did her best to follow this. She knew that she needed to get to grips with it. She worked hard to focus. On a more basic level she also needed to know how much money she was going to need to get herself to Mumbai on that train. She wanted a number, an actual number, so she would know how it compared to the pieces of paper in her envelope. From the way Vikram had been talking, she didn't feel that a bag of herbs would equal a train to a city.

'Train to Mumbai – maybe a thousand rupees?' said Gita. 'Plane to France – more like forty thousand. You see?'

A thousand rupees for the journey she needed to make first. Forty-one thousand to get to France and rescue Zeus. She was nearly halfway there.

Arty felt reckless. Nothing was tying her down any more. She could afford to get to Mumbai at least, and when she got there she would find the airport, and some more money, and catch an aeroplane to Paris.

She sat on the bed after dinner and counted the money again. She had to do it five times over, six times, seven times, because she had to be sure she had it right. However many times she did it, it was still twenty thousand rupees. She could easily get to Mumbai.

Arty said she was going to bed early, and packed her bag. She had her three keys on her mother's chain round her neck, and Venus's note and her book and bear in her bag, and she packed her money, all the clothes she had, and her toothbrush. She made sure she had Florence's address and phone number and email, and Joe's too.

She sat on the bed until the house was perfectly quiet, listening as Gita and Vikram went to bed. She felt bad about them because they were kind, and she thought they might get in trouble for losing her, so she decided to leave them a note.

Sorry to run away. I do actually have some money. I will be fine. I think I will go to France. Thank you for looking after me. You are good and kind. Blessings to you. Arty.

She hardly dared to breathe as she edged down the stairs, hanging on to the wall, terrified of falling, and crept out of the back door. She clicked it shut, and then tiptoed round the side of the house and on to the street.

It was dark, and the moon was nearly full. The world was full of night sounds and possibilities.

The last full moon, she realized, had been Kotta day. Every single thing had changed since then. Arty had lost everyone. The moon didn't care.

This was the 202nd moon of her life.

She walked to the end of the road, and followed the route she had memorized earlier on the way back from the cafe, heading to the woods, where she walked deep into what Pia had called 'the government forest', found a place in the middle of some trees and sat down to wait for morning.

Being here was like being at home, apart from the fact that she was alone. She listened to the sounds from her other life. She talked to a lizard who stood still on a twig, pretending to be a stick, and watched a snake slither past. It was a poisonous one but she didn't bother it and it ignored her back. She listened to the crickets and the other insects, letting their sounds fill her with home. She let herself dissolve into it and it gave her strength. She was the goddess of her own life all night. She had to be.

She stared at the trees, remembering her childhood dreams of the Lorax coming out and playing with her. She willed him to come back now, to say 'Arty, let's play!' as he had in her dreams, to sing and laugh and throw her in the air. She missed those dreams, and she concentrated as hard as she could on trying to bring them back. It was easier to long for an old dream than for her old reality. It was less brutal.

As soon as it started getting light, Arty walked back to the road and started heading towards, she hoped, the train station. She thought she knew where it was, but she was very tired so when a little car with open sides buzzed to a halt beside her she turned to it gratefully.

'Rickshaw?' said the man.

'Can you take me to the station?' she said in Hindi.

He nodded, and she got in. This rickshaw was a new thing but she hardly noticed that. As they rode, the sky got lighter. The man asked her for some money and she concentrated very hard and reached into her envelope and brought out one of her notes. She held out the money as a token of a thing she was exchanging for a ride in a rickshaw, and the man gave her some other money back. They thanked each other. It was a huge milestone for Arty, and normal for the rickshaw man.

The station was quite busy, even though it was early. Its building was shiny and cool, with the floor and walls and ceiling all made of the same cold stone. Arty liked it. It was easy to find the ticket office, because she followed a sign that said TICKET OFFICE. The office was busier than she had thought it would be, so early in the morning, but she just stood in her first-ever queue, hoping that she was doing it right, and before long it was her turn.

She said, in Hindi: 'Hello. I would like to buy a ticket to Mumbai.'

The man nodded. He had a pointed face with sharp cheeks and he looked bored. 'Second class?' he said.

'Yes.' She had no idea.

'Twelve hundred.'

So she handed over one that said 1,000 and two others that said 100 each, which had come in her change from the rickshaw. That added up to twelve hundred. The man gave her a ticket. When she wasn't holding her money any more she wiped her fingertips on her trousers to get the evil off her skin.

She had used money and it worked. The note and coins had come to her for a while, and then moved on, sloshing on their evil way around the world.

'Where should I go?'

'Platform two,' the man said.

Arty saw that people were walking up the steps and crossing a bridge to the other platform. Other people, however, were jumping down on to the train tracks and crossing that way, pulling themselves up on to the platform at the other side, and that looked easier, and there were no trains coming, so she did that, and then she was on platform two.

She noticed the way people were standing around as if this were a completely normal thing to do, and she did everything she could to look like they did. No one really seemed to look at her and she just stayed there, attempting to blend in, trying to calm her heart by doing the right breathing. She was disguised as an ordinary person who had always lived in this world, standing in the early-morning sunshine waiting for a train. She even found the part of the platform that said CARRIAGE A and stood underneath the sign, because her ticket also said CARRIAGE A. A man came and stood close to her and breathed on her neck, so she hit him and he said she was a whore and went away. That was the only bit of bother.

She waited for Vikram and Gita, for Pia, for the police to get here before the train, but none of them came, or if they did it was after Arty had gone. When the train arrived it was so huge and so noisy and scary that she gasped, but she managed not to scream or to run away.

She stared at it as it slowed down and people started to jump on and off. So *this* was what a train was. It was a monster. An angry metal monster, completely different from the friendly train in her head. Still, it was a good-hearted monster because it was letting all the little humans climb on and off it and it was giving them a ride to Mumbai. It was blue with lots of carriages. It didn't have steam coming out of its funnel, or a face on the front, so it wasn't at all like a train from a book. Now that Arty knew what a train was like she wished she hadn't walked across its tracks. Next time she would use the bridge.

There was a big step to get up on to it and she had to hang on to a pole to pull herself up, but she did it, and there she was, in Carriage A, breathing through her mouth because of the smell of dust and people and old food that was seeping through the train in little clouds.

She showed her ticket to a woman passenger, and asked in Hindi and English if she knew where she should sit. The woman found Arty's seat (number five), and gave her a little cake thing that was perfectly spherical from a tin of them she'd brought with her, and it tasted of things Arty didn't know. It was wonderful.

'This is my favourite thing ever,' she said as little crumbs went all down her front. She felt bad for the Dairy Milk, but right at that moment she liked this more. It was a symbol of kindness. Someone had been kind, and it was someone who wasn't being paid to look after her.

'Thank you!' the woman said. 'It's butter and sugar. Fennel seeds. Turmeric.'

'It's perfect.'

It really was. It made Arty's mouth dance and sing. Fennel seeds and turmeric. She made a note in her head. She thought determinedly about fennel seeds and turmeric to block out all the other things that were inside her.

There was a man opposite her but he was frowning at some pieces of paper on his lap, writing on them with a pen, and he took no notice of Arty at all.

Everything jolted as the train began to move. She pressed her face to the window and stared at the disappearing station. She just stared and stared. She hung on to the edge of the seat with both hands because it felt so strange. She closed her eyes and tried to get used to the way her stomach felt, then opened them to concentrate again on the outside. It was different from travelling by car. It was bumpier but also calmer, and when she got used to it she thought it was better.

The hills out there were green, and there were people on the train tracks working with stones. Quite often it all went black and then, after a little bit, the outside world came back again, but no one else seemed to think that was odd.

She missed Zeus. She missed Venus and Vishnu. She missed Luna and Hella and Diana and Kali and Hercules and Inari and Odin. She knew she would miss them every day. They left a gaping hole inside her with jagged edges. She pushed it away. She had to focus.

She could smell the strangers around her and they all smelled of sweat and Wasteland things, and that was because they lived here, and this was the real world and now Arty was part of it too.

A man nearby was reading a book, which looked nice, so when Arty was able to stop staring out of the window she got out *Woman on the Edge of Time* and started reading. She stroked its pages, knowing that she would treasure it forever because it belonged to Venus. It was a thing that had gone from Venus to Arty, from mother to daughter. It had come from the clearing.

133

She lost herself in it. The outside world in this book was worse than this one, and strangely that was a comforting thing. She lived with Connie, saw everything through her eyes, threw herself into that life. She longed for Connie's other world just as much as she longed for her own.

Every time the train stopped she looked around, but it was never Mumbai. It was just another station. After quite a long time she waved at the man opposite to attract his attention.

'Do you know if we're nearly at Mumbai?' she said. 'I didn't miss it, did I?'

He shrugged and looked at his watch. 'You certainly couldn't miss Mumbai!' he said. 'And, besides, it's the last stop. Another hour, more or less.'

'Thank you.'

He was picking up his papers again, then stopped and leaned forward. 'Hang on a moment,' he said, 'haven't I seen you online? You came out of the woods, yes? Forest girl?'

Arty looked at him. She had no idea at all what he was saying.

'I did come out of the woods,' she agreed. 'But how do you know?'

'I saw it on social media,' he said. 'Hold on a sec. Here we go.' He got his phone out of his pocket and pressed things on it.

'You were in hospital?' said the man. 'Someone put your story online. It's been very popular because you came out of the woods. The account is called . . .' He looked at his screen again and said, 'Joeonthego.'

He held it out to her. There were the photographs she had seen on Joe's phone, of Arty and Zeus in the hospital. She stared at them.

'Joe. Joe did that.'

'Looks like it,' said the man. 'How are you now?'

'Fine,' she said, and she got up and moved to an empty seat further down the train, because she hated it that this man knew about her.

JUNE

She jumped away from me and screamed.

'How dare you?'

She pulled the plastic out of my hand. I had hurt her. A line of blood was running down her cheek. She had a hand over her eye, but I knew. I knew that I had hesitated just a bit at the last minute so I hadn't pushed my weapon all the way in, but I had still done it.

I had done it but not enough.

'You did that wrong,' said a bearish voice, but she looked at me in alarm, and I could see she thought I had said it.

'Push her!' said the rabbit, and I did. I pushed her as hard as I could. She fell completely to the ground, and I ran through the open door and up the stairs.

The door up there was locked. I had known it would be, but all the same this was further than I had been for a very long time. I hammered on it and shouted. I shouted, 'Help me! Help me! Let me out! It's not fair!' and other things as loudly as I could. All the animals came too and joined in. I kicked the door. I threw myself at it, my whole body. I shoved the handle. I tried to pull the door off its hinges. I went wild, attacking it, fighting it as the only thing that stood between me and where I needed to be.

I thought I heard something on the other side. I redoubled my efforts, slamming into the door over and over again, screaming at the top of my voice, right up until the moment when she pulled me from behind and pushed me all the way down the stairs.

I lay at the bottom and knew I had messed this one up completely.

10

At Mumbai she got off the train with everyone else, jumping down to the platform and feeling the solid ground beneath her feet. She stood, her legs shaking, and stared around.

There were other trains, and Arty tried to picture them leaving, all setting off for different places, going across India and maybe into other countries too, because she knew India had borders with Pakistan, Nepal, Bangladesh and other places. The world had opened up, and Arty was here, with money, and she had nothing to lose because everything had already all gone.

There were two women lying down, looking as if they were asleep, with brightly coloured bundles of maybe laundry next to them. There were wooden carts with wheels. People were taking boxes off the part of the train that said LUGGAGE AND BRAKE VAN. The sun was hot on her head, but the air was thick and she struggled to pull it into her lungs.

She wondered how many of these new people knew who she was.

Everything was loud. Arty took a deep breath and walked through the middle of it, and only once had to tell a man to leave her alone. She just walked, finding herself in a place where people waited looking at brightly lit screens with places and times on them, and then she walked past a few shops (one of them was a pharmacy, and she looked in case the shop man was the round-faced man who'd had to go to hospital because of her, even though she knew it couldn't have been). Then she was outside the station, and her ears were filled with cars shouting at each other, and a man was asking if she wanted a taxi.

'No thank you,' she said, and she walked past him, walked past a lot of yellow and black cars that were all waiting in a line (taxis, she supposed) and stood at the side of the road.

She couldn't move. The cars. She took a step to one side to stop herself falling over. The air was impossible to breathe because it was filled with pollution from hundreds of cars. Thousands of cars. She gasped and struggled for breath. It felt so different inside her.

And everything was so loud.

The cars were honking at each other constantly, driving round each other, ducking into spaces, taking up the whole road. If they could have, they would have driven over the top of each other to get to wherever they were going more quickly. They were like a swarm of bees, crawling over each other. Arty looked, and she knew it was too much for her. She had no idea what to do. She had thought the roads in Lonavala were busy.

She watched an old woman crossing the road by ducking into spaces and letting the cars go round her. She watched a man walking along in the traffic, heading in the same direction. It was all too much like the crossy road game that Zeus had played on Joe's phone, and that game always, always ended with you being flattened.

She stepped out all the same, just to see what happened, and several cars blasted their horns at her. She stepped straight back again. She couldn't do it. She didn't even know where she was going. She stood and stared for quite a long time, just standing still and letting the city – her first city! Mumbai! – move round her. She looked back at the front of the station, which was bright blue with a picture of a big building and a blue sky, with writing in maybe Hindi; if it was, that meant she didn't understand Hindi when it was written down.

She only knew one person in Mumbai, and that was Joe. She knew he had come here yesterday, and that his retreat would start tomorrow. He was here today. He must have arrived at this station. He had to be here somewhere.

But he had told everyone about her coming out of the woods. She had never told him not to, but she hated it that he had done it. It made it harder for her to run away.

'Taxi, miss?'

A man was beside her. She looked at him, and looked behind him to the line of cars. He was about Vishnu's age, and he was thin, with a moustache. She thought his eyes were kind.

'Do you know if there's a Nepalese boy from Germany here?' she said.

'A Nepalese boy? From Germany?'

She switched into Hindi because it felt like that would be easier. Or Hinglish, rather. Someone had called it that, but she couldn't remember who. When she didn't know a Hindi word she said it in English.

'I'm looking for a Nepalese boy staying here. He's from Nepal but his family live in Germany. He came here yesterday. Do you know where he might be? His name's Joe.'

'You want a hotel? German person would stay at hotel.'

'Yes please.'

He looked at her for a long time.

'I'll take you to Colaba,' he said. 'That is where tourists go. We'll go near to the Regal Cinema. Leopold Cafe. The Gateway of India. The hotels around there, that would be your best place to find a German boy, I think.'

He smiled at her, and it was a lovely smile that changed his whole face.

She smiled back and committed those words to memory. Regal. Leopold. Gateway.

'Thank you so much,' she said. 'You are kind. Let's go there. Don't worry – I have some money.'

The man looked at her. 'Maybe one, two hundred rupees on the meter?'

She thought of the eighteen and a half thousand in her bag.

'Yes,' she said. 'That's OK.'

She sat in the back of the taxi, clinging on to the door with one hand, holding the seat beneath herself with the other, and could not take her eyes off the scenes outside. At first she had to take herself away from her body and do controlled breathing, but whenever she closed her eyes to concentrate she had to open them wide again because she couldn't not look. It was the most incredible thing.

Mumbai was huge and it had everything in it. The world was here, all of it, right here. Hundreds of people, thousands of cars, and that was just on this bit of this road. The sky was hazy and everything faded away in the distance, as if she were in a dream, a little bit of sharply focused world surrounded by sleep and mist.

'First time in Mumbai?'

He pulled her back to reality, if that was what this was.

'Yes! First time. Definitely.'

'Which country?'

'Just India. I came on the train from Lonavala. My mother is English. My father is . . .' She thought of Vishnu's different countries. 'Indian,' she said.

'Welcome, welcome!'

'Thank you.' She gasped as he squeezed the taxi into a tiny gap. Arty had no idea how he'd done that. He just used his horn to tell everyone he was there, and somehow there had been space for him. 'What about you? Where are you from?'

'Me? From the north of India. A little village. I had no education there. I got married at seventeen because my parents said so. Then divorced. No children. I came to Mumbai alone and learned English. I was like you when I arrived here. Very shocked. Very, very shocked.' He chuckled. 'Like you. Don't worry, my dear. You will get used to it.'

Arty wanted to know all about his story, and he told her. He told her how he had worked and saved the money, then run away. He had travelled third class to Mumbai, riding on the roof of the train.

'The *roof* of the *train*?'

'Indeed!'

She gasped at every bit of it. She would never have imagined that people other than herself found it scary to arrive here, and it all made her feel a bit better.

'I always dreamed of Mumbai,' he finished, 'and now I'm here.'

'Why did you always dream of Mumbai?'

He turned round and grinned, while driving into a tiny space and round a corner. Arty closed her eyes. She listened to the cars blaring at them.

'Bollywood!' he said. 'It was Bollywood of course! I am a big, big fan of Bollywood, and particularly of AMK. You know?'

'What's your name?'

'Me? Salman.'

'Salman. I'm Arty. The thing is, Salman, that I don't know *anything*. I don't know what Bollywood means, or anything else, and I have no idea what AMK is. Is Bollywood like . . . Hollywood? I've heard of that.'

He laughed. 'You don't know Bollywood? Wow. You are in for a treat! You must go to Bandra. You can see AMK's house there. And many others. But AMK. He is the greatest movie star who ever lived. That is a true fact.'

'The greatest movie star that ever lived!'

'Indeed he is. Very wonderful man.'

'Wow. I'd love to see him. Can I watch . . . movies . . . at the cinema you said?'

'The Regal Cinema. Yes! Very famous cinema. Best in the world.'

'That's good.'

'This is it here now. See? Regal Cinema.'

She looked out of the window. They slowed down and stopped, right outside a building that did indeed say it was the Regal Cinema. Arty stared.

Her legs almost gave way as she got out of the car. 'That was a *scary* ride,' she told Salman. 'But thank you for bringing me here. And thank you for talking to me. Have you seen me on your phone, by the way?'

'It's normal for Mumbai,' he said, 'not scary. And it was a pleasure to talk to you. I haven't seen you on any phone.' When she started counting out the money he said, 'No. No, it's a present from me to you. You remind me of me. Good luck to you, Arty.'

'Really? Thank you for the present. Thank you, Salman!' She wished she had something she could give him, but she didn't have anything at all.

'Go to Bandra.'

'Bandra. Yes. I will. I promise. Thank you. I'll find AMK. Thank you, thank you.'

She watched his car vanish into the traffic. Soon she couldn't tell which one it was. She stood on the pavement and looked around. This was where tourists went, and it was where she might be going to find Joe. She wasn't sure where to start. A man came over and said, 'Would you like beautiful shawl from Kashmir?'

'No thank you. Do you know if there's a German Nepalese Buddhist boy here?'

'Beautiful shawl?' he said. 'Handmade. Excellent price.'

Arty really didn't want a beautiful shawl. She thought she might have liked one, now that he said it, but she didn't want to spend her money on it. She needed this money until she could find a job, and she wasn't really sure how to do that. Needing money for everything certainly made life complicated.

'Is cashmere what it's made of?' she said, because he was still standing there. She had heard of cashmere. In books it was really expensive and special. She thought she would like to touch it, just to see.

'No. Kashmir. From Kashmir. In the north. It's a very beautiful place. Come into my shop!'

She thought about it, but she could see that his shop was empty.

'No thank you.' She walked away. Everything about this place was breathtaking. The cars were speeding past, beeping at each other. People were laughing, talking, arguing or walking along in silence. Some of them, she thought, would be families. Some would be friends. Some would like each other and some would probably hate each other. The scale of it blew her mind and she tried to focus on the tiny things.

A jasmine bush that she could just see down a less busy road.

An ant walking up a wall.

She stood in front of the Regal Cinema and wondered what it would be like if she watched a film. She had thought everyone sat on chairs and watched a big screen together, but now she knew that phones had screens (some of them with her picture on them), and that trains didn't puff, and that cars were like bees, so she was sure she had the cinema wrong too.

All the same she had done it. She stood still for a moment next to a stall selling gold jewellery, and she appreciated the fact that she was here. She was in Mumbai and, even though she knew that Gita and Vikram would guess she had come here, it felt like the biggest place in the world, and she was sure no one would find her in the crowds. She would hide among the people.

She was in a place that she had never imagined. A part of the world that was not so far from the clearing, but that might as well have been Mars. A place that was by the sea, though she hadn't seen it yet.

She had gone from being one of eleven, to one of two, to one of seven billion. It felt like all seven billion were right here in Mumbai, all of them trying to squeeze along this pavement right now.

'You like some pretty earrings?' said another man. There were so many men. She looked at this one, hoping that he didn't know she was the girl from the woods, but he didn't seem interested in her, just in whether she wanted earrings.

'That's kind of you,' Arty said. 'But I don't really. Thanks, though.'

Lots of people were offering her stuff. She walked along, saying 'No thank you' to everything, because she knew it would be rude to ignore them. She looked at every person to see if they were Joe but all of them weren't. She pretended she was Venus, before Arty herself had been born, walking along here not much older than Arty was now. She wished she had asked her mother every single thing about her old life, rather than almost nothing.

When she noticed that a sign said LEOPOLD CAFE she stopped because she knew that Salman had said it was a place she could go. Joe might be in there. She stood in the street and looked in, because it had a big wide doorway.

There were lots of people, and those people were eating food. Arty realized that she was hungry.

A little crowd was standing outside, and a woman in uniform was in charge.

'One person?' she said when she saw Arty looking.

Arty nodded. Now there was just one of her.

The woman wanted to look inside Arty's bag, so she showed her, and the book and the bear and the other bits and pieces in there seemed to be all right. She called out to someone inside, and the man nodded and beckoned for Arty to follow him, so she did. She stepped into the cafe, pleased that she had been to one before so she didn't need to panic about what to do at this particular point. Though this one was much bigger and more clattery and echoey than the previous one. He showed her to a little table with two chairs. Arty sat on one of them and noticed the menu on the table under a glass top.

Almost every table had people at it. They were eating, and talking, and laughing. Some of them had pale skin and some were darker, and everyone seemed busy. She watched two men at a nearby table drinking from huge bottles of beer that weren't Kingfisher, but which looked the same. She stared at the list of things to eat.

Gita and Vikram must be looking for her. She could picture it. Vikram would probably have gone to work before Gita went to wake Arty up. She must have found the empty bed and the note. She would have told Pia, and everyone would be wondering where she was. And she was here, sitting in a cafe in Mumbai, all on her own.

The woman at the door was looking at her and talking to another woman. A man joined them and they all looked at Arty together, and then away.

She felt her heart pounding and turned her attention to other people's plates instead. Those two men were just drinking beer. Some women at another table were eating something that was sizzling and brown, and Arty was pretty sure it was meat. The thought made her stomach clench and she looked away, though her eyes kept stealing over to it. There was a woman on her own on the other side of her, an old white woman with short white hair. She had a plate of green sauce, with, Arty thought, vegetables, and a piece of bread.

That looked all right.

She could see that the waiter was coming and she could feel that she was breathing quickly as she tried to work out what she was going to say to him, and hoping that he wasn't going to say anything unexpected to her. She planned it in her head. Talking to a new person was still weird. Her breathing was getting faster and faster.

The old woman saw her looking. 'Everything OK there?' she said.

'What is that you're eating?' said Arty, her words tumbling over each other. 'Because I don't know what to order. And that looks nice.'

She laughed. 'It's bloody amazing, sweetie. Do it. Palak paneer with a roti. Perfect.'

'Palak paneer with a roti. What shall I get to drink?'

'What are you after, darling? Masala chai? Coffee? Mango juice? Lassi?'

Arty smiled at her. 'You are so kind,' she said. 'I *love* chai. We used to drink it a lot.'

'There you go then. Get that.'

The waiter was standing beside her. Arty had never spoken to a waiter. When they were in the other cafe Pia had done all the ordering.

She took a deep breath. 'Hello,' she said. 'Could I please have a palak paneer and a roti and a cup of masala chai?'

He nodded. 'Sure you can. Anything else? Maybe a bottle of water?'

'Yes please.'

'Right away.'

He went away and Arty turned to the woman and smiled. She couldn't help it.

'I've never ordered from a waiter before. And it worked! Thank you for helping me.'

The woman looked at her. 'You did good. The first time in your life? How old are you, darling?'

'Seventeen.' She told the lie on impulse.

'All alone?'

Arty closed her eyes. Everything was dark red and that was good. Red was the colour of blood, and blood meant life. That meant she was all right. This woman was making her feel alive by talking to her. Her words were travelling through the air into Arty's ears, and Arty's brain was taking meaning from them. She was here. She was present. *I am present in the universe.* Her feet, in their green flip-flops, were on the ground. She felt the floor of the cafe through them, and she knew there was earth beneath that, and that it went down and down to the liquid centre of the planet.

'Yes,' she said. 'Yes. I'm alone.'

The woman patted the other side of her own table. 'Join me? We lone wolverines should stick together.'

'Thank you.' Arty moved herself and her bag across to the other table. The woman made some signal to the waiter, and in no time at all two more people (they looked like a couple, and they were talking in Hindi about a wedding they were going to) were seated where Arty had just been.

'So,' said the woman. 'Tell me about it. First, are you OK? How does someone so young as you find herself alone in Mumbai? And sorry – you talk kind of like the Queen of England, and you look like you could be local, maybe. Not that it's any of my business. Are you a tourist, I guess is what I mean? Backpacker? Though I imagine you'd have ordered from a waiter before.'

'I'm not a tourist,' Arty said, and time stopped for a moment.

She saw in a flash that what she said now was going to be the thing that defined who she was out here. This woman had clearly not seen her on 'social media' like the train man had. She didn't need to know.

She remembered Diana in the clearing saying that there were some things that you could call into being just by naming them. She froze as Diana's voice spoke, clear and real, in her head. It was so real that she wondered why everyone in the cafe hadn't stopped what they were doing to listen.

It was a lesson they were having, sometime before the last Kotta.

'You might not understand this now, Arty,' Diana's voice said, 'but at times the words are the thing itself. You make it happen by speaking it. The police, out there, they would say, "You're under arrest," and the words made it true. The same applied to weddings, for what *that's* worth. You say the words to the right person. You're married. The thing you speak can become your reality by the fact that you've spoken it.'

She remembered her mother saying, 'Look at the world out there. See it for yourself . . . You could have an adventure and come back.'

Arty put those two things together. She reframed her life. She was going to make a new reality by speaking it.

She turned back to the woman. 'I don't think I'm a backpacker,' she said. 'I don't really know what one is. I've never been anywhere apart from India. I live in a community with people from lots of different countries, but I've lived in the same place all my life.' She took a deep breath and went on. 'I'm seventeen and I've come to Mumbai on my own because it was time for me to see the real world. I've got some money, and I'm here for a year. My family are all at home waiting for me. This is my year of learning.'

It sounded good. She liked it a lot.

'Ohhhh-kaaayyyyy,' said the woman. 'Kind of like a gap year?'

'Yes.' That was nice. 'It's my gap year. That's exactly what it is.'

'But,' said the woman, 'you're coming to it from a place where you've been . . . sheltered?'

'Yes.'

'And your community – is it far from here?'

'It's in the forest. It's very, very far away. I came on a train. I have lots of money. It's here, in my bag. Eighteen and a half thousand rupees.'

'Oh, God,' she said. 'Be careful what you say to random people in cafes, darling. I'm all right. And that's lucky. And eighteen and a half thousand rupees sounds fabulous, but please tell me it's not supposed to last you an entire year?'

'No. I need to get a job.'

The woman sipped her wine and looked at Arty with eyes that seemed to see everything.

'Your community,' the woman said. 'Would it be a religious one?'

Arty relaxed a little. 'No. At least, not really. We're all gods and goddesses. My mum is called Venus. She had a different name when she was in the world, but her name's Venus now because everyone at home has god and goddess names. Venus is the goddess. She's in charge. We do yoga, and stretches, and breathing exercises. We say mantras. We thank the land for feeding us and we thank the water, and we thank the forest and . . . things.' She stopped, overwhelmed.

The woman changed. Her eyes were interested.

'A *matriarchy*? Now you're talking my language. You live in a functioning matriarchy? So they didn't throw you out? It sounded for a moment as if you were living in some awful religious place. I was picturing a patriarch who expelled you for refusing to know your place, or for being pregnant or something. It's not that?'

'It's the opposite of that. I'm here because it was time for me to see the outside. There are eleven of us in the clearing. I was the first child born and I'm the only one who's completely grown up there. I've never met anyone my own age. The adults set it up twenty years ago, so they've all come from out here and they know what it's like and how different we are. But I didn't. I have little brothers and a sister but they're younger.'

Arty felt swamped with relief. She had spoken everyone back to life, and now they were alive inside her and inside this woman's mind too. She had plucked Zeus away from Florence, erased her existence, and sent him back to the clearing to be happy. It felt good.

'I'm Cherry.' The woman extended her hand and Arty reached back, not quite sure what she was meant to do. Cherry held her hand and shook it up and down.

'I'm Arty. Are we *shaking hands*?'

'Good to meet you, Arty. Yes, we are. So you chose to do this?'

'I did.'

'They let you go? You didn't run away?'

'They let me go. I sold our herbs, and that's how I got this money. I have to find my uncle Matthew or maybe our friend, Persephone, because she used to live with us but then she left. I think she's in London. Matthew might be there too but I'm not sure. I'm going to spend a year here, living in the world, working, seeing how it all works, and then I can choose whether to go back, or to stay here, or to do a bit of both.'

'Oh my God,' Cherry said. 'Just – wow. I'm surprised they'd send someone so vulnerable out like that. It's harsh, but I guess if you're going to your uncle or a friend of the family . . . Still. Mumbai, alone?'

Arty felt defensive. 'I wanted to go. It's not as if I can't go back if I need to. I can go back any time.'

'When did you arrive?'

'In Mumbai? Today.'

'And where are you going to sleep tonight, my darling?'

Arty hadn't expected to be anyone's darling, here.

'I don't know,' she said, feeling a little bit warm. 'I know one person in Mumbai. He's called Joe and I met him in Lonavala. He was kind to me. He helped me a lot. He's going to a meditation thing tomorrow, but I don't know where he is today. I thought he might be in this cafe but he's not.'

He had also, Arty now knew, put photos of her up on the internet. She didn't understand how that worked, but in some weird way he had made people know about her. That was what the man on the train had said. She didn't like that, so she didn't tell Cherry. She would forget about it. She was making an effort not to think about it. Even if he had done that, he was still her only friend. She still wanted to see him again. She wondered why he had disappeared.

'You got his email? His cell phone?'

Arty nodded, took the paper out of her pocket and unfolded it. She pushed it across the table to Cherry.

Cherry took out her own phone. 'Want to call him?'

'Yes! Yes please!'

She watched Cherry tapping her phone. Cherry put it to her ear then passed it to Arty.

This was another new thing. She was using a phone. She had a phone pressed to her ear like people did in books, and it was making a sound that was definitely not Joe's voice. She listened to it for a bit, and then it stopped and a woman's voice asked if she'd like to leave a message.

'Do I want to leave a message?' she said to Cherry.

Cherry nodded. 'Just say whatever you want to say to him and he'll hear it later.'

'Hello, Joe,' she said. 'This is Arty. I'm trying to find you.'

'Tell him to call back on this number,' said Cherry.

'Call back on this number,' Arty said. Then she said, 'Love from Arty,' and hung up.

'You are *adorable*,' Cherry said. 'Well, let's hope he calls back soon.' She put the phone down on the table so they could easily answer it if it rang. 'So, let me get this straight. Your plan was that you would walk around and hope to run into him?'

'Yes.'

Cherry grinned. 'Mumbai has a population of around eighteen million. I looked that up before I came here. You're not likely to find him by happy chance. Good thing we called him.'

'Eighteen million?'

'I know, right? Me too. And I'm from San Francisco, and there are enough of us there. Let alone growing up in a community of eleven.'

Arty knew she couldn't imagine that many people, so she put the thought from her head. 'So what should I do?' she said. 'And then how do I get to London?'

Cherry had a kind face. Arty had never spoken to anyone as old as she was before. She stared at the lines

156

around her mouth and nose. They were nice, she thought. They showed all the ways Cherry had moved her face for her whole life.

'I'm not sure how you get to London,' Cherry said. 'Like you said, I guess you'll need to gather a bit more money. Or could you contact your uncle or your friend? Give me their numbers and I'll call them for you. They'll surely send you the funds you need.'

'I don't have their numbers,' said Arty. 'We don't know what they are.'

'OK. Emails then?'

'No.'

'Hmm. What are you supposed to do?'

Arty forced a smile. 'I'll find a way.'

'Darling,' said Cherry, 'do you have an ID card of any sort?'

'What's that?'

'ID. Identification. A passport or anything like that?'

'No. I don't.'

'In the countryside you were OK with finding accommodation? I guess it could be different out there. Here you're going to find it difficult to find a room without ID. At the very least, a photocopy of your passport and visa – that's what I always need. They all ask for that if you're foreign, or for your ID card if you're an Indian national. Which would you even be? An Indian national, I guess. We can't have you sleeping on the street, but hotels are breaking the law if they let you stay without ID, and they won't do it. You don't have anything at all?'

'Nothing. I've never had anything with my name on it.' Arty tried to think about it, but she was still excited about the fact that she had brought her family back to life for Cherry. 'I stayed with people in Lonavala. I think I'll get a train back out to the forest and sleep there. I know how to sleep in forests. I'm just . . . not good when there are people around.' She looked outside. 'I don't think I could sleep *there*. But isn't there just a room I could stay in? One someone's not using?'

Cherry sighed. 'You'd think, wouldn't you? Welcome to the modern world. Out here we have outrageously rich people, and people dying of starvation. People sleep in the streets while huge luxury apartment blocks are empty.'

'Why can't the people in the street sleep in the luxury places?'

She shrugged. 'Exactly. Why can't they? Because somehow the system has stopped that happening. We, the people at large, are given television and iPhones and celebrity gossip to stop us thinking, while corporations screw us over again and again and again. The media pushes its own narrative, which is that homeless people are bad and scary and brought it on themselves, and the rich deserve to pay no taxes because they've worked hard, and then everyone's happy to shove out the poor, the disabled, the women, the people with differently coloured skin . . . to push all of them, anyone who can be reframed as "other", under the bus.'

'Push them under the *bus*?'

'Oh, not literally, sweetie. I'm so sorry. I'm an old Marxist and I started to rant. Your mother would be with me on this, I imagine. The bus was a metaphor.'

Arty was a bit scared. 'So I have to find a place to sleep. I'll go to the forest.'

'No. You're not getting a train to some random patch of woodland. Safety, for one thing. Hmm.'

She looked at Arty, and Arty understood for the first time the phrase 'a twinkle in her eye'. She had never actually seen anyone with that before, but now she could see it in Cherry.

'Your eyes are twinkling,' she said. 'Like someone in a book.'

Cherry laughed very loudly. 'It's because I'm plotting,' she said. 'Also like someone in a book.'

She stopped talking when the waiter tried to deliver Arty's tea to the wrong table, before bringing it to the right place. Arty wasn't comfortable yet with someone doing something for her, without her doing something nice for them in return, but she supposed she was paying the money as a token that would allow him to do something nice. Still, it felt awkward.

'Thank you very much,' she said to him, and he told her she was welcome and that the food would be along in a minute.

She turned back to her new friend. 'What are you plotting?'

'Well,' said Cherry, 'I shouldn't. But anyway. Just for tonight I think I can give you shelter. This is my last night here so if they throw us out in the morning, who cares? I'm in an Airbnb in Bandra and, although I shouldn't have anyone else staying on pain of all kinds of dire things, I think we'll find a way. I have a huge room and enough cushions to make you a spot on the floor. Obviously I'm not suggesting we share a bed or anything so don't worry about weirdness. The landlady is a sweetie, so I feel bad, but I can't ask her because she'd have to say no.'

'Did you say Bandra?'

'I did. It's across town from here.'

Arty couldn't believe that she had said that word.

'That's where the Bollywood people live.'

'It is! Two of them on my street, apparently.'

'Can we go to AMK's house?'

Cherry was laughing. 'You've never ordered a drink from a waiter, yet you know who AMK is?'

'Salman told me about him. The taxi driver. AMK is the greatest movie star who ever lived.'

'Salman the taxi driver? How much did he charge?'

'Nothing. He said it was a present from him to me.'

'And he didn't . . . ask you for anything else?'

Arty shook her head. 'Like what?'

'Never mind. Just wearing my cynical hat.' She saw Arty's face. 'Oh, not a real hat. Though I'd love to know what a cynical hat would be like. In one of my previous lives I worked in fashion, and I would love to make you a cynical hat, my dear, to guide you on this gap year. Yes, we can go to AMK's house. Of course we can. But first tell me more about your society, Ms Goddess.'

Arty's food arrived, and she ate it while telling Cherry about the way life in the clearing worked. Her current life. Her happy life. She pretended with all of her might. It was hard to talk about it, but she did it. She brought it back and made it real with her words.

'So you'll come to stay with me tonight,' Cherry said when she had finished. 'That's settled. My room's in the basement. Kind of underground, though there's a window of sorts. One night only, but it's something, isn't it?'

Arty nodded. 'Thank you very much,' she said. 'I've never been underground.'

She remembered Venus saying, 'Don't go into the basement,' but she thought she couldn't have meant this one.

'That's OK,' said Cherry. 'It's a gorgeous room. You'll like it.'

JUNE

It got worse, because now I was in more trouble. After I hurt her and ran up the stairs she was a lot meaner with me. She was furious. But it wasn't as if she could do much, because she could hardly make my life any worse than she already had.

The days went on. I sank into despair. I looked to my cartoon friends for help, but they were lethargic too, lying around in the corners of the rooms, sleeping or staring into space. For a long time we just watched television and did nothing. I lost track of the days and weeks.

I had my list of ideas. I knew that the next thing on my list was to try to attract attention from the world outside, but I had already hammered on the door at the top of the stairs and that had done me no good at all. I had tried to make a sign for the window but I couldn't get it up high enough even with the bluebirds helping me lift it, and anyway I knew that there was a little wall between that and the pavement. I threw some things at the high window but nothing happened, so I moved down the list.

Next: convince her I was sorry. That one wouldn't work so soon after hurting her.

I was down to my final option.

When I had the energy, when I felt the time was right, then I was going to start a fire.

11

Cherry's room was inside the front door, then down some stairs. Arty wasn't good at stairs, and she went down them slowly, feeling ahead with each foot, lowering herself gently. It was different from going up and down the two broad steps in the clearing or a ladder. She had had to concentrate hard on the stairs in Vikram and Gita's house, and in the hospital they had used a lift, which had made Arty feel sick. She kept a hand on the wall and concentrated.

Ahead of her Cherry turned round. 'Are you all right, sweetie?' she said.

Arty couldn't look at her. She had to look at her feet. But she nodded, knowing Cherry was watching.

'Haven't done this much before,' she managed to say, frowning, and made it to the bottom of the stairs.

Cherry breathed all her breath out at once in a big huff.

'Of course you haven't,' she said. 'Wow. Yes. That makes sense. Take your time. It takes as long as it takes.'

The walls were white, with a picture of an elephant on one of them. The floor was cold, with rugs on it. The last rug Arty had seen had been in Venus and Vishnu's bedroom. There was a bed, the same sized bed that Arty's parents had slept in. There was a little light next to the bed. It had a black wire snaking around the floor and into the wall. There was a photo of a man beside the bed, a man with much darker skin than Cherry's, and Arty didn't know who he was. Next to him there was a photo of a woman, who was old, like Cherry. She had dark skin and white hair. There was a book on the table, some clothes on a chair, a suitcase in the corner.

She felt her heart pounding. Arty gasped for breath, forcing it into her lungs, forcing it out again. No breath was quite enough.

'I need to do something,' she said quietly, then gasped for air.

'Sure.'

Arty stood in the middle of the room and managed to say: 'I see the white wall with a picture of an elephant.' Her voice was a hoarse whisper. She breathed in and out. 'I hear the traffic outside.' In, and out. 'I smell the chemicals from the house, I think. I touch my shoes with the soles of my feet, and the soles of my shoes touch the floor of this room and the floor touches the earth. I taste the traffic and the chemicals. I am present in the universe. I am here, in Cherry's room. I'm Artemis and I am here in the outside world, with Cherry. Cherry is my friend. I am present.'

She breathed slowly in, held her breath, and breathed out again.

After a while she felt a touch on her shoulder.

'You OK?' said Cherry, and Arty took Cherry's hand and held it very tightly. The meditation had worked, just about. It had calmed her enough. She nodded.

'I'll show you what I do,' said Cherry.

She took two pillows from the bed and put them on the ground, then took a candle from a shelf and put it between them and lit it. Arty looked at the box of matches she used, the way she swooshed a match across the side of the box and made a flame appear. She watched her light the candle and breathed in the smell of jasmine that filled the room. Cherry took a little bell and rang it. It made a tinkly jingly noise.

Cherry took Arty's hand and started chanting. '*Om*,' she said, and she kept it going until the vibration of the word went right through Arty, through the middle of her. She joined in. Then Cherry changed it to '*Om mani padme hum*' and Arty joined that too.

She closed her eyes, but the candle still flickered. She sank into the moment, losing herself, finding herself, letting go. *I see the flame through my eyelids. I smell the candle. I hear our chanting. I feel the pillow and Cherry's hand.*

After a while she felt all right, so she stopped chanting and opened her eyes.

Cherry carried on for a bit then stopped and laughed. 'How was that?' she said.

'So much better!' said Arty. 'Thank you. Thank you for letting me come to your home. Thank you. Can I just do one more thing?'

'Sure you can, darling.'

'Right.' Arty kept hold of Cherry's hand and put her other hand on the top of Cherry's head. She had no idea what to say so she made up the words, trying to make them sound right. 'As a goddess of the clearing I use my power and the strength of the universe to pass it on to you. You, Cherry, are now an honorary goddess because you have shown kindness and love to me. We welcome you.'

She couldn't think what else to say, so she sang a little bit of 'Respect', and to Arty's amazement Cherry actually joined in. Her voice was lovely.

'You know the words!' Arty was astonished.

'It's a famous song. A wonderful one.'

'Oh. I thought it was just ours.'

'It's everyone's. It's amazing. Here – do you want to hear it?'

Cherry went and fetched her phone and fiddled with it for a moment. Then she put it down and smiled at Arty.

The song started to play. It was huge. There were sounds in it that Arty had never heard before. It made her skin shiver. It made her heart beat faster. She couldn't breathe. She had never heard anything like it. It was the song and the words she knew, but bigger, bolder, wildly exciting.

'Oh,' she said. 'I had no idea. I could never have imagined.'

'And thank you so much, my dear. That means more than you can possibly know. I am honoured to be a goddess. Tell me – just how remote is your clearing? It seems like it's a million miles away from this late capitalist world, but it's clearly not. Not in miles at least.'

'It is remote,' said Arty. 'It's a place you can live in for sixteen or seventeen years and only sometimes see an aeroplane and nothing else. It's behind a fence with a sign that says "Danger Radiation", but I think we must have put that there to stop people going in. It took me all day to walk from the clearing to the fence. Then we went in a car to Lonavala. It was horrible.'

'Fascinating,' said Cherry, and there was something in her eyes that she didn't say.

Arty looked at the photographs beside her bed. 'Who are they?' she said.

Cherry glanced over at the photograph, then away. 'That man is my stepson, Barney. The woman is Alisha. We were together for twenty years, and she left me.' They were still sitting cross-legged on the floor.

'Did she die?'

'No. She really did just leave. She had enough of me.'

'Oh. That's mean.'

'It wasn't really. It was just time to go separate ways. We'd been clashing for years. But Barney's my son in all but biology and I miss him more than Alisha. So my path brought me to Mumbai. Which I'm OK with. Well, this is my home for today, and it's your home too now that you've chanted in it and made me a goddess. We'll make you a bed on the floor with these pillows. I think you'll be comfortable.'

*

Late in the afternoon they went to stand outside AMK's house. It was easy to find. Cherry just typed into her phone to ask where it was, and the phone directed them there. It was a six-minute walk from Cherry's room.

Arty loved it: it turned out that the other people outside his house were friendly to her, and they all agreed with her that AMK was the greatest movie star of all time. His house was huge, though it was hard to see it because there was a high wall and there were tall trees with lots of flowers on them. Still, she could count six floors, and the idea of all those stairs made her dizzy.

There was a sudden commotion.

'Look!' shouted a man, and everyone was pointing and getting their phones out.

'What?' said Arty to a woman with lovely food. They were all excited by something in the house but Arty didn't know what.

'Someone at the window!' the woman said, gazing intently.

Arty could see it if she looked very hard. The outline of a person standing at a window on the nearly top floor.

'Is it AMK?'

'Maybe one of the family. Or staff.'

Arty was excited as any of them by that. She could see that Cherry was enjoying herself too. She asked Cherry if she could leave another message for Joe; when he didn't answer again she said: 'Hello, Joe – it's Arty again. Please come and find me in Mumbai. I'm outside AMK's house. You can easily find that. Love from Arty.'

She ended the call carefully by pressing the red circle and handed it back.

When Cherry said it was time to leave they walked down to the sea. Although she had glimpsed it in the distance when they arrived in Bandra, this was the first time she had been able to concentrate on it.

'Oh my God,' Arty said, staring at the waves, just as Cherry's phone rang.

She looked at the screen and said, 'Sorry, darling. It's not Joe, but I do have to answer. Hey – Barney!' She made some kind of gesture with her hand that Arty thought meant she wouldn't be long.

Arty nodded. She didn't mind how long Cherry was on the phone. She just wanted to be near her, and she would stare at the water for any amount of time.

So much water in one place moving around. If she stood in this spot staring forever, she still wouldn't understand it. Sometimes she tried to turn away and pretend it was normal, like everyone else did, but she couldn't help spinning back and looking again. It was as big as land, but it was made of water. If you stood on it, you would fall through and get wet. It made the air smell different. It was a place where they couldn't make buildings or shops. She pictured the wind blowing across the ocean, picking up bits of water and salt as it went, blowing them into her face.

A bird landed on the water and sat there, bobbing around.

There were stones and rocks leading down to it, and then there was sand.

Cherry punched the air with her right arm, even though the person on the other end, *Barney*, wouldn't be able to see that. Arty only heard a few words, when she almost shouted, 'Well, maybe your biological mother?' And another time: 'Actually I'm with a friend. No, not like that at all.'

Even though the bottom of AMK's house wasn't beside the sea, Arty could see his top windows. She waved just in case he was watching and wondered whether AMK could control the ocean like gods could in stories. She knew he was a human, but she still wondered.

Cherry stopped her phone call and started another. Arty looked at her in her red trousers and her black T-shirt. Cherry was much older than Venus. Maybe she was what a *grandmother* would be like. She thought that one day she should get her own hair cut short like Cherry's. She liked it that, out here, you could make your hair be however you wanted it to be, that there were people whose job was changing other people's hair. She had found that fascinating, walking with Cherry earlier, and had made her stop so she could stare at people casually snipping other people's hair with scissors, letting clumps of it fall to the floor.

She walked along the path that went beside the sea, away from Cherry and away from AMK's house. She sat on a rock on the beach, her bag beside her, and looked out at the water. After a while she stood up, her lungs full of the salty air, and picked her way back up the beach to the path. She turned and set off back towards Cherry.

A few seconds later she heard someone shout, 'Excuse me! Stop please!' and when she looked over her shoulder there was a man who she thought was a policeman running after her.

She could not let this happen.

They were not going to take her now.

She took a deep breath of fresh air and ran as fast as she could. She ran and ran, and she could hear that the policeman was running after her. She ran towards Cherry, who was still on the phone, and past her. Lots of people were in her way and she ran past them too, but she could hear the footsteps getting closer and then there was a hand on her shoulder, pulling her back, and she had to stop.

It was a man in uniform, so he had to be a policeman, she thought. He pulled her round so she was facing him. He was tall and skinny, and for some reason he was laughing a bit.

It flashed through her brain the way things might go from here. She would be in trouble for running away. She would be taken to a new foster home and they would watch her all the time, and lock her in at night so she couldn't run away, and the people wouldn't be as nice as Gita and Vikram. She took great gulps of air and tried to shout to Cherry to come and rescue her.

'Sorry to scare you,' the policeman said in Hindi. 'You dropped this.' And that was when she saw that he was holding her bear.

Her precious bear from the clearing, with 'Love You Loads X' written on the heart it was holding, was squashed in his hand.

She grabbed it and looked at him. 'Are you a policeman?' she said, because she was too scared to say thank you.

'Me? No, not a cop,' he said. 'Just on my way to work. I'm a security guard. Why? Why were you running so hard from someone you thought was the police?'

Arty forced her mouth to smile at him.

'No reason,' she said, and then she saw that Cherry was there and she let all her breath out at once and clutched the bear and leaned on Cherry and pretended to think it was all funny.

JUNE

Once there had been camping stoves here, but now there weren't. There was nothing to use for fire. I was going to need to find a way to make it, or else I was going to have to steal something from her, some matches or something, and start it with that.

A cartoon firefly flew past me, humming a tune. I put out a hand to catch it. I had wanted to talk to this one for a long time. For the first time it flew straight into my hand. It stood on my arm, its feet tickling me. I wished I could use it to start my fire, but I knew it didn't work like that.

'How do I make a fire?' I said.

It smiled at me. It had a human face. It had my mother's face, in fact. I looked away, then forced myself to look back at it.

'Electrickery,' it whispered.

I nodded. It was right: the only thing that was fiery down here was electricity, but I didn't know how electricity worked. I certainly didn't know enough about it to pull it out of the wall and get a spark from it.

Starting a fire was going to be the most dangerous thing of all. I needed to give myself the best chance possible of being rescued. I decided that, when I had a way of starting it (when I managed to steal something from her, somehow), I would try to do it when she was down here. Otherwise she was probably mad enough just to let me burn.

I watched a television programme about electrical fires. I looked at pictures of people's houses, all black and sooty after the fire had been put out, and I wished they would be more specific about how those fires had started in the first place.

I started making a pile of stuff that would be good to burn. There were books, some shelves, some blankets that I didn't need. I put them under the window so the people outside would notice the flames as soon as they began.

I waited. Sooner or later she would bring something down here that would help me.

12

Arty had a nice evening with Cherry. Cherry took photos of the two of them together too, but she promised she wouldn't show them to anyone, and Arty believed her. She slept better on Cherry's floor than she had since Kotta day.

Cherry only asked her once why she had run away from the security man, and Arty said, 'Because I was scared,' and Cherry didn't ask any more. In the morning, though, Cherry said Arty had to go to the police station.

They had an argument about it.

'You *have* to, sweetie,' she said. 'I would never forgive myself if I left you fending for yourself in the city. You could come with me on the train to Dharamsala, but again that's not straightforward without ID. The police will help you get documents and then everything will be open to you. I think they'll be on your side, darling.'

'I need to stay in Mumbai,' Arty said. There was no way she was going to the police.

'You need an ID card of some sort. You just do.'

'Why does everyone have to have a piece of paper to say who you are? Why can't we just exist?'

'That's a good abstract philosophical point, but we can't change the way the world works *today*. You can't have the law adjusted to suit you *right now*.'

They were having breakfast, sitting on the wall looking out at the sea. Cherry had agreed that they could go to AMK's house for a bit after this. Her train was at five past four in the afternoon. Arty had the basis of a plan: she was going to let Cherry think she was going to the police, and then run away.

Arty put a piece of pakora into her mouth. That was the name of the food the woman had given her yesterday. She wanted to eat it every day. The sun was shining on her head. She was eating nice food. She had slept deeply and that made her mind feel sharper. She was considering jumping on the train with her friend and going to whatever Dharamsala meant. Cherry said she was going to be on lots of trains for a long time. Arty thought that sounded fine.

'OK then,' said Arty. 'But how about if I come to the train station with you, and then go to the police? I can say goodbye to you properly. You're a goddess. You should have another goddess waving to you.'

Cherry grinned. Arty loved the way her face crinkled when she smiled.

'Nice try, miss. I'm taking you through the door of the police station myself, and that's final.'

Arty shrugged and looked away.

They watched the sea breathing in and out, the waves on the shore, the washing drying on the rocks. The wind was blowing salty water into her face. Arty wanted her old life back, but she also wished she had not been quite so isolated from all of this.

After standing outside AMK's for a while (a car went in! But its windows were blacked out), Cherry said, 'Right. We've still got a few hours. I want to show you one more place.'

'Yes please!' said Arty.

They caught a rickshaw to Bandra station and Cherry bought them return tickets to a station whose name Arty didn't catch.

It was nice seeing things with Cherry. Arty knew she was safe.

Arty loved it on the train. She loved being crammed in with the people, because she and Cherry were both goddesses.

They got off at a station called Mahalakshmi.

'Come on,' said Cherry. 'Just a quick look, and then we'll head back. You said you liked doing laundry, right? It makes you feel like Rumpelstiltskin?'

'I did.' Arty remembered doing the laundry with Zeus, when Hercules was ill. She put it from her mind again, and calmed her breathing, and stayed in control of herself as she followed Cherry out of the station and round to stand on a bridge.

Cherry pointed and Arty looked out and saw that there was a little city there, below where they were standing, and that it was filled with washing. 'The Dhobi Ghat,' said Cherry.

Arty stared and stared. There was a rooftop full of white shirts hanging on lines. A lot of sheets, all pinned up in rows. She could see people doing the laundry, scrubbing at things in vats of water. Everywhere, washing was hung up to dry. It was on every rooftop, and there was a vat of washing water in every space. This was a whole town of laundry.

Arty stared. 'I could do that!' she said. 'I could get a job here, Cherry! I could work here, and then they'd pay me money and I could use that to buy my ticket to London. I wouldn't have to try to grow herbs in secret!'

'Oh, darling.' Cherry put an arm round Arty's shoulders. 'And that is why I'm taking you to get official help. You absolutely *cannot* start growing weed. Did your friend Joe explain why it had to be secret? Because it's highly illegal, here in particular. That is the worst idea I've ever heard, and I've heard some bad ideas in my time. Also, I think you'd have to wash a hell of a lot of sheets to buy a plane ticket to London.'

Arty could see there were stairs going down into the Dhobi Ghat and she set off carefully, holding the wall beside her with both hands.

'Arty!' said Cherry, but she followed. Arty had known she would. Down at street level there was a row of shops, and they walked along past them all without looking. At the end people started saying, 'Tour of the Dhobi Ghat?' but more to Cherry than to Arty, and she said no to all of them.

At the end of the path there were stalls selling food. A very small breeze blew a stench into Arty's face and her stomach turned over. She had to sit down, and then to put her head in her hands and try to breathe. She could feel pakora in her stomach churning around. She was going to be sick. That was not the smell of food.

'Oh shit,' said Cherry, and she sat down next to her.

Arty couldn't turn her head. Every part of her was writhing. She thought she had the plague. This was how Venus had felt, and Hercules and Hella and Luna and the others. She turned her head aside. It was too much. The world went sick round the edges, and Arty was back in the clearing. She could see dried sick, blood, bodies in her home. Most of all it was bodies. Now it had finally got her too.

This was the smell of rotting flesh.

She could see the bodies of all her family. They were right there. In her head she saw her parents' bodies, even though she had never seen them in reality. She saw her mother's dead eyes. She saw her father lying like Hercules had, a shell with none of his essence there. She remembered Hercules, Diana, Hella, Luna. She could not bear it.

'I am present,' she muttered. 'I am here in Mumbai. I'm in the Wasteland. I see nothing. I hear nothing. I feel nothing. I smell death. I am with Cherry.'

I am with Cherry. That was the part that pulled her back. She opened her eyes and saw a table with severed animals' heads on it (sheep or goats – something like that) and there were cats underneath licking up the dripping blood. That was the thing that smelled.

She was sick, noisily sick, on the dusty road. A dog ran over and started eating it up.

'Oh, darling.' Cherry was cradling her in her arms and Arty succumbed, leaning into her, feeling her heartbeat. 'Oh, sweetie. Come on. Let's get you out of here. Sorry. Oh God, I'm so sorry. I only wanted to show you the laundry because I thought you'd like it. I had no idea . . .'

A few people were nearby, and Arty thought from the tones of their voices that they were being kind. She couldn't do any more breathing or meditation because everything smelled of death, so she took shallow breaths instead and forced her legs to stand up so she could get away.

'That went well,' said Cherry later. They were in a rickshaw, with Cherry's backpack on the floor, on their way to take Arty to the police station before Cherry's train. 'I'm so sorry, darling. I had no idea there would be a table of goats' heads. I just thought you'd like the laundry city.'

'I did like it.' Arty was largely recovered now. 'It was amazing. It's like a whole city all about washing. It was so interesting. I really loved it a lot. Thank you. I suppose I should stay away from dead things.'

She stopped. She hadn't meant to say it quite like that.

'You should really. Those goats' heads were . . . intense.' Cherry smiled. 'I know. I stopped eating meat about twenty years ago. I was vegan for a long time too, but that paneer kind of tempted me out of it since I've been here. People still see animals as being there for humans to do what they like with. It's not fair.'

'It's really not.'

'Sorry.'

'Stop saying sorry! I'm sorry. I was sick on the road. That was pretty horrible.'

Cherry grinned. 'You gave a stray dog a meal. You know what, Arty? I'm going to miss you very much. I know we only met yesterday, but it's one of the most fortuitous encounters I've ever had. You must solemnly swear to keep in touch with me, one goddess to another?'

'I solemnly swear. Goddesses.'

'Tell me what happens next. What the police do. When you get to London. We will meet again. I know it.'

'I know it too.'

'As soon as you're in a place with technology, what will you do?'

'I'll log into my email: *artyvenus@gmail.com*. Password: *goddesses*.'

'Good. There will be plenty of messages from me waiting for you when you do. I promise you that.'

They had set up the email on Cherry's phone, trying different combinations of important words until they found one that hadn't already been taken by someone else. Arty hadn't got her head around how it worked, but Cherry said all she needed was her email address and password, which she shouldn't tell to anyone else, and she would be ready to go.

The rickshaw stopped. 'Police, madam,' said the driver.

'It's just me getting out here,' Arty told him in Hindi, knowing that Cherry wouldn't understand. 'So drive her to the station as soon as I'm out. Whatever she says, she has to get to the station quickly. Thanks!'

'Of course.'

She and Cherry hugged. Arty said, 'I'm fine. I promise. Go and get your train and have a lovely time in the north.'

'You promise?'

Cherry did not want to leave her. Arty could see that. But Arty had made sure they left late, so there wouldn't be time for Cherry to come with her.

'Yes.'

'If this doesn't work, you can go back home.'

'I will.'

She walked into the police station until she heard the buzzing of the rickshaw's engine and knew that they were driving away.

A promise wasn't one of those things that became true just by being spoken. It was just a word. There was, Arty thought, nothing binding about it. Nobody's world had changed when she said 'Yes'.

'Can I help you, miss?' said a young man behind a counter.

Arty's heart started pounding again. She did not like being so close to the police.

'No thanks,' she said. 'Sorry. I was just feeling a bit ill and I came in because I thought you might have air conditioning.' She had no idea where that came from, but it seemed to work.

He smiled. 'Sorry. No air con here! Maybe one day!'

Arty smiled back and left.

Cherry's rickshaw had gone.

She was alone.

JUNE

I only had to wait a couple of days, and then the moment arrived. By this point I had an excellent collection of flammable things in the corner, and she hadn't realized that was what I was doing. She thought I was pulling the silly books apart and piling the pages up because her stupid prison had driven me mad, and I could see that she liked that. She liked breaking my mind.

My friends had started to talk to her, and she always thought it was me. We enjoyed that, me and the teddy and the rabbit and the kitten and all the mice and the birds and the monkey and the pigs.

'She doesn't love you,' the bear had said one time, and it turned its heart towards me, the embroidery saying 'She Hates You Loads X'.

'I do love you,' she'd said with a sigh. 'And please stop talking like that.'

I had moved the box that the toys had been in over to the door, and they were going to jump into it when the fire started so I could rescue them. The others, the cartoon ones, would just vanish and meet us on the outside. The box was up against the wall, covered in a T-shirt, looking like a bit of mess but not one that you would particularly notice. There was nothing else in here I cared about. In fact, I couldn't wait to burn every single bit of the prison to ash.

She came in huffing away, and she sat down next to me on the mattress. She looked at me with her one watery eye and touched her hair, which was looking thin. She touched the piratey patch over her other eye. She hadn't lost her eye or anything. She'd just hurt it a bit. She was wearing a necklace that said MUM on it.

All the animals had put patches over their eyes too. They stood behind her copying everything she did.

'You do know that this is because I love you,' she said.

'You do know that this is because I love you,' mimicked the animals.

'Oh, stop that,' she said, and she started to cry, then made herself stop. I pulled my hair across my face. I was going to cut my hair as soon as I had scissors.

'Can I cut my hair?' I said. 'Look at it!'

She made a tutting sound. 'Of course not. You think I'm going to give you a pair of scissors after this?' She touched her eyepatch.

'A pair of scissors after this?' said the chorus, and they all touched their eyepatches.

'It'll be better soon,' I said.

'I know it will, but you'd do it again, wouldn't you?'

'I wanted to get out.'

'And you'll be allowed out when you're ready. You're not ready. Not at all.'

We sat there together for a while, and I zoned out while she told me about people I didn't care about, and as she spoke I noticed that the rabbit was dancing round to the side of her, pointing at her apron pocket.

There was a thing in there, and I recognized it as the thing she used to use to light the ring on her cooker. You clicked it and a little spark came.

'Tell me about Mrs Bourne,' I said. 'When did you stop being friends?'

She looked at me with her one eye and gave a wicked little smile. 'That's harsh. She's a good neighbour! How can you accuse me of not liking her?'

'You don't, though, do you? Does she know I'm down here?'

'Of course not.' She told me all the things she'd disliked about Mrs Bourne for ages. 'It was when she got the new washing line,' she said. 'You remember that.'

As she spoke I moved my hand closer and closer. In the end she didn't notice me pulling the thing out of her pocket. I moved my hand without looking at it, staring into her pale eye as she spoke, watching her face contort as she talked about her friend and neighbour. I moved the thing over to my sleeping bag and pushed it underneath.

The animals cheered and danced.

She didn't notice.

'You seem a little bit better,' she said as she left. 'A little more rational.'

I took the cooker thing and practised clicking it. There was a spark inside it.

13

Arty had done something bad. She had stolen something from Cherry and she hoped that when Cherry noticed she wouldn't mind too much. Arty had picked up Cherry's passport when Cherry was in the shower. It was interesting. It was a little book filled with pages, which was not at all what Arty had expected.

It was dark blue, and unsurprisingly it said 'PASSPORT' on it, and '*United States of America*'. Arty had flicked through the pages until she found a photograph of Cherry looking cross. Surname / *Nom* / *Apellidos*, it said. ARMITAGE. Given Names / *Prénoms* / *Nombres*: MARGARET CHERYL. Not Cherry. It said she was born in 'Wisconsin, USA'. There were four pieces of paper folded and tucked into it. Two of them were copies of the page that had her photo on, and the other two were copies of the page with her visa on. Arty had stolen one of each copy and put the passport back.

If she needed a document in order to be allowed to stay anywhere, then she would use this one. She would pretend to be Cherry. The only thing that worried her was the date of birth, because she knew she couldn't pretend to be the same age as Cherry.

Arty didn't look like the photo, but neither did Cherry, and if Arty cut her hair she thought she might be all right. She didn't know what year she was born, but she worked out what it might have been by asking a tea seller what year it was now and subtracting sixteen from that. She caught a train to Churchgate and went back to Leopold's to work it out.

Leopold's cafe was the same as before except that it didn't have Cherry in it this time. It still didn't have Joe. Arty looked around, checking every person in case they were him. She did not understand why he had disappeared. She wanted to see him. She pictured his face, and she tried to imagine it into being. She needed him.

Arty was better at ordering at least. She asked for a drink of Coca-Cola (it was the best drink in the world), and borrowed a pen from the waiter to change the year of birth. It took her a while to work it out, and she had to ask the people around her some questions, but she ended up sure that Cherry's birthday was September the twenty-first, so now that was going to be Arty's birthday too. She just changed the year as carefully as she could.

When that was done she asked the man who was still trying to sell her a beautiful scarf from Kashmir where she could find somewhere cheap to stay, and he told her that she should go to the Austen Hotel just round the corner, as long as she would consider coming back to buy a scarf from him.

The hotel was a white building with cracks in the front, but Arty felt it looked friendly. On the inside it had a strong smell, but not a nasty one. There was dust and food and cleaning stuff in the air. It smelled like a place that had given travellers shelter for many years.

When she got to the desk in the main entrance they just wanted her to sign in with her passport number and nationality, so she wrote down all of Cherry's information, and pretended to be her. Margaret Cheryl Armitage. It was an odd spiky name. It didn't suit either Cherry or Arty.

'Your passport and visa,' said a man. 'I need a copy.'

'I have a copy,' she said, and she passed him the pages. She had scratched the photo with the pen lid a bit so it didn't look like anyone in particular. The man looked at it for a moment, and her heart beat very fast so she worried he could hear it, but then he put it aside without really seeming to have looked at it at all.

'Room six,' he said, pushing a key across the counter. 'Breakfast included. It will be brought to your room in the morning at eight. Veg or non-veg?'

'Veg please,' Arty said. 'Definitely veg. Thank you very much.'

A few hours later she was walking by the sea on her own, trying to keep herself whole. Maybe, she thought, she should have done what Cherry said and gone to the police. Joe had never called back, and now Cherry had gone, with her phone, which meant that Arty's link to Joe had gone too. Florence had refused to take her. No one wanted her.

I could go back to Gita and Vikram.

It was true that Gita and Vikram had seemed to want her, though they might not any more. She examined that thought, as a small child waved to her from its father's arms and she waved back.

She could live with Gita and Vikram if they would have her back. She could go back to people looking after her. People who were being paid money to look after her. Back to a place in which she was confined, given a set of rules. Nice people, but she didn't want that.

She had to get to Zeus, and she had to get to Matthew and Persephone. That was her mission. Sometimes she felt like a child, and at other times she felt older than anyone else, because she was looking at their world through different eyes. She was about sixteen, which was not a child, and so she was going to be an adult. She could do it. She would do this her way.

She was wearing a pair of red trousers that matched Cherry's, because she had seen them for sale outside Leopold's and had bought them with her money. The green flip-flops were still on her feet. She smiled down at them, a sad smile. A pair of shoes were the most constant thing in her life.

All she really wanted to do was to stand exactly where she was now, here in the tourist part of Mumbai surrounded by other people who didn't really know what they were doing, with the hot sun on her face, the people walking by as if Arty were one of them and not worthy of comment at all, the waves coming and going. The sea was a huge space in the city. It was the most calming thing to stand and stare at it, here even more than Bandra because the city was more intense.

Across the road there was a big expensive hotel and Arty imagined being in a room up there with the waves outside her window. She pictured herself lying in bed, listening to the sound of the sea as she slept. It would be the sea and traffic. All the beeping didn't scare her any more. In fact, the different tones the cars used made it sound as if they were talking to each other. You could never count to more than eight before you heard the beep of a car.

Over to her left was a big stone archway that didn't lead to anything. Arty didn't know why it was more interesting than anything else, but lots of people were walking round it and taking photos, so she took a deep breath of car-and-sea-flavoured air, and felt the salt vapour of the sea going into her lungs, and she let that power her along as she went to investigate. Perhaps it was some kind of portal, like in a story.

Arty was astonished by people. She was constantly surprised that there were so many of them and that, actually, they didn't have fights and wars and point guns at each other and rampage around stealing and killing. They just milled around each other, talking.

No one in the clearing had told her that most of the time people being together worked. She had imagined that she and her family were hiding from wars and bombs and danger, taking shelter like refugees in books.

Why didn't you tell me? she asked them. *You never mentioned the good things.*

You couldn't just walk over to the archway. You had to go through a little building first, and put your bag through a machine, and step through a rectangle that beeped or didn't beep depending on whether you were good or bad (or something like that). It didn't beep for Arty, but it did for the man next to her and she gave him a hard look. She picked her bag up again from the other side of the machine, and then she was able to go to the archway.

She looked up to the top of it and read:

ERECTED TO COMMEMORATE THE LANDING
IN INDIA OF THEIR IMPERIAL MAJESTIES
KING GEORGE V AND QUEEN MARY
ON THE SECOND OF DECEMBER MCMXI.

She had once known Roman numerals. As far as she could remember, M was a thousand, C was a hundred, so a C before an M would be nine hundred. And of course X was ten so XI would be one more than that. That should mean 1911. That was even before Cherry was born. Arty knew that for sure.

The arch was to celebrate a British king and queen arriving in 1911. An invasion. Arty was vaguely aware of the fact that the British had liked to invade places some time ago, and that India had been one of their conquests. She pictured a boat pulling up, and a man and woman in what she imagined historical royals might have worn stepping grandly on to the land and walking under this arch and into India. It was a weird thought. She wanted to walk under it herself, but she couldn't because it was blocked off with metal fences.

She smiled as she realized that she already knew about this place. She remembered Gita telling her about it. 'The Gateway of India is there, on the coast where the British monarchy first landed.' That was what she had said. Arty had not pictured this at all: she had imagined a real gate in a huge fence, like the one to the forest with the padlock round it, with kings and queens in gowns and crowns unlocking it and walking through to India as if it were theirs to take.

She walked around. It was busy here. A man tried to sell her a metal stick, and she wanted to stop and ask him what it was for, but she remembered just in time something that Cherry had said: 'Darling, if you start up conversations with people selling things, then they'll think you want to buy them and you'll leave them more disappointed.'

So she just said, 'No thank you,' and carried on walking, and sure enough the man just went to try to sell it to someone else. He didn't look disappointed at all.

She watched some people taking photos together, holding their phones out in front of them so they were all in the picture. That was a selfie. She knew that because she had taken selfies with Joe, and with Cherry, and everyone at AMK's house had taken selfies all the time. She was in some of them. She watched two women asking some foreign tourists for a selfie, and having a photo taken with them. She saw a family using one of those metal sticks to get their phone further away, and understood why the man was selling them.

She walked and looked and breathed the sea air. She calmed the voice inside her that said, *I don't know what to do.*

I can see the people and the sea and the Gateway of India.

I can hear the waves and the traffic and the voices.

I can smell the cars and the sea.

I can feel the soles of my flip-flops and the ground beneath them and the core of the Earth beneath that.

I can taste fear, because I can see a group of young men coming towards me and I don't like the looks in their eyes.

She turned to walk away but they came after her. She walked faster and they did too.

'Hello, miss,' shouted one.

The others giggled.

She walked so fast that it turned into a run. They ran after her.

One of them sprinted round to look her in the face. 'It *is*!' he said. 'Ninety-nine per cent sure!'

He was wearing jeans. So many of the men in the outside world seemed to wear jeans. They must have been hot. He put his phone up to her face, so she supposed he took a picture.

'Excuse me,' she called to the nearest people, who were a man and a woman walking hand in hand. 'Can you help me?'

They looked over and started walking towards her. 'Is there a problem?' said the man.

'Yes,' said Arty, but at the same time one of her pursuers said: 'Look! It's the girl who came out of the woods!'

She stared wildly around. Every cell in her body yelled 'RUN AWAY!' She looked for a place to go, but more people were around them now and there was no path. She was surrounded.

'I am not.' She spoke very quickly. 'Please leave me alone!'

'You vanished into thin air! The police are trying to find you!'

'No.' She spotted a space between two people and set off fast, running away from all of it. She thought of the man who had recognized her on the train from whatever Joe had put on his phone. These men had seen her on their phones too, but Cherry hadn't. She didn't understand any of it, but she knew she had to get away. She ran as fast as she could, pushing between people when she had to and yelling 'Sorry!' over her shoulder.

She looked back and saw phones held up everywhere, and then other people were coming closer just because there was a commotion. People in front of her had their phones out too and Arty wondered if this was a nightmare because everything had changed so fast.

She was not going to be taken away by the police.

She was not going to be treated as a child by people who didn't understand.

'The girl who came out of the woods!' someone shouted behind her.

'Hey, do you like the twenty-first century, Artemis?'

She ran to the security place. She was hot and her T-shirt was sticking to her armpits, and the only place she wanted to be was in her room in the hotel with the door locked behind her.

The woman security guard was watching people step through the magic beeping doorways. Arty tugged on the sleeve of her pale brown suit. The woman was annoyed, because she was trying to do her job.

'Please!' said Arty. 'Please can you make the men stop chasing me?' The woman looked round and her face changed.

'Yes,' she said. 'Yes, I can certainly do that.' She motioned Arty away with her hands and turned to shout at the crowd.

Arty went back through a rectangle and ran as fast as she could, as hot and dirty and smelly as could be, to where she thought the hotel might be.

It was easy to vanish into these streets. As soon as she was round a few corners she slowed down, because she thought a girl running was probably easier to remember than a girl walking. She walked in circles for a bit, but then the streets rearranged themselves around her and she was there, exactly where she wanted to be, on the corner of the right road.

She walked slowly up to the Austen Hotel, hoping they hadn't discovered that she wasn't Margaret Cheryl Armitage, looked behind to check no one was following, and then took a deep breath, summoning the strength of Zeus in France, and Joe wherever he was, and Cherry on her train, and her family in the clearing, and walked through the door.

She crossed the tiled floor and checked the face of the man behind the desk, hoping that he wouldn't say,

'You're the girl from the woods and everyone is looking for you.'

He didn't. He looked up, smiled a little smile and carried on writing in his book. 'One second,' he said. His name was Amir. It said so on his name badge.

'I like your pen,' she said, and she did, because it was an old-style one that could have been a feather.

'Thank you,' he said, and he put it down and reached behind him, taking the key from the hook with the number six next to it. 'Here's your key, Miss Armitage.'

'Thanks,' she said, and she smiled a very true and grateful smile; she'd forgotten she'd left her key at the desk when she'd gone out. Arty went upstairs to room six, where she closed the door and locked it with the key.

She leaned on it and breathed. She was safe again. This was her room, her own place, her piece of the outside world.

The shower was down the corridor, and she took the towel that had come with the room, and some of the little sachets of chemicals they'd left there, and spent ages getting clean. She knew that you had to smell of chemicals or people thought you were dirty, and so she made sure she did. She washed her hair twice, and washed all her body, particularly her armpits, which she had to admit were absolutely stinking.

Then she sat on her bed with wet hair, her body wrapped in a towel, and tried to work it out. This was definitely time for her to choose to be an adult. She tried to be Venus, to work out what her mother would have done.

Get ahead of them, darling, Venus said in Arty's head. *Don't let them catch you. You can do it.*

What about the social media? Arty asked her. *The phones?*

Sorry, darling, said Venus. *I don't know anything about phones. Just get to London and find Matthew and Persephone. Rescue Zeus. Kali hated her sister, you know.*

It didn't matter that the conversation was in her head; it gave her the support she needed to keep fighting.

Joe had shown Arty and Zeus that phones were not the things she thought they were.

He had taken a photo of her and done something with it, and the man from the train had shown it to her. This was where it went murky. She knew that a thing called a phone was really a camera and a map and a way of writing letters to people. However, Cherry had said, 'I don't do social media. Stopped a few years ago and, oh my God, do I feel better for it.' Arty knew that *social media* was the key. If people on *social media* knew her, that would explain why Cherry hadn't but everyone else had. Because Cherry wasn't on social media and the rest of these people were.

She wondered whether Joe had said on social media that Arty's family were dead. She wished she had a phone herself, so she could find that out, and call Cherry, and try again to find Joe. But she couldn't do any of those things.

Maybe her money could buy her a phone. She felt that she probably needed one.

She got dressed in her red trousers and T-shirt, even though they were dirty now, and washed her old clothes with soap as best she could and hung them out to dry on the rail in her bedroom. They dripped on to the floor but the floor was tiled and Arty didn't think it mattered. She considered hanging them out of the window, but that felt like a flag and she didn't want to make anyone look.

Her stomach cramped and she sighed. Her period was the very last thing she needed. She checked the bottom of her bag and found that she was at least prepared. Somewhere in the hell of the plague sweeping the clearing, her mother had remembered to pack their moon cups.

That took her almost to the edge. She screwed her eyes up. She thought of Venus packing everything she thought they might need. She realized that, in preparing for their periods, Venus had acknowledged that they were going to be away for a long time.

She lay down on her bed and tried to cling on to her mother's strength.

There was a knock on the door and it took her a while to realize where she was. She was naked on her bed, tangled up in sheets and a towel.

She put on her clothes as quickly as she could and opened the door.

'Good morning,' said Amir, and he handed her a tray that had tea and breakfast on it. She managed to thank him and take the tray, which rattled in her hands.

It was morning. She must have been asleep for a very long time. She put the tray on the floor and sat and ate her breakfast with her fingers, wrapping vegetable curry in bread and eating it as if she were at home. She was starving and the food was perfect. There were boiled eggs, and that reminded her of home because although their poor chickens had been eccentric, when they were in the mood to lay there would be eggs all the time.

She hadn't thought about the chickens. They were probably still alive, scratching around for food, wondering why no one was collecting their eggs.

She drank the tea and licked the plate. Her strength was back; now she was ready to set off to catch a train to Mahalakshmi to ask for a job in the Dhobi Ghat.

'See you later, Miss Armitage,' said Amir as she handed in her key.

'Yes,' she said. 'See you later.'

She stepped out of the hotel and no one looked at her. She started to walk towards where she hoped the station might be. It was hot and she was soon sticky. She walked around the streets a bit, and then, when she passed a place that said COMPUTER, EMAIL, INTERNET, she decided on a whim to go inside.

She hired a computer and sat down in front of it. It was surprisingly easy.

JUNE

I gathered my friends around me and we all gazed at the clicky thing. They sat at my feet and we marvelled that we had done this. She had brought a thing with a tiny spark of a flame inside it into our room, and we had stolen it.

I was feeling better. I would never admit it to her, but in myself I was beginning to feel more grounded. That was why those old demons had become my friends, I supposed.

'We need to pick a time when we'll get rescued,' I said. I was including them even though all of them but the bear, the rabbit and the monkey could fly through walls.

'We do,' said the bear. 'Daytime.'

'Daytimes,' said the rabbit, 'and busytimes.'

'Yes,' I said. 'It needs to be busytime outside, doesn't it? We need someone to call the police straight away.'

We had to start this fire as far away from the door as possible, and I had to understand that I might not get out.

I was very aware of the fact that I might actually be going to die and that the bear and the rabbit and the monkey might be going to go with me. That was a clear consequence of starting a fire when you are locked into the world's most secure basement. I was ready for that to happen.

'We don't mind,' the bear said, stroking my knee.

We tried to work out when it was busiest outside. The trouble was it was almost never busy. Still, the morning, when people were going to work, or the afternoon, when they were coming home – those were the times to go for, I thought. I kept the television on because it would occasionally tell me the time, although only on a few of the channels.

'We must do it,' said the rabbit, 'before she notices the fire thing has gone.'

'Yes,' I said. 'We must.'

It was still light outside. There were people out there, however impossible that seemed, and I knew that some of them might have mobile phones in their pockets and would be able to call for help as soon as they saw the flames.

If they saw the flames. This place was so secure, so fire-proof and bombproof, that I knew the window wouldn't smash. It had been built to keep the danger out, but instead it was going to keep the danger in.

We had a bit of a plan. I filled every container I could find (and there weren't many of them) with water, and stood them by the door. In reality this amounted to the plastic bucket she'd given me and a few plastic cups and bowls, but it was better than nothing. I would stand by the door, holding the toy box, and if no one came I would try to put the nearest flames out. I had considered standing in the shower and fending the flames off by running the water, but I didn't think that would work. I had to be by the door. All the same, I left every tap in the little bathroom running just in case.

14

Arty was terrible at typing. She wished the alphabet was written in the right order on the little squares because she had no idea how to find the letter she wanted and it took her forever to work it out, every single time. The internet place was a tiny room in a basement with three chairs and three computers.

This is a computer, she whispered. It was just a box but somehow it could link her to everything in the world.

There was no one else in here so she couldn't copy what they did. However, the screen said 'Google' on it, and when she pressed a letter a picture of it appeared on the screen, so after some time she managed to write 'girlfromthewoods'. (Later she would discover how to put a gap between the words.) The computer said: 'Did you mean *girl out of the woods*?' So that was all right. She said that was what she meant.

And then she was looking at herself. She was in the computer. There was her photograph. There were NEWS RESULTS. There were pictures of her at the Gateway of India. There was a lot of stuff about AMK's house. People knew she had been there. They were sharing photos with her in them. A caption said that AMK had offered a reward for anyone who could find her and take her to safety, but that didn't seem to make sense. One of the results said that '#girloutofthewoods is trending', whatever that meant.

And then there was a photograph of her with Zeus at the hospital.

She touched the screen, stroking Zeus's face with her finger, and she held her breath and stared at him for a very long time. His huge dark eyes. The way he was pressed into her. She had hated the hospital and yet she missed everything about that time now with all her heart, because Zeus had been with her and now he was in France.

Control it.

She could not leave this picture here in the computer. She held on to that fact.

'Excuse me?' she said to the boy who was in charge here. He was about her age.

'Yes?'

'Is there . . . is there a way of getting this picture out of the computer so I can take it away with me?'

'You want to print?'

'Do I?'

'It sounds like it. Can you pay extra?' She nodded, and he came and stood behind her and pressed some buttons. 'There you go,' he said. He pointed to a plastic box in the corner and a piece of paper came out with herself and Zeus on it. He handed it to her.

'Thank you.' She stared at it, then folded it in half and put it into her book. The boy went back to his desk, back to his own computer.

It was easy to work out how to move the little arrow around the screen and click on things, and she discovered that the police were looking for her since her escape from Gita and Vikram's house. Even AMK wanted people to find her, and she was annoyed by that. She skimmed past the words because she didn't want to read what people were saying, but she saw enough to understand that the whole world knew about the sickness, and that they knew it because Joe had told them about it when they were in hospital. Just like the man on the train had said.

She had thought she was so clever constructing her alternative world, but actually everyone knew. Everyone knew what had happened. No wonder Joe hadn't called her back.

She typed 'Gmail' into the bar at the top and filled in 'artyvenus' and 'goddesses', and then she was looking at her own email account.

That was a brand-new thing. She wished Venus and Vishnu could see her now.

There were four emails in it. Three were from Cherry and the fourth was from Gmail telling her that she was welcome to their service. Cherry's first one was about the train, the second one was sending her lots of goddess things, and the third just said: 'Oh my god Arty – email me!!!' Before she could think about replying to that, she knew what she had to do.

She typed in Florence's email address and wrote:

> Dear Zeus, I miss you so much! I think about you all the
> time. I hope you're all right in France. I will write more
> when I can use the computer better. I love you. We are all
> gods and goddesses. Your sister Arty xxxxxxxxxxxxxx

Then she typed in Joe's and wrote:

> HELP. I NEED YOUR HELP. You told everyone about me.
> This is my email so tell me why you did that. Help me.
> Please Joe. I thought you were my friend. Arty

She was reading Cherry's first message properly when
the boy who worked here put his hand on her shoulder.
She turned round, wondering what else she didn't know,
and found that it wasn't the boy.

It was the police.

They were a man and a woman wearing brown uniforms.
Arty was so scared she almost wet herself. She had seen
police in the distance, but she had kept as far away from
them as she could. And now there was just her and them in
this tiny room. Her, and them, and the boy.

She looked over at him. He made a strange face.

'Sorry,' he said. 'I recognized you at once. That photograph, if I wasn't already sure, I was then. I called them.'

'Why?'

'For your safety. Everyone is worried about you. Also,
AMK wants you found.'

'But I'm fine.'

The policeman looked cross.

'You caused a lot of worry to a lot of people,' he said. 'You ran away from a safe home, and now you're living under a stolen identity. This is a serious business.'

'It's not a stolen identity!' Arty was furious. 'I didn't steal anything. Just one piece of paper, and that was from my friend. Two pieces of paper.'

'You are not Margaret Armitage,' said the woman. 'She is sixty-four years old. You, on the other hand, are sixteen or so. Your name is Artemis. You were placed in an excellent foster home with people who took great care of you, and then ran away from those people who were looking after you in the dead of night. They were distraught.'

Arty felt sorry for them. 'They were really nice,' she said. 'It's not their fault. I just needed to come to Mumbai once that woman took Zeus to France.'

'You were not at liberty to do that.'

They led her out towards a police car, which turned out to be a car with POLICE written on it, without a blue light or a siren or anything else that Arty thought a police car would have. There were people on the pavement holding up their phones again. She wanted to run past them, but then she had a better idea. If they were so interested in her she would use them to help her.

'This is a message for Joe,' she said loudly to them all. 'He's Nepalese and from Germany too. Joe, I know you put my photo everywhere. Come and talk to me unless you're too scared. And, AMK, why do you want people to find me? That's not fair.'

'Come *on*!' The policeman was cross, and the woman pulled Arty's wrist so she had to go with her.

She got in the car. 'Am I under arrest?' she said, knowing that she wasn't because being under arrest was one of those things that only happened when you said the words to activate it, and no one had said them to her. She thanked Diana for that. Otherwise she would have been scared, but now she was only angry.

'No,' said the woman. 'Of course not. We're taking you back into care.'

'I can care for myself.'

The woman didn't answer.

The police station had a blue arch over its entrance and writing in yellow. Arty was ready for a fight. There was no way she was going 'back into care'.

She asked for the bathroom and locked the door and screamed and screamed and screamed. Then she took deep breaths of toilet smells until she was sick. After that she pulled every part of herself together and marched out there to find out what was going to happen next.

It turned out that everyone had easily worked out that she was in Mumbai, as she had suspected they would, but that after that she had successfully vanished. No one knew what she had done from the station or beyond. When Joe had listened to her messages from Cherry's phone he gave the police the number, and that was why Cherry had emailed

Arty sounding panicked. It had taken him a while to listen to them because he had been on his meditation thing.

When he heard her message saying she was outside AMK's house he had put it on the internet. Which, Arty thought, had not been very meditative of him. Joe, she decided, was not her friend after all. He was not her friend at all. She put her hands in her hair and pulled. This was horrible. Joe was the first friend she had in the outside world, and he had done a horrible thing to her. He had done a thing that made her life much worse, and that was not what friends did. She drew in all her fury and focused it on him. At that moment she hated him. She had never hated anyone before, and now she did, and the feeling was shocking and almost thrilling.

Then she realized that there was a mean thing she could do to him, in return. She remembered what he had said about the herbs, and went over to the policewoman, who was sitting at a desk writing with a pen.

'I gave Joe a bag of herbs that we grew in the clearing,' she said. 'He sold them for me and gave me money. He said he could go to prison if anyone knew about it.'

The woman wrote that down.

Arty said it again later, by which time they were in a little room. Arty was sitting on an uncomfortable chair and looking at the walls. They were too close. The police man and woman talked but Arty didn't say anything about anything except the herbs. She didn't care. She only half listened to what they said to her. They were concerned for her safety. She was a minor, too young to be out like this on her own. She had been through a terrible time. She needed an official identity, a surname, guidance, looking after. She needed documents. Cherry had said that too. Did she want to apply for Indian nationality or British or both?

'Both,' she said, because she wanted to keep both her mother and her father alive.

Then she stopped speaking. She pretended she was her sister, Luna. She said nothing, and wondered whether the cream walls really were coming closer, and looked at the floor, which was tiled with black. If she screwed her eyes up a bit, she could imagine it was a deep pool, and that if she got up from her chair she could fall into it. There was a fan on a table that blew into her face every time it swept round to point at her.

She thought about ways to escape, but she knew she couldn't. People in books escaped from prisons by tunnelling out through floors or behind posters, or by crawling through sewers, but she didn't have any idea how to do any of those things.

'Can I go now?' she said after a while.

'No. You can't leave until we're satisfied you have somewhere to go.'

'I've already paid for tonight at the hotel.'

'No.'

'Where shall I sleep then?'

The woman sighed. 'We're looking for an emergency foster home. Just wait here for now.'

'Have you got a book I can read?'

'There might be one somewhere.'

She came back a bit later and handed Arty a copy of *Great Expectations*. She started reading it and immediately relaxed. That, it turned out, was exactly what she needed. She loved every word of it. The shell of her stayed in the police station in Mumbai, while the little Arty inside went off to the freezing marshes. She read and read and read. She ate the lunch they gave her. She carried on reading.

'Someone is here to see you,' the woman said, at some point in the afternoon.

Arty followed her, hoping against hope that it would, somehow, be someone from the clearing, even though she knew that there was no chance whatsoever of that being the case. It was hardly going to be Zeus, and it was even less likely to be anyone else.

She just really wanted her mum. Maybe, she thought, it might be Cherry.

'Joe!' she shouted, and she ran right into him, the joy of a familiar face overpowering the fact that she hated him. She wasn't sure what to do with her energy; in spite of everything she was happy to see him because she had known him longer than anyone else out here. He was still wearing his orange T-shirt, and his hair was a bit longer than it had been before.

'Sorry,' he said. Arty could see that he didn't want to be here at all. 'So they found you. I have to say this first: I'm sorry for putting your picture on Instagram. I'm sorry for telling everyone you were at AMK's house. Sorry, Arty. I didn't expect you to be pleased to see me.'

'Why did you?'

He looked at the policewoman. They were in a big room with people answering phones and tapping at keyboards, but Arty was pretty sure that everyone who was close enough was listening to them.

'I didn't think I'd see you again. I thought your story was interesting. I was cooped up in hospital for ten days and I thought you and Zeus were amazing. To be completely honest, I thought you'd get me lots of likes on Instagram and that's my weakness. I had a story to tell, and that was exciting. I'm really, really sorry.'

Arty looked away from him. 'You should be sorry because I was doing well. I thought you were my friend. You've spoiled everything.'

'You know, when I got your messages I called the number back but I couldn't get through. So I put it out there that you were in Bandra at AMK's house because I wanted you to be safe. Everyone was looking for you.'

'Well,' she said. 'Now they've found me.'

JUNE

It turned out that it was difficult to set a house on fire. In films it was easy. You dropped a match and everything went up in flames. Now, though, the basement filled with smoke, but the flames didn't catch on anything. That man Jeremy Clarkson's face turned to ash, but he wasn't flammable enough. I couldn't make the room catch fire.

My friends were no use to me at all. They were just waiting by the door.

I coughed. The smoke was horrible but there weren't enough flames to do what I needed it to do. There were no curtains. I walked over to the pathetic little fire and offered it the edge of my sleeping bag, but that just smouldered and made the smell worse. I had wanted to start the fire when she was here, but now I knew how impossible that would be. She would have put it out easily, over and over again.

I stood and watched.

'Come on,' I said to it. 'Come on! We need some petrol or something. You have to do it fast.'

I looked round at the bear and the rabbit for backup, but they were just standing there, looking like toys. The other creatures had already left.

I spread all my clothes, all my bedding, everything I could around the fire, and offered it the edges of everything. I couldn't put the whole lot on there because it would have put the fire out straight away. I vaguely remembered learning that flour was flammable because of its surface area. Obviously I had no flour.

I gave the fire every page of every book I had, and I added all the wood I could find. It didn't burn.

It didn't burn. It didn't burn. And then it did.

I believed in fire gods because one moment I had lots of things mildly melting, and then I had a fire. The fire god pointed at my basement, and fire leaped up into the air. It was up the wall. It was licking everything, coming after every single thing in the room. The smoke was intense, and I dropped to the floor. I hammered on the wall. I watched the window crack, which I hadn't expected to happen at all, and I begged the people outside to notice.

I had done it. Whatever happened now, this part of my life was over.

15

'I'm just so sorry, Arty,' Joe said.

'You've said that too many times,' she told him, and leaned back and kept her eyes on the cricket.

'But it's true. I don't know what comes over me. I'm addicted to it, I think.'

That was more interesting. 'Addicted to what?' she said. 'Is it like drugs?'

'I guess it's a better addiction than drugs. But I feel it taking hold of me and it's like I can't do anything apart from upload the picture and count the likes.'

'Count the likes?'

'I know. It's pathetic, isn't it? I won't do it again. I won't do it today.'

She looked at him. 'I think you will. The man on the train said that the story was very popular. And now you know what I'm doing this evening. I think you will.'

He screwed his eyes up and shook his head. 'I won't. I know I'm not allowed to tell anyone about this evening.'

Joe and Arty were sitting in the shade at the edge of a field that was in the middle of the city but with all the roads hidden by trees and railings. Arty was lying back, propping herself up with her elbows on the ground to watch several games of cricket all at once.

'Don't talk about it any more,' she said. 'Tell me about the cricket instead.'

The sun was hazy, as usual, and she liked the shade, but she was finding it difficult to concentrate on anything. Joe was sitting a little way away from her, uncomfortable even though they were kind-of friends again. Some part of her that she didn't really understand wanted him to sit closer, in spite of what he'd done. She wanted to be near him. It came across her in waves, fury and then something different, something that was the opposite of fury.

The police had let her go out with him as long as he promised to let them know where they were and not to leave the area. She shuffled a bit closer to him. They were filling in the time until her evening appointment, which was possibly the scariest thing that had happened since she arrived in the outside world.

'OK,' he said. 'Well, watch that little guy over there. Watch the way he's holding the ball. I've been watching him. He thinks he's Harbhajan Singh. He's trying to bowl a doosra. I think he can do it, but he hasn't done one yet.'

'*Doosra*? That means "the other one" in Hindi.'

'Does it? It's a cricketing thing too. It's where you bowl the ball and it spins the way you're not expecting. See, he's using these two fingers –' he held up two of his fingers, the middle one and the ring one – 'instead of these, which you usually use.'

She watched. The man threw the ball – bowled it – and the batter hit it.

'Not that ball then,' said Joe.

'That was the same one,' said Arty. 'Not the other one at all.'

Cricket was new to Arty. She had seen a lot of games in the street but had thought it was people messing around with a ball and sticks of wood. Now, though, she had discovered that it was a real game. She was starting to understand the rules, and she was trying hard to concentrate on it to block out all the other things, because thinking about cricket stopped her thinking about everything else.

Joe had explained batting and bowling, and then other things as she'd asked more and more questions. Arty liked the words: silly mid-on, corridor of uncertainty, googly, cherry. Particularly cherry. And now doosra.

'Waiting for the doosra,' she said, without knowing what she was looking for at all.

'Always,' said Joe. He turned to her. 'Ready for tonight? Honestly I won't tell anyone about it. You can depend on that. I'm not having AMK on my case.'

'Oh,' she said. 'A scary man will stop you, but not a girl? Isn't that a bit sexist?'

'Sorry.' He smiled, and it did something odd to her.

'And I'm not ready at all. How could I be?' She was feeling fluttery inside. She had done a good thing for him today. She had stopped him going to prison.

'These herbs,' the policewoman had said. 'You said you gave them to Joe and he gave you money. What exactly were they? What name did you know them by?'

Arty knew some other names for the herbs now. They were called grass, and cannabis, and weed. The policewoman was looking at her very intently.

Joe had told the whole world about her because he wanted the attention. He had told them about the plague and the clearing. He had pretended to be her friend, but he had not helped her at all. He had just used her and Zeus to get lots of attention on social media. It had messed up a lot of things for her.

However, he had also given her money, and without that money she would still be in foster care. If she'd given the herbs to anyone else, she would have been in trouble. He had told her a lot of things about the outside world. He had been nice to Zeus. And she was pleased to see him.

She had met the policewoman's gaze.

'Coriander,' she had said. That had been the end of it.

Everyone forgot about that quickly, because someone nearby answered the phone and called out, 'AMK's people are on the line!' From there it turned out that AMK was very interested in Arty. He wanted to meet her. He wanted to meet her for dinner tonight. They were going to the restaurant of a smart hotel, and after that he was paying for her to stay there for the night in a luxury room.

Even the police had been very excited by that. AMK had offered the reward that had made the computer boy call the police. He had offered it because he had been worried about her safety, and now he was so delighted that she had turned up safe that he wanted to meet her. Everyone established that he was going back to his house after dinner, and she was staying in the hotel alone, and then they all agreed that she could go.

'Dinner with AMK,' she said now, as someone hit the ball over their heads. 'I won't know what to say to him.'

'You will,' said Joe. 'Look! There it was! The doosra.'

Arty hadn't seen it. 'Can we go to Bandra? I want to tell the people at his house.'

'No. You heard them. You're not allowed to disappear again. I've had to leave my passport with them as security.'

That was why they were here, at the Oval Maidan, a big field not far from the police station.

'They're going to make me go to another foster home after that,' Arty said. 'Aren't they? I'm allowed one night in the smart hotel and then I'm going to have to go and pretend to be someone's daughter. Someone I've never met before.' The idea of foster parents made her feel weird in lots of ways. It was the way the word 'parents' was used so casually. The adjective 'foster' didn't distance it enough from the idea of her real parents.

'Yes,' said Joe. 'You're at a terrible age for the system. There are girls who are married at your age, so in lots of ways it's ridiculous to keep you under lock and key. That's why I'm allowed to take you out. And it's why you're allowed to stay at the hotel, thanks to Mr AMK.'

Someone from a different game hit the ball hard, and it came towards them. Joe pushed Arty down, but she shoved his arm away and leaned over, caught it with one hand and then threw it back.

He was surprised. 'Where did you learn that?'

'At home. We played a lot of ball games. You have to keep fit.'

'You do. Yes.'

'Joe?'

'Yes?'

'Can I see the things on your phone? The pictures of me and everything? I know you said before that I shouldn't. But I saw things on the train, on that man's phone when he knew who I was. I want to look properly. I want to understand what it is that people know about me. I . . . well, I asked those people outside the internet place to tell you to come, and then you were there. I need to see how that happened.'

She watched Joe thinking. She reached out her hand to touch his head. It was fuzzy. Strange sensations went through her.

Joe was nineteen. She was sixteen. That wasn't very different.

He took her hand in his and looked at her. 'Are you sure?'

And suddenly she didn't care about the phone. She felt his hand on hers, and she didn't feel alone any more. She had the strangest feeling that she wanted to kiss him. It was in every cell in her body all at once.

She looked at him.

He was looking at her too. They looked into each other's eyes, and then he turned his head away and tapped at his phone screen with his thumbs in the way that people did.

'Are you sure?' he said, as if that moment had never happened, and she longed for him to look at her again. 'OK. Don't freak out. You've got your own hashtag. It's hashtag girloutofthewoods.'

Arty sighed. 'I saw that,' she said. '*Hashtag girloutofthewoods*. I saw it but I didn't understand it.'

He talked, explaining it all to her. All she could think of was the feel of his hand on hers, the feeling that had gone through her when he looked at her that way. Was that love? Did she *love* Joe? She was pretty sure she didn't even like him very much, except that he was her only friend. So why had he made her feel like that? She looked at his fingers as he showed her things on his phone. She liked his fingers. She liked his arm. She liked the way he smelled of himself rather than of chemicals.

He told her about phones and she ignored him until she got interested. When she started to understand she found it interesting, then horrible, then fascinating, and then so awful that she wanted to throw all the phones in the world into the sea. The way social media worked was something that her recent self would have thought of as magic. She found it hard to understand that all the people who stood around tapping at their phones were secretly doing this. They were looking at photos of Arty and clicking on her hashtag. Girloutofthewoods. They were writing about her, laughing about her. They were making things up about her. Someone was pretending to be her, and someone else was pretending to be her red trousers, writing things on the internet to pretend they were baffled by everything in the world.

Someone else wrote, 'Me, when I wake up and can't remember what day it is,' and put a photo of her looking confused at the Gateway of India and the hashtag girloutofthewoods. There were lots like that.

It was really, *really* stupid.

'OK,' she said. She regulated her breathing. She stared at the people playing cricket. She watched a boy wearing blue waiting for the ball, then stepping forward and holding his bat out at just the right angle to hit it. It made a pleasing noise. He started running. Arty stared at it and breathed deeply. 'OK,' she said again. 'And people think *I'm* the strange one. Does everyone do this?'

'No. But lots of people. Most people your age. Most people my age.'

'People who are clever still think this is funny?'

He looked embarrassed. 'It has different uses. Some people watch videos of kittens. Some people organize politically. Some people listen to stories to fall asleep at night. But, yes, lots of clever people still think it's funny. Plenty of people live through their phones. Including me. I have to admit that. I do. But, Arty – look. I didn't write about the plague really, but people have put it together. They're trying to get to your clearing. Don't worry – anyone who gets close is being stopped. The fence is locked and there are guards. I think there was a woman who got through but that was dealt with.'

Arty closed her eyes and fought it all down inside herself. She had put the clearing out of her head, and now it was coming back. People were actually trying to go there. It was all wrong. Everything about it was horrific.

'I hate them all,' she said. 'I hate those people.' Joe didn't reply. 'I don't want a phone,' she said after more time had passed. 'I'd like to talk to Cherry and Zeus, but I could use the normal kind of phone for that. I hate all the rest of it. I will never, ever, ever be part of it.'

'I know. It sucks. Again, sorry. I uploaded the first picture of you and Zeus on our first day in hospital because your story was so incredible. And I did want the attention. I couldn't help myself. It's the opposite of being a good Buddhist.'

She looked at him again. He looked into her eyes and then away. Then he looked back.

'Arty,' he said, and his voice was different. 'You're sixteen. I'm nineteen. Some things would be a terrible idea and can't happen.'

She nodded. They would never speak about it again.

The boy in blue was running. It said BABU on his back, and Arty thought that was a nice word to say. *Babu*. She mouthed it. She wanted to think about anything other than Joe.

'They'll forget about you soon,' Joe said after a while. 'It's a social media storm. They don't last. The next thing will be along.'

Arty pushed the phone away. They stayed there not saying much, just watching. Someone caught the ball and Babu was out. The next person to come up to bat was called, according to his shirt, Ankit.

Arty didn't want to watch the cricket any more.

'I've never seen a movie, Joe,' she said, shifting around. 'Can we do that?'

He looked at his phone. 'Maybe,' he said while tapping. 'Let me see.'

'I'm scared about meeting AMK. I've never met anyone like him. I mean, I've never met anyone. But particularly not like him. He feels like a god to me. Does he look like a person?'

'He does. He *is* a person, Arty. Just a person. He's never met anyone like you either.' He looked hard at his screen. 'So, we can't go and see one of *his* movies, but we can go and see *a* movie at the Regal Cinema, which is nearby, in an hour. How about that?'

'I know where the Regal Cinema is!'

'We leave here in maybe twenty minutes?'

'Twenty minutes,' Arty said. 'One third of an hour. One seventy-twoth of a day. Seventy-second, I mean.' She was getting to grips with the way the time worked out here.

'Can we have a photo together?' Joe said. 'I'll email it to you, and you can keep it to remind you of today. I'll only send it to you. To prove myself as a friend.'

She didn't answer. The photo he took showed Arty wincing and looking away. She felt awkward because of her strange feelings. She wanted to be close to Joe and far,

far away from him at the same time. She did not want to be in any of his photographs because she knew what he would do with them but he had promised he would only show it to her and she wanted to believe him. She very much wanted him to prove himself.

JUNE

It was a wall of flame and it went from the floor to the ceiling.

It was hell. It was like being in a painting of hell, but it was real.

It was hot. I was scared.

16

The seats were red and warm. Arty stared up at the screen. The cinema was different from the way she had expected it to be. First of all, it was an enormous amount bigger. Arty had expected a small room, and she thought they would be sitting on a row of chairs to watch the film, basing her ideas on the television at Gita's house. In fact, this was a huge space with hundreds and hundreds of comfy chairs to sit on. The screen was gigantic. And the lights were off, so you had to look at the film because you couldn't see anything else.

The movie was confusing at first. It was like watching a book, but seeing it in the moving pictures rather than in your head. Arty loved watching books play out in her own brain as she read them, and it was very strange seeing it done on the outside. The movie was called *1921* and it turned out to be incredibly scary. She grabbed Joe's arm as they watched the story of a man in London cutting his wrists, and then saw him as a boy in Mumbai, and followed the story of how he came to do that.

She was transfixed and astonished by everything about it. She forgot all about everything else. She forgot about hashtags and selfies. She forgot about the fact that the greatest movie star of all time wanted her to have dinner with him that very day. She forgot all of it. She wanted to stay in this cinema and watch films forever and ever and ever.

She loved reading. She loved looking at the sea. She liked cricket, and now she loved movies. All of them could hide the bad things for a while. She wanted to gather her family around her and show them. *Look!* she told them in her head. *Look at this! There's a way of telling stories on a screen and it's really, really amazing.*

But of course the adults already knew that. They must have been to cinemas before they went to the clearing. She told the children instead. *Hey, Luna,* she said internally. *Look at this! I know! It's the most spectacular amazing thing. You could sit and look and no one would want you to talk to them. Hey, Herc. See?* She pulled the two of them on to her lap and watched it with them, which was the best she could do. She imagined Zeus watching a film in France and hoped he would find it as wonderful as she did.

The story was full of ghosts, like Arty's head. It made her feel scared in the same way that books could make her feel scared. She was sitting perfectly safely in a chair in a comfortable room next to Joe (not thinking about his arms, his hands, his kiss), but she was terrified of the ghosts terrorizing poor Ayush. It was a safe terror. She sank into it, and the real world stopped meaning anything at all.

The film ended and Arty sat there for a long time. She needed to pull herself out of it, back into the other world, but she had no idea, for quite a long time, which was real.

When they stepped out into the sunshine, Joe laughed. 'That wasn't the greatest movie to start your viewing career. Are you OK?'

'Are you joking? It was amazing! It was the most incredible thing. I want to watch it again. Oh, the ghosts. The music. The . . . everything. I loved it so much!'

'You did seem to be invested.'

'Yes. It was brilliant and awesome.'

He looked as if he thought that was funny, and Arty was annoyed at him all over again. 'Good. Glad you liked it. Movies come much better than that. So now you can ask the greatest movie star who ever lived all about cinema.'

'Yes. I'd better go to the hotel.'

Joe took her photo outside the cinema, which was annoying again because she didn't trust him. He walked her to her hotel and into the part that was called the lobby. Her things had been taken to the hotel already, but she hadn't been there yet.

It was the most astonishing place. There wasn't a ceiling. It just went up and up. It made her head spin to look at it, even though she had looked up into outer space from the clearing, and *that* hadn't made her dizzy. The rooms were all in corridors round the edges of the open space.

The lobby was completely shiny. The people who worked here were kind. They all stopped to say hello to her. It was different from her other hotel. This one was full of air and light and plants and space. It was like being on a spaceship, she thought. That was how other-worldly this felt.

'Hello, Miss Artemis,' said a nice man. 'How are you?'

'I'm very well, thank you,' she said, and collected her key so she could go up to her room, with one of the hotel people accompanying her. Joe told her to have a nice time, and she wondered, as she said goodbye, whether she would ever see him again. She was sad and happy to see him leaving. Life as a girl in the outside world was so difficult.

'No social media,' she said, and he smiled and waved as he walked off. His phone was already in his hand before she stepped into the lift and she knew that he would post the photos anyway because he was addicted to the 'likes', as he had said. She hated that.

The hotel man pressed button eleven to get to her room. He opened the door for her with a white card, and then she was there, in a room with an enormous window and a view over Mumbai. The bed was huge. The bathroom had a bath and a shower in it, and there was water and chocolate for her.

When the man left she ran a bath and emptied so many chemicals into it that the bubbles made mountains and valleys of white (perhaps like snow), and then she lay in the perfect warm water and tried not to think about the fact that she was having dinner with AMK tonight at this hotel. The police had let her take *Great Expectations* with her, so she got out and went to fetch it from her bag, but it turned out that reading in the bath wasn't a very good idea. First the pages went wavy and then she dropped it in.

She lay still instead and tried to calm herself. She didn't like being alone with her thoughts. The way she had felt with Joe had been strange, and now she found she missed him and was angry with him, both at once, but she knew that if she couldn't trust him then he couldn't really be her friend.

But he had taken her to the cricket and the cinema. Without him she would have spent the afternoon at the police station. He had made her feel excited and happy, and then told her nothing could happen with those feelings. It was complicated.

All that, though, was a distraction. Her real thoughts were about her family, about Zeus. She had no idea where he was or how he was, but she was sure he was crying for her and for their family. She longed for the beat of his heart closer to hers, for the feeling of his little hand in hers. She was adrift without him. And behind that was the gaping jagged hole where the rest of her life had been ripped to pieces.

She lay in the bath for a while, thinking about her parents and her family and the clearing, letting the tears roll down her face into the water, and then she got out and had a shower too to wash her hair properly. She got dressed in the purple dress that a woman at the hotel had brought to her, saying it was a gift from AMK's wife. It was soft and pretty and it fitted her well. It was a long dress with gold thread in it, and there was a pair of baggy trousers that went underneath.

While she waited for her hair to dry she sat on the bed. She turned on the television and flicked through the channels, but there was nothing she wanted to watch.

In the end someone knocked at the door. When she opened it, a hotel man was standing there.

'Miss Artemis,' he said. 'I have the great pleasure of announcing that Mr AMK is waiting in the restaurant for you.'

He was sitting at the table, a big man with a white beard and black hair. She walked towards him, feeling self-conscious. She hoped she was wearing the dress and trousers properly. She hoped she had washed enough. She had no idea how she was going to use the right table manners for this, because she had no idea what they were.

She wasn't really scared of AMK, because she didn't care about anything. This was her post-life, she thought; her real life had been at home, and everything that came after didn't matter. She gave him a wary smile and he stood up to kiss her cheek.

'You smell wonderful,' she told him, and he laughed.

'You're very kind,' he said. 'So, Artemis, we meet at last. I hope you didn't mind my getting involved in your life as I did. I was captivated by you. A girl alone in Mumbai, having walked out of the woods. I'm so sorry for your losses, my dear girl.'

His voice was deep and wonderful. Arty liked him at once. Joe was right: he was just a human being when you got up close. Their table was by the window, and she looked out at the blackness where she knew the sea was hidden by the night. There were lights of cars going along the road off to their right and left far below.

There were several knives and forks on the table next to each other.

AMK saw her looking at them. 'Don't worry, my dear,' he said, smiling and patting her hand. 'No need for ceremony here. This is a welcoming and accommodating place, and anyway you are perfect. You are a shining example to all humankind.'

Arty smiled. 'Well, you're the greatest movie star of all time.'

He loved that. 'How can a girl who came out of the woods be aware of the work of a humble Mumbai thespian, let alone speak of it in such glowing terms? Can my fame travel so far as that?'

AMK had ordered the vegetarian menu for them both. They stopped talking while a woman put a bowl in front of Arty. It was chaat with lentil ice cream, she said.

'It sounds unusual,' she added, 'but you will find it delightful. I hope so. Let me know if there's any problem.'

'I've never had ice cream,' Arty told her, 'but I've read about it in books.'

AMK roared with laughter at that. 'She's never had ice cream,' he said to the woman, 'and her first taste of it is lentil flavour. You tell *that* to your chef!'

The waitress, Arty thought, was trying not to stare at AMK. 'I'll make sure she's informed,' she said, and she laughed too.

'And you, my dear,' he said to Arty, 'you must go to Chowpatty Seaface and try some more conventional ice cream before you leave Mumbai. Though I think right now it would be as hard for you as it would for me to go there incognito. All the world knows that you watched some cricket and then went to the cinema this afternoon.'

'Did he put up a photo of me at the cricket?'

'I don't think so. There was one of cricketers, and then the cinema, but not with you in it. He still said he was with you, so same difference really.'

She was pleased that Joe had, at least, kept his promise not to use her photo. Still, it hadn't stopped him telling everyone about her, and that was nearly the same thing.

'He's not my real friend, is he?' she said.

AMK sighed. 'I fear not.'

Arty looked around. Her head was spinning. She wanted to go back and to try to explain all this to everyone in the clearing, but there was too much. She could never make them understand that she had become famous, that the greatest movie star in history had taken her to dinner, that she had gone to the outside world and found cricket and cinema and lentil ice cream. And that she had met a boy who told the whole world about her on his phone. In the clearing they had thought that phones were for talking to one person at a time.

Maybe, she thought, she had died. Perhaps this was her afterlife. Maybe the plague had killed her too, and this was the weirdness her brain had spun for her for eternity.

She pushed those thoughts away. The room was quite dark, with candles on the tables, so even though it was an expensive restaurant it felt cosy. There were other people here, but their tables were far away, and it didn't seem like the kind of place that would let anyone come over to ask for a selfie. Even if they did, they would want them with AMK rather than with Arty. That made her feel happy.

'You were going to tell me,' he said, 'where you found your extremely flattering appraisal of my modest talents.'

'It was truly one of the first things anyone told me when I came to Mumbai,' she told him. 'I'm afraid I hadn't heard of you in the clearing, because I'd barely heard of cinema. But when I got to this city I met a man called Salman. He was my taxi driver. He moved to Mumbai because of you. He said I had to go to Bandra and see your house because you are the greatest movie star in the history of the world. So I did.' She smiled at him. 'I agree with him.'

'But you've seen none of my movies?' He leaned forward. He did not look annoyed that she hadn't seen his films.

'Not yet, but I promise I will. How many have you made?'

'I've starred in seventy-three. I've directed six.'

'Can you tell me about it? I went to the cinema today. You know that. I went because I was meeting you and I wanted to know what it was like to see a film so that I'd understand a little bit. But we went to see *1921* because it was on at the Regal Cinema. Do you know the Regal Cinema?'

'Of course! One of the finest. It is a very historical place. From the nineteen thirties. So those bastards weren't showing one of mine?' He was saying angry words, but he was laughing.

'Not today, but probably all the other days.'

'Probably. I expect you were *very* unfortunate with the schedules.'

'So how do you act a story and then it becomes a film? What's . . . I don't know. What happens?'

He settled back and sipped his glass of wine. It was red wine, but really it was dark purple.

'It's a long and complex process. Are you sure? I'll tell you while you eat that lentil ice cream.'

Arty picked some of it up with the little spoon that had come with it. When she put it in her mouth she jumped a bit on the inside because she had never expected that. She knew it would be cold, but the way it kept its coldness so small, so pinpointed on her tongue, so it spread slowly through her mouth, that was not something she had expected at all.

She swallowed. 'Oh my God,' she said. 'That's amazing.'

She saw his eyes laughing as his mouth stayed serious. 'I'm glad to hear it. So fervent an assessment.'

She took some more. There wasn't enough of it here but she thought she wouldn't ask for more because that would be rude and she didn't really know the rules. 'Go on then.'

'Well,' he said, taking some of his cauliflower on his fork, 'the first thing that will happen these days is that a script will arrive. By the time I see them, enough of my people will have read them for me to know that they will be worth a bit of my time.'

'And that's all the words you'll say in the play written down? Like Shakespeare?'

'Yes, and I have played my share of Shakespeare in my time, my dear. I did *Lear* last year.'

'*King Lear*?'

'You know it?'

'I do! I've read it. I'd love to see it.'

'I'll get you a DVD of my *Lear*. It's far from definitive, no doubt.'

Arty didn't know what a DVD was, but she decided to find that out later.

'I bet it *is* definitive,' she said. 'Thank you. So then . . .'

'So then, let's say I read it and think, *Yes, this is an excellent script and very much what I would like for my next movie* (generally I don't think that). Then my people will work out terms, and all the paperwork and financial things. Don't worry about that. Fast-forward a little, and it's the first day of filming. Indoor scenes will all be shot on set, in a studio, with tight security. Outdoor ones in a carefully chosen location.'

'What if it's on the street?'

'Then the street will be closed off, and the general public are not allowed in. Anyone you see in the background of the shot will be an extra, that is, someone employed by the production for that purpose. Otherwise people see a camera and smile and wave, and that is, of course, untenable.'

He explained cinema to her all the way through dinner, and Arty couldn't believe she had worried that she wouldn't know what to say to this man. It turned out she could ask him anything she wanted about himself, and he was happy to talk and talk and talk. He explained everything. He was very kind. She added him to her list of friends. Joe was off that list, and AMK was on it.

Arty had had no idea there were starters and main courses. She was glad, as it turned out, that she hadn't asked for more lentil ice cream, because there was a massive plate of food still to come. It was paneer and spinach, with cauliflower and all sorts of bits of sauce. She had never had cauliflower before, and its taste was a bit weird, but everything around it was delicious and so she dipped it in the sauce and ate it anyway. Her drink was Coca-Cola, which was the best drink ever. She drank two of them, and then switched to the water that was already on the table, because she was worried that the Coca-Cola might be costing too much money.

'I know you hate beer,' he said when he saw her looking at his wine. 'But have a sip of this. It's very different. You're too young to drink really, but one sip when no one's looking and no harm will be done.'

He handed her his glass and looked around. Arty noticed that the only two empty tables were the ones on either side of them.

She sipped it. It coated her tongue and tasted bitter and strange, but a moment later it was nice. She sipped again. 'That's much better than Kingfisher,' she said, and she drank it all, then handed the glass back to him.

When the puddings arrived she was astonished all over again. Hers was made from pineapple and coconut and it came with some special cardamom ice cream in a bowl on the side, which the lady said was a gift to Arty from the chef – 'So you can try something more conventional with regards to the ice-cream world.'

AMK had something with cream and nuts, and a glass of a different wine.

Arty tasted the ice cream and couldn't believe anything could be quite that delicious. The sugar danced in her mouth and made her head spin and sing. She wanted to stay here forever. She loved it that they had talked about movies and not about her life, but now she wanted to tell him.

'Where I grew up,' she said, picking her words carefully, 'we have a celebration once a year. This year.' She swallowed. It took a lot of work to say this. 'This year was the twentieth one. Anyway, every year Hella, who is our shaman, which means she's the only one who goes into the outside world, she would bring us treats for that day only. And the biggest treat in the world was a chocolate bar. Dairy Milk. You know it? In a purple wrapper.'

He nodded. 'Sure I know it. Who doesn't?'

'And we would unwrap it so slowly. And lick it, and savour every moment. To me, for all of my life until a little while ago, that was heaven. It was blissful. It was like magic. We thought it was rare and special. I never, ever imagined that this could exist.' She gestured with her spoon to everything and dripped some ice cream on the table.

A M K dabbed it with his napkin. 'It was rare and special to you, my dear. It sounds a lot more sane. We have so much excess out here.'

'And people with nothing too.'

'And far too many people with nothing. I try to use my money for good. I have a foundation to help street children, and I sponsor a programme to get education for girls.' He drank the rest of the wine in his glass quickly. 'But I also know that's not enough. I have been lucky with my success.' He paused.

Arty thought she was meant to say something, so she said, 'You're lucky to be the greatest actor there has ever been.'

'Thank you. And, really, I should take as much as we need to live a comfortable life, me and my family, and give everything else to those who need it. But then you need security – you've seen that. What are they like, those fans at my gate?'

'Oh,' said Arty. 'They're so friendly. They pass around food and take lots of pictures in front of your house. They're amazing.'

'I owe it all to them and yet I can't stop and talk to them because it would never end. Oh yes – I brought you these. Signed photographs of myself, for you to give to any fans you meet.' He handed her an envelope. 'But nonetheless, when they wait outside one's house, security is required. I am both grateful and wary. Then you need a driver. You know why I first got a driver? It was when a fan jumped in front of my car and I swerved to avoid her and hit a cat. It was a street cat, and it didn't die straight away, but that was it for me. It was a cat, but it could have been a child. So then you have a driver and then you need blacked-out windows for privacy because they take photos of you all the time, and then you're expected to have the right lifestyle, and I got married and my wife couldn't be expected to work. The spotlight would have made it impossible for her. In fact, she gave up a promising career in medicine for me. So I am eternally grateful, and she is a wonderful, wonderful woman. She wishes to meet you too incidentally – for me to invite you to our home.'

'Please say thank you to her for my clothes.' She patted her dress.

'Of course. Then children come along, and education is expensive, and then they grow up and want to move to New York and London and some such. And I suppose the expectation of it all mounts and mounts and mounts, and then you find that you're never away from it. I choose to come to this restaurant because they are discreet, but you can be one hundred per cent certain, Artemis, that one of the other patrons at least is snapping or filming us here, and you can be certain that it will appear on the internet later tonight.'

'Do you look at that stuff?'

'Oh heavens, no. That way madness lies. You mustn't either.'

'No. I agree. Madness.' She was warm inside, filled with gratitude that he understood these feelings. 'Joe showed the hashtag stuff to me today and I hated it *so much*. Just so, so, so, so much.'

He took a deep breath and looked as if he were about to say something, then stopped.

'What?' she said.

'Well – like you said, Joe isn't your friend. If I were your father, I would forbid you to see him again. He has proven himself to be exploiting you for his own gain and notoriety.'

'He's not a very good Buddhist, is he?'

'Indeed he is not. And for another thing you're a teenage girl and he is a man of, what? Twenty?'

'Nineteen.'

'Exactly. He's an arsehole. I know boys of that age are arseholes because I've been one myself.'

'Don't worry. I don't think I'm going to see him again.' She thought about the feelings Joe gave her. She certainly wasn't going to discuss them with AMK. Anyway, nothing was going to happen between them. Joe had said that.

'Good. I wouldn't trust him an inch.' He put his glass down and sighed. 'And again I hope it was OK that I got involved in your life. I felt responsible when I heard that you'd been to my house. I wanted to know you were safe and sound. I wanted to take you to dinner and hear about your life. And now I believe I have to pay some money to a boy who works in a computer centre.'

'You do! Thank you for caring about me.'

'But of course. Now I want to know more about your clearing. I'm fascinated by the Dairy Milk. Would you feel up to talking about it? Not the bad things. But your childhood. You grew up in a matriarchy?'

'Yes. My mum was the goddess. I'm a goddess now too.'

'I would say you are, my dear. Yes. You are.'

Arty took two sips from his wine because it made her feel braver, and she told him all about the clearing, about the rules and the ideals. After a while he asked the waitress for a pen and paper, and started writing it all down.

'Would you mind if I got someone to write a film about you?' he said. 'I would like to direct this myself.'

'I wouldn't mind at all,' Arty said. 'As long as you put in the bits where I'm waiting outside your house with your fans. Can you be in it?'

'How meta!' he said. 'Yes of course. I would like you to entrust me with your story, Artemis. I promise to consult with you at every stage. I may even have to make a cameo appearance playing myself. What do you say?'

Arty grinned.

'Well,' she said. 'Of *course* I say yes.'

Later, as she lay in her huge bed and stared up at the ceiling, her head spinning with the strangeness of it all, she realized that her story would involve actors pretending to be her family, and dying, and she cried and cried and cried. She didn't want there to be a movie about that at all.

In the morning she noticed that there was a telephone on the table in her room, half hidden by a vase of flowers. She found the piece of paper with Cherry's phone number on it and decided to call her and tell her about AMK. However, just as her hand touched the smooth plastic, it rang, which made her gasp.

She picked it up, and two days later she was on an aeroplane.

JUNE

No one was coming. The rabbit was just a toy rabbit. The monkey was a stuffed monkey. Only the bear was still talking to me. Only the bear had been with me through all of this.

'Come on,' it said. 'You can do this. Let's throw the water. We haven't come this far just to give up, have we? Hey?'

I threw my bucket and cups of water at the flames, with the bear jumping up and down on its little legs, encouraging me, but it was so pointless that it made us both laugh a kind of despairing laugh in the end. The fire had eaten half the room. Everything was fuel. The whole thing was out of control. I pushed myself back against the door and watched the flames coming closer.

I watched it eat the world I had lived in for so many days I had lost count. I was glad to see that go.

I had thought I could use fire to my own ends. Of course I couldn't. When people think they can have any kind of control over anything, the universe laughs at them.

It was licking the wall opposite me. It was coming closer every second. Everything smelled of smoke. Everything was closing in. There was a locked and bolted door behind me and a greedy fire eating everything in front of me. There was only me in the zone between the two. Me and the bear.

I couldn't get out and so it was going to eat me too, and my clothes and my hair and my bear and everything that had ever made me, me. All my atoms would be rearranged and used as something else, and my energy would be transferred into the fire's energy, and I hoped it would eat the whole of this house and the other people in it while it was at it.

'Don't worry,' said the bear. 'Don't worry.'

I knew that your life was supposed to flash before your eyes, and I tried to make it happen, but all that was in my head was white-hot terror. I tried to remember good things, but I could only find the bad ones. I was a ball of fear, and the flames were strengthening it and making it real.

If I get out of here, I said, *I will lead a good life. I will devote it to doing good to everyone.*

The flames were at my feet. I didn't care any more.

I stepped forward. My hair was smoking. I held the bear behind my back, out of harm's way. This was it.

PART TWO

17

As the aeroplane wheels touched down, she closed her eyes and hoped it was meant to be that way. She was using all her powers of self-control not to scream and pull her seatbelt off and run for cover. Air travel didn't feel like a thing that could reasonably happen. But it had worked, and here she was, landing in London. She was on a mission. Now it was time to find Matthew and Persephone and, most of all, Zeus. She had AMK supporting her, and the fact that he was supporting her gave her strength. She had emailed him to thank him for the dinner and to tell him she was going to England, and he had replied wishing her luck. He'd made her promise to tell him how it was going and said he would send her anything she needed. That gave Arty a little warm feeling inside. She had just got thousands of miles closer to Matthew and Persephone and Zeus – and Matthew at least should be easy to find now. And she had the greatest movie star of all time telling her: 'This story has a happy ending. I know it.'

She remembered sitting in the clearing and looking up at the lights that passed overhead. They were *aeroplanes*,

Vishnu had said, and she had gazed at them with a vague interest, not really caring. Aeroplanes were the same as shooting stars in her world. Arty had seen pictures of planes in books, but she had never really thought about the fact that those lights in the sky had represented people inside metal boxes flying through the air.

She had never, ever thought she might be in one. Even when she had run away to follow Zeus, she had never properly imagined the aeroplane. It had been an abstract thing, and now it was real. As the plane bumped along the runway, she hung on to the armrest next to her and held her breath. No one else was screaming. Even Arty wasn't actually screaming. If she was screaming, it was on the inside. She checked; her mouth was closed.

No one else seemed to feel that flying was an impossible thing. It was just Arty. Even Zeus had been on a plane by now, and he must have been through all this. She knew that he would have tried to hide how scared he was, would have reached out for her and found she wasn't there, and that broke her heart.

All she could see through the window across the aisle was a patch of grey sky. They really should have bigger windows on planes.

This was England. She was pleased that she was here to follow her mother's quest, but what she didn't want was to have to stay with the grandparents who had come forward to claim her. Venus had hated them. Arty remembered her saying, *Be careful of the rest of my family. Don't go into the basement.* She didn't know what Venus had meant by

250

that, but she was keeping that advice in her head at all times. It was precious; one of the last things her mother had said to her.

No one had given her a choice. Her mother's family had seen her on the news and come forward to claim her, and now she was going to live with them. So here she was with an emergency passport and a piece of paper with '*Matthew Jones & Tania Roswell*' written on it in her bag, and two unknown keys round her neck. The only thing she could do was to get on with it.

'Excuse me,' she said to the man next to her, just as he clicked his seatbelt open. He took it off even though the sign was still lit up.

He looked round. 'Mm?'

Arty had ignored him for the flight because that was what everyone was doing. Now she needed information.

'What's London like?' she asked. 'Are there eighteen million people?'

'Not eighteen million,' he said. He had grey hair and he had spent the whole journey watching episodes of a programme called *Veep*. He smelled like old wine. 'More like eight?'

'Smaller than Mumbai.'

'Indeed.'

'But still a bit big to walk around and hope you find the right person.'

He laughed. 'Yep. You'll need a more focused strategy than that.'

'Thank you.'

Arty turned her face away so he knew not to talk to her any more, and closed her eyes so she could pretend to be somewhere else. She didn't want to go to wherever it was that her grandparents lived. *Clevedon*. She wanted to go to Persephone's house. She wanted to find Matthew. She was very much hoping that he would be at the grandparents' house.

She knew that her grandparents were going to be there to meet her, and she knew they had paid for her to go on the plane. Perhaps she would get used to England at their house and as soon as she could she would go to London. She had been trying to prepare herself to meet them, but it was difficult because all she had in her head were monsters. Her mother hadn't been happy at home. She had been so unhappy that she had run away to India and never spoken to them again. She had never said anything good about them. 'It wasn't a happy place.' Arty could hear her saying that now. It wasn't a happy place. Arty was arriving at an unhappy place.

She could see that there was grass here. The sky was still grey. It didn't look very different from Mumbai even after all that flying. The aeroplane stopped moving, and then people were queuing so they could be the first to get off. Arty waited for every one of them to go because she found that she didn't want to get off the plane. Then she stood up, took her bag from beside her feet and put *Woman on the Edge of Time* into it. She touched the keys round her neck for luck. She was the last off the plane because she had to do some meditation and breathing before she could make her legs stand her up and walk her towards the door.

The nice plane people were standing there saying goodbye to everyone. When Arty went past, the very last of all, a woman with pink-painted lips said, 'Good luck, Arty. I hope it works out for you here, darling.'

Arty turned and looked at her face. She was kind. She knew Arty's name. She felt her eyes fill with tears.

The woman rubbed her arm and then, as Arty started properly crying, she hugged her.

'Do you live in England?' Arty said.

'No, no. I'm Delhi based. Working this route today.'

'My dad comes from Delhi! Can I come and stay with you there?'

The woman laughed. 'Oh, sweetie. It doesn't really work like that, I'm afraid. I wish it did.'

'Well,' said Arty, 'thank you for being kind. You're really lovely. I wish it did work like that too.'

'Oh, darling.' The woman wiped under her eye with a finger, and the lady next to her was sniffing too. 'You take care of yourself, all right? Tell me – what was AMK like?'

Arty stopped and felt her face smiling through her tears. 'He was wonderful,' she said. 'So kind and funny. He's going to help me.'

'You lucky thing. I'd give *anything* to have dinner with him.'

'Oh! I've got something you can have.' Arty felt inside her bag. She had his envelope of pictures in there, so she gave one to the woman. 'There you go. He said I could give

these to people if I wanted to. That's for you, from him.'
She handed them to the others too.

The woman gasped and clutched it to her chest.

'Thank you so much,' she said, and as Arty walked
away she could hear them talking about him.

She walked without knowing where she was supposed
to be going, as the other passengers had vanished. Actually
she managed not to get lost because she never had to
pick a way to go. It was all right there for her, like a path
through the forest. She just went the way the yellow signs
showed her, in the same way that she had followed Hella's
path and come out of her whole world. This path took
her to passport control, and she stood at the back of a
queue that said REST OF THE WORLD because that had to
include even her, and she liked it that it moved slowly
because she was in no hurry to get out. She wouldn't have
minded staying in the airport for a long time, and never
actually being anywhere.

In the end a woman looked at her emergency passport
and nodded and said 'thank you' and told her she hadn't
needed to queue because this still counted as a British
passport but it was fine, and then she was there. The next
stop was a place to collect bags but Arty didn't have a bag
to get, so she walked, very slowly, under a big green sign
that said NOTHING TO DECLARE.

She had quite a lot to declare actually. Mainly she
wanted to declare that she absolutely did not want to meet
these grandparents, who had driven her mother away and
who had a basement she must avoid.

Then she was in a wide open space with huge windows, and crowds and crowds of people. She wanted to run away, but she had nowhere to go.

She saw them before they saw her. The woman was holding a sign that said ARTEMIS JONES on it, and she supposed that must be her own name. She had never known she was called Jones. It didn't feel like a word that was hers.

The woman was the palest person she had ever seen. 'Jones' was a word that suited her. She should have been called Jones Jones. Her skin was grey and her hair was grey and she was wearing a grey skirt and a greyish blueish jumper. The man had his arms folded and looked grumpy and purple. He looked like a Crosspatch Jones.

Arty walked to them as slowly as she could. When they saw her, their faces changed in slow motion. The woman fixed on a smile, but her eyes were sad and she flinched a bit. The man just made his lips thin in something that wasn't a smile at all, then looked away and kept his arms folded.

Arty saw that they didn't want her any more than she wanted them. She saw they wanted Venus, because she was their daughter. She thought they wished Venus had been the one to walk out of the clearing and come on an aeroplane to see them. They were waiting for Arty in case she had turned out to be an exact copy of her mother, but they could see at once that she wasn't.

Arty wanted Venus too. She missed her more than they did. She tried to imagine what a nice granddaughter would do now, and she smiled, even though she meant it just as much as they didn't.

'Hello,' she said, and she tried very hard to pretend to be nice. 'I'm Arty.'

'Artemis,' said the woman. This was her grandmother. If she'd been eaten by a wolf, Arty wouldn't have told it she had such big teeth. She would have gone back outside and eaten the cake on her own. 'Well. Here you are. How was the flight?'

'It was weird,' Arty said. 'It wasn't like I thought.'

'If we get back to the car now,' said the man, 'then we'll come in under an hour in the car park. Lucky you landed on time or it would have cost us a bloody fortune, though you took your time getting out. We wondered about getting the bus here, or maybe just your grandma coming up to meet you, but we weren't sure if you had bags. Often you see them with hundreds of bags, all taped up and what have you.'

He looked quite cross about the fact that Arty didn't have hundreds of bags all taped up. She had no idea what she was meant to say to him. He turned and hurried away and she followed.

This did not seem to be the sort of grandfather who would be kind and come to rescue his grandchild from a predicament. He was the sort who would leave her in a forest alone because she was too expensive to feed.

The grandmother (Jones) walked fast, and Arty ended up trailing. She lost sight of them altogether in the end, and then she didn't know where to go, so she stood still and let the airport happen around her.

It was not so different from the airport at Mumbai. Everything felt blue, but not soft or gentle or relaxing blue.

The airport blue was harsh and cold, like metal. It was quite exciting, though. It was the way she thought a space station might be. A place to go to if you planned to be shot away into the sky.

But all the people here were in their own worlds; they were on their own space stations. They walked round her looking at their phones and Arty quite liked that. She was almost pleased when she noticed a couple of people on the escalator pointing their phones towards her, because that let her be her Indian self.

She smiled and waved. The people waved back. A woman in a sari came up to her and said, 'You are friends with AMK – can it be true?'

'Yes it can!' Arty said, and she reached for a photo. This was the last one she was going to give out, because she was keeping the final picture of him for herself.

'Here you are,' I said. 'It's from him. For you. He said I should give them to friends and that you are his friend too.' She embellished the last bit.

'Thank you! Thank you!' said the woman, and she took Arty's hand and stared into her eyes.

Arty's grandmother turned up on her other side and tugged at her other arm.

'Artemis,' she said. 'For goodness' sake! Don't talk to strangers! Keep up. The car park!'

'*You're* a stranger,' Arty said, and her grandmother pretended she hadn't heard.

They went out of the door, and it hit her.

The cold.

The cold.

The freezing cold. All the hairs on her arms stood up and she trembled all over. She had never known that it was possible to be so cold.

'Oh my God!' she said. 'Why's it so cold? What happened?'

Her grandmother huffed a bit. 'It's actually quite mild,' she said, and Arty could see that somehow by feeling cold she had offended her.

She sat in the back of the car and didn't say anything. Jones talked a little bit in a small voice, saying things like: 'It was quite a shock when we discovered it was you, Artemis. The girl in India on the news. Our granddaughter.'

'Did you know I existed?'

'No. This is completely new to us. We never imagined we'd have grandchildren.'

'So how did you find out?'

'Oh, the Indian authorities found out the names of everyone who lived there, and we had a visit from the police telling us what had happened. We were astonished.'

'What about my uncle Matthew?'

'Yes?' said Jones. 'What about him?'

'Can I see him?' Now she felt wide awake.

'Not for a long time, I'm afraid.' Her voice was tight. Arty looked to her grandfather, but he was staring straight ahead, not saying anything either.

'Why not?'

'He's in Africa. Doing his *good works*.' She said 'good works' as if that were a bad thing.

'Doing what?'

'Oh, he works in a refugee camp. We never see him.'

'We do,' said her grandad. 'He comes back.'

'Yes, but as little as he can. He's living in Uganda. Once or twice a year we get a visit and he's impossible to get hold of. You'll meet him one day.'

'Can I talk to him on the phone?'

'Once in a blue moon.'

Arty thought about this. Uncle Matthew was alive, and living in Africa doing 'good works'. She might be able to speak to him on the phone and she would meet him one day. That was something. She knew that Uganda was a long, long way from here, but the fact that he was alive, and that she knew where he lived, was a huge thing.

'We've missed Victoria terribly,' Jones was saying. 'Matthew has too, of course. And then this happens –' She stopped talking very suddenly.

'Don't upset your grandmother,' said Crosspatch as if Arty had done that.

'I'll try not to,' she said.

She wanted to ask her grandfather about patriarchy but she thought she'd probably better not because all the feelings she was getting from this man were that he hated her, and also that he probably loved patriarchy. After that she just stared out of the window while they talked to each other about people she didn't know. At one point Jones offered Arty a sweet, and she kept it on her tongue for a long time, loving the sugar in spite of herself, letting it melt as slowly as it could.

The roads were orderly and less bumpy, and no one seemed to use their car horns at all. Everything was straight and smooth. The houses were different, the road signs were different, the writing was different, and there were no people walking around. It was quite boring.

The inside of the car smelled like nothing she had ever imagined. It was like chemicals, and it hurt her throat to breathe it. At one point she thought she was going to be sick, but it passed.

Arty didn't really care about this place. She didn't want to be here. She wanted to be in Mumbai, and then back in the clearing. She was only here, she told herself, for Persephone and Zeus, and for Matthew when he came back.

She was thousands of miles from everything and everyone she had ever known, apart from Zeus. She felt sick with longing for him. She leaned against the window and imagined herself going to France until she fell asleep.

The house, when they got there, was not in a clearing in a forest as she had secretly hoped it might be; it was a square house in a street of other square houses that all looked the same. However, at the end of the street there was the sea, and that was something Arty had not expected at all. It was grey and soft on the horizon, close enough to the Mumbai water to be the same thing, and she loved that.

'The ocean,' she said, walking up the road towards it. The hairs on her arms were standing up again. She was trembling with the cold, but at least she was looking at the waves. There was land on the other side of it.

'*Ocean* is a bit of a stretch,' said Jones in a brisk voice, following her to bring her back. 'It's an estuary.'

'Is that France?' She pointed to the land, and waved, just in case Zeus was over there looking at her. She would build a boat and go and find him.

'France!' She laughed. 'No, of course it's not France. That's Wales. This way, Artemis.'

Arty didn't know what an estuary was, though she knew that Wales existed, thanks to her lessons with Diana. The house had a garden path like a house in a book and a green front door. Clevedon was a place with houses in it, by the ocean, across from Wales.

Jones stopped, looked Arty up and down, and smiled.

'I've got you some suitable clothes,' she said. 'They're in your room.'

'I like my clothes. AMK's wife got me this dress.' She was not going to let Jones say anything against her purple dress. It was beautiful. 'He's the greatest actor in the world.'

'I'm sure it's just the thing for India,' she said. 'But be sensible. You need something warmer, don't you?'

The carpet was so thick that it tickled Arty's feet when she stepped out of her green flip-flops. Her grandmother looked a bit surprised by her taking her shoes off.

'That's nice,' she said. 'Your mother always did that too. She left them right there, the same as you.'

That made the world stop.

Venus had lived *here*. Arty had come through a portal and traversed a universe, and ended up in a place Venus had known too. That had not felt real until now.

'Did she . . .' Arty took a deep breath. She had to say it. 'Did she live here? In this very house? With you? And . . . Matthew too?'

Jones nodded without looking at Arty, and walked off. 'She lived here until she stormed off to India and never came back,' she said as she went. Arty wasn't quite sure what to do, so she waited for a bit until Jones said, 'Come on. Into the kitchen.'

On the way she passed a door that was locked. She didn't know what made her stop and stare at it, but Jones looked back at her and said, 'Not in there. That's not a place for you to go.'

Arty said, 'Is it the basement?'

Her grandmother didn't answer.

'This is the kitchen,' she said.

Arty's eyes darted around. She felt like a small animal that had come to the wrong place and needed a way out. This was *not* a kitchen. Everything in it was bright white. Every surface was shiny. The smell was not a food smell. It was a chemical smell: in fact, this room was the way she expected a science laboratory would be, rather than a place in which you made food.

There were cupboard doors, all closed, and a few machines were tucked away on shelves. There was one book, called *Delia's Complete How to Cook*. Two little bowls and two spoons were drying on a rack by the sink, and that was the only sign of anything to do with eating. There was a white table with three chairs at it, and Arty wondered whether they had got another chair out for her.

'Is this where you . . . cook?' she said, and for a few seconds she was back in the clearing, sitting in the cooking area with Vishnu. He was boiling up the vegetable peelings to make stock. There were bags of rice and lentils next to him, and a pot over the fire. That had been real cooking. Here she felt it was more likely that her grandmother would hand her a pill and that she would get everything she needed from that, like in space stories.

The clearing kitchen could never have gleamed like this, because it had been packed-down earth. It had shone for Arty, though, because it was the place where things from the ground were transformed to nutrition that gave them all the energy they needed. She had sat with Vishnu for hours at a time, while he told her about protein and carbs and vitamins. He explained what they got from which food. He kept them all as healthy as he could, by growing and feeding them the right things.

He would have been horrified to see this, and at first Arty was glad he hadn't had to. Then she remembered that he was from the outside world too (not England, but still) and that he had known this stuff well enough to decide to leave it all behind. Her heart overflowed again. Her family had seen this, rejected it, and made something different instead. She appreciated it all now like she had never done before. She didn't say any of this aloud.

Her grandfather shouted, 'Back in a bit,' and the door slammed.

Jones rolled her eyes a bit at the place where his voice hung in the air, put her bag on the back of the door and sighed.

'Yes,' she said. 'This is where I cook.' She clicked the button on one of her machines and it started to make a noise. 'Welcome to your new home, Artemis.'

Arty picked up a thing from beside the cooker. It was white plastic and had a button on it.

'You can call me Arty, Jones,' she said. 'Everyone else does.' She hadn't meant to call her *Jones*, but her grandmother didn't understand what she meant anyway.

'Arty Jones,' she said. 'Yes. All right. Put that down.'

Arty pressed the button. The thing made a clicking sound and inside it, at the tip, there was a tiny spark.

'What should I call you?'

'Oh, call me Grandma. I always thought if we'd had grandchildren I'd be Grandma. And now here you are.'

'What's this for?'

Her grandmother took it out of her hand and put it back in its place. 'It's for lighting the hobs. Don't fiddle with it. Sit down.'

Arty picked up one of the spoons and looked at her face in it. It was upside down. That was right. She *was* upside down. She sat down, the spoon still in her hand. 'There are no other grandchildren?' she asked. 'Matthew doesn't have any children?'

'Of course not. He's never in one place long enough. He's not a family man, your uncle.'

'When's he back?'

'A couple of months, perhaps? Artemis – Arty – I can see you're excited about your uncle Matthew. I suppose your mother talked about him.'

Arty could hardly say the words. 'She spoke about him all the time. She . . . she didn't know if he was still alive.'

'Yes. Well. I'm surprised she spoke of him fondly, given the way things were when she left. She hadn't seen him since he was in a terrible state. She told you about the drugs, I suppose?'

'Yes.'

'He's long past all of that now. We're proud of him. It hasn't been easy for him. So she spoke about him – I daresay she spoke about us too?'

'She did,' Arty said. The words *she told me to stay away from your basement* were jumping around, wanting to come out, but she decided she had better not say them. 'She missed him,' she said instead. 'And you,' she added, even though that was a lie. She could see that Grandma needed to hear it.

'Well,' said Grandma. 'If she'd got in touch, we would have welcomed her with open arms. And you too.'

'So, Grandma?' The word felt strange to say. It was a storybook word. 'What should I call . . .?' She didn't even know his name, so she couldn't ask. She pointed at the place where his *Back in a bit* was still hanging in the air.

'Oh, Grandad, dear.'

'OK. And will he call me Arty?'

'Yes. Arty Jones. Would you like a cup of tea, Arty Jones?' She smiled as if she were being a bit mischievous. 'And then I'm sure you'd like to freshen up after your journey.'

'Yes please.' She saw that the noisy machine had boiled some water very quickly. She liked that, and she watched her grandmother putting a little square that Arty thought had tea in it into a cup that she took from the cupboard, and pouring the water over it. She wanted to tell her how they had made tea in the clearing, filling the urn with mint and whatever else had grown that was edible, and topping it up with water throughout the day. She had a feeling, though, that her grandmother wouldn't have liked that.

She watched Grandma put milk into the tea (which Arty didn't want), and take out the square things with a spoon and put them into a bin that she actually opened with her foot. Arty had no idea whether the 'freshening up' she was meant to do next involved washing her hands, or having a shower, or doing a wee, or something entirely different, a new English thing that she didn't know about.

They sat at the table. The tea was horrible and Arty wanted to spit it out like she had the Kingfisher in the clearing but she felt she couldn't do that here. She had to try to be the sort of granddaughter Grandma wanted.

'This tea is so different,' she managed to say, wanting to scrape the slime of the milk off her tongue. She knew the masala chai she had had in Mumbai had been milky, but it had also been filled with spice and flavour. This tasted of slimy milk and dust.

'Oh,' said Grandma. 'Did you want some sugar?'

It turned out that sugar made it better.

'Does Uncle Matthew know I'm here?' she said.

'We've tried to call him,' said Grandma. 'No luck so far. He's like that. We'll keep trying.'

'I can't wait to meet him.'

'He struggled with his twin taking off like that all those years ago. He went out to India looking for her. He was a bit cagey about it, but he came back saying he thought she would be all right.'

'Matthew and Venus were *twins*?'

'Venus!' Grandma stopped talking for a long time. When she did speak her voice was different, and she said, 'Your mother's name is Victoria, dear. And to us, whatever she went on to call herself, she will always be Victoria, or Vicky.'

'Sorry.' Arty had known that. She pictured her mother with her long straggly hair and flowing skirts and made herself apply the word *Victoria* to her image. It was just a word. It wasn't the right word, though it had been once. It was a word that Venus had rejected for herself. But Arty could see that she would always be Victoria to her mother. It was what her parents had chosen for her.

Grandma spoke quickly. 'You know, Matthew is Matthew Arthur, so I wonder whether you're partly named for him.'

Arty didn't know what to say. Arthur. Artemis. They were both Art. Maybe Grandma was right, but Arty would never know.

Grandma clearly wasn't very good at silence and soon she started talking again.

'Now, I've been looking into your options, Artem . . . Arty.' Arty smiled her thanks, and Grandma did a tiny smile back, just with the very corners of her mouth. 'You're sixteen, aren't you?'

'I think so. Though we didn't measure things like that very much.'

'You're sixteen. That's what they said. Do you have a birthday?'

She remembered the date of birth on Cherry's passport and said, 'The twenty-first day of September.'

'September the twenty-first? Goodness, you'll just fit into that academic year then. Right. That's good. I'm glad we have a birthday for you. Is it on your passport?' Arty nodded. 'That's very good. We need to get your passport made official too, because that one they gave you was just an emergency travel thing.'

'OK.'

'There's a social worker going to come to see you too, but don't worry about that for now. So in September you can start at sixth-form college, just before your birthday. Now it's May, so you've got a few months to get up to speed. I got you a prospectus for sixth form. Have a look. See what you think.'

She stood up and went to open a drawer. The prospectus was a glossy book with a picture of girls and boys smiling on the cover. Arty leafed through it, gradually working out that Grandma wanted to send her to a place where she would be able to study.

Arty knew all about school. She remembered their own lessons in the hut in the clearing, where Diana and everyone else (but it had mainly been Diana) taught the children to read and do sums, and all the other things they thought they would need to know. Arty had learned to read and write, to do things with numbers, to look at maps, sitting out in the fresh air during the winter, and undercover in the rainy season. She had loved learning.

'Do I have to study everything?'

'Of course you don't! Oh – you do know how to read, don't you? Yes, look at you reading that. You'll be all right, I daresay. Three subjects would be the norm, if you want to go to university, which you should, though you'll have to get a loan for your living costs. Or stay here with us and go to Bristol, I suppose. The bus would still cost, mind you. What are you interested in? Have you studied before? My friend Mrs Bourne from down the road recommended a tutor to get you up to speed between now and September. Normally there would be entry requirements for some GCSEs but under the circumstances . . .'

Arty stopped listening properly and leafed through the pages. Psychology. Maths and further maths. Chemistry. She didn't know anything.

'English literature!' She said it triumphantly when she found it, stabbing the page with her finger. 'That's what I like. I like books.'

'Good. What else?'

Arty didn't know. 'What did . . . What did my mother do?'

Grandma sighed.

'Oh, she did English too, and history and economics. Two As and a B. Clever girl. She did much better than

Matthew, of course. He was a lost cause at that point but he caught up later.'

'Can I do the same as her? English, history and economics?'

Grandma paused.

'Read up on them a bit. If those are what you really want to do, then I suppose you could. Economics is complicated, I think. I could never understand a word of what she was on about, and you – well, you've never even known shops really, have you?'

'I know shops now. I've been to loads of them. I've been to Mumbai shops and cafes. I learned how to use money.'

Grandma smiled properly.

'I'm sure you have. Rather you than me with those Mumbai shops. Well, if that's what you want, you should have a go. You've got time to find out.'

Arty flicked to the economics page and read the description. It made about as much sense as the rest of it, which was not very much at all, but she was interested in money, and she thought she could give it a try.

Her bedroom was her mother's old room and that was just too much. Everything was new and different, and she was supposed to stay here now for years and years. She needed to work out how to fit into her mother's old life, the one she had given up to become goddess of the clearing.

She didn't know anyone. Matthew was in Uganda and she didn't know him anyway. She had no idea how to find Persephone, and Florence and Zeus hadn't replied to her emails. She didn't want to cry in front of anyone, but she did actually need to cry.

There was a bed with a thick blanket kind of thing on it, which was pink. There was a pillow with a pink case. The walls were pale pink, and there were spots on them where, Arty thought, pictures had been taken down. She looked at the books on the shelf. They were definitely Venus's books: there was *Anna Karenina*, there was *Cat's Eye* and there was a book called *The Second Sex*, which she picked up and flicked through. She would read that.

She stood at the window and looked at the other houses that were out there with other people inside them living their strange English lives. She watched a cat walking along a wall. It was fatter than the cats she had seen in Mumbai. The garden here was a square of grass with some flowers round the edge and two trees by the back wall. One was small and the other one was big with thick branches.

She knew about this tree. That tree was the place where Venus and Matthew had sat and she had played at being goddess. That was where the clearing had begun.

She walked over to the bed and sat down because her legs could not hold her up for a second longer. She reached into her bag and took out her special bear from the bottom of it. It was holding out the heart that said 'Love You Loads X' on it, and Arty clutched it to herself. That bear had been with her for her whole life.

She buried her face in the pillow and thought about the fact that she had made her mother's journey in reverse, from the clearing to Lonavala, to Mumbai and back to

Clevedon and the tree. It had unravelled. She was in a weird dream, living Venus's old life. She would be going to her mother's old college, doing her old studying, sleeping in her old room, and all of it without being able to discuss it with her.

She missed her mother so much. The only person who would understand this was dead.

She buried her face in the pillow, even though it smelled weird, and cried and cried and cried. She kept it as quiet as she could so Grandma wouldn't come in. Nothing happened. She heard cars going past sometimes. She cried until she couldn't cry any more, and then she just lay there and stared into the bleakness.

This was her new life. And there was nothing she could do about it except wait for a long time and meet her uncle Matthew, if he ever answered his phone.

After a while she picked up the towel that was on the end of the bed and opened the door quietly to check that no one was out there. Then she ran into the bathroom and locked the door.

It was bigger and shinier than any bathroom she had used in India apart from the one at the AMK hotel (it was a lot smaller than that). She stared at her puffy face in the mirror for a while. She never knew she had a big brown spot on her cheek until she came out of the forest. She didn't mind it. Her hair was knotted and she thought she looked messier than other people did.

She turned the shower on and let it run hot before she stepped under the water. She washed her body and hair for a long time, using the shampoo and conditioner and the shower gel, and rubbing her face to make it look normal again. She brushed her teeth, with the new toothbrush Jones had given her (it had a little button on it that made it vibrate! She loved it so much that she brushed them twice), put some cream on her face, and wrapped the towel round herself, ready to run back to the bedroom.

Her grandfather was standing on the stairs. Arty stopped, not sure whether she was meant to say something to him, but he just looked at her for a few seconds, then turned away.

She dressed in the clothes Grandma had left her. They were black and blue like bruises. She put on a pair of the blue jeans that everyone else wore but they felt weird, so she tried a skirt instead and that was better. She put on a blue shirt that buttoned up the front, and because she was so extremely cold she added a jumper. Jumpers were also called sweaters and pullovers. Arty had read about them in books, but never worn one. It was scratchy.

She stared at the girl in the mirror. She looked like an English girl. It almost made her laugh. She hung her purple dress on a hanger and brushed her hair even though it was still wet. She put it into a plait so that it would dry wavy.

Her grandfather was back on the landing when she came out.

'Must have been quite a thing,' he said as if he had been waiting for her, planning what to say. 'Finding that we were here. Flying over.'

'Yes,' Arty said. 'Yes, it was. Quite a thing.'

He grunted.

'Must be strange for you too,' she said.

He actually smiled. 'Yes,' he said. 'Yes. Strange. Good that you're here.' And he went down the stairs.

JUNE

I stepped back again and pressed myself against the door. No one was coming to rescue me. The fire was coming closer and closer and I knew that this was it. I pushed myself back as far as I could. The smoke was heavy in my throat.

I kept the bear behind me, squeezing it to reassure it. It said, 'Thank you,' in a tiny voice. We waited.

I thought of everything I'd done. I screamed for my mum.

'I'm sorry, I'm sorry, I'm sorry!' I shouted to the whole world. I really was sorry. I was sorry for everything. I was sorry for surviving when I shouldn't have.

If they let me out, everything would be different. I could see a life in which I helped people. I would never do anything but good deeds. I promised it to the universe.

The door swung open and there were hands on me. I wasn't sure what had happened, but I could breathe the air out here. I wasn't on fire. I gulped down the air as if it were a glass of water.

Someone picked me up and carried me right out of there. And I was free.

18

'We need to have a funeral,' Arty said, fiddling with her cup of tea. She hated saying the words but they were necessary. 'I don't even know what happened to. To. To her body. And the others' bodies too. No one said.' She remembered how confused she had been during that time, how absent she was from her self. 'Or maybe they did but I didn't hear properly.'

The fog was clearing now that she had been here for a few days. She didn't have to worry about money, or about where she was going to sleep or whether she was going to eat. A stressed social worker had come over to check that she was all right, and was satisfied that she was. Arty was officially living here. With survival taken care of, everything else was flooding back.

She was sitting in the kitchen with both grandparents, drinking tea. There was a plate of biscuits on the table. Arty wanted to eat them all at once, but she knew it would be rude. She had already eaten three in quick succession.

'Can you help me find out?' she said when they didn't reply.

'Well,' said Grandma, 'from what we understand, everyone involved was . . . cremated. Because of the infection. I know you don't know much about everything that happened on that front, and I'm glad you don't, but I know it was taken very seriously.'

'We expect to have the ashes delivered to us at some point,' said Grandad, looking into the corner of the room. He picked up a pink wafer, looked at it and put it back.

'When Matthew's here,' said Arty, 'can we have a funeral? A blessing? Otherwise nothing is quite finished. Venus – Victoria – deserves a ceremony.'

Neither grandparent said anything for a while. Arty sipped her tea. Now that Grandma was letting her drink it black, with one sugar, she liked it.

'Of course she does,' said Grandma. 'Yes, Artemis. We'll have a nice ceremony. And of course Matthew will come.'

'It feels a bit odd to us,' said Grandad. 'We hadn't heard from her for so long . . .' He looked as if he wanted to explain more, but he stopped speaking.

Arty nodded. Grandma stood up and Arty took a pink wafer in case she was about to take the plate away.

'Yes,' said Grandma. 'We'll do something nice for Victoria. And we can do it your way, even if your grandad and I might find it odd. Now, the laptop should be charged up, so do you want to get ready for your Skypie thing?'

Arty smiled. 'Yes please! I'd love to.'

Her grandparents had produced a computer after she'd begged them for it. They had plugged it into the wall a while ago, and had promised that she could use it to call

Zeus. She had emailed Florence to ask if she could call, and Florence had actually replied, and so they were speaking at half past eleven, which was very nearly now.

Grandma cleared the table, and Grandad helped Arty set the laptop computer up so that the camera was on. She hated it when her face appeared on the screen, but then she got used to it when she realized this image of her would be on Florence's screen for Zeus to see.

At twenty-eight minutes past eleven she ran upstairs to fetch her bear. She wanted to show it to Zeus. She sat at the table with the bear on her lap, and stared at the screen, and waited.

At exactly eleven thirty the computer made an electronic sound again and again, and she clicked the green thing to answer it. A few seconds after that a picture appeared on her screen, and it was a picture of Zeus.

It was actual Zeus. His hair was much shorter, and his teeth were white, and he looked different in lots of tiny ways, but it was him. Her little brother. Her other self.

'ARTY!' he yelled, and she saw his face get suddenly bigger as he tried to climb through the two screens on to her lap.

'Zeddy!' She knew she couldn't climb through, but she stroked the place where his face was on the screen. 'Oh, Zeddy, darling. How are you?'

'Arty, I can see you!' he said. He was bouncing up and down.

'I know, darling,' she said. 'And I can see you too.' She stuck her tongue out at him, and he did the same back to her. 'How is it in France?' She saw him look round and knew that Florence must be out of shot. 'If we talk in Hindi,' she said in Hindi, 'then no one will understand.'

'Yes,' he said, switching languages. 'I don't want to be in France. I want to be at home.'

'Me too,' she said. 'Oh gosh, I miss you so much, darling.'

'I miss you so much too.' They were both crying. That was no good. Arty picked the bear up off her lap and held it up so he could see it. 'Hello, Zeus,' she said in the bear's voice in English, making it move around. 'It's very nice to see you again. Have you been reading some books?'

'Hello, library bear!' said Zeus, cheering up at once. 'Yes, I have, because Arty did teach me reading in English and now I go to *la grande section* and I do some reading in French too.'

'Well,' said the bear, 'that is quite something. You are a very clever young man.'

Out of the corner of her eye Arty caught sight of her grandmother leaving the room quickly. That was good. She turned her attention back to Zeus. They talked about books, about his nursery school, about his sisters. They switched between languages often, and she noticed how much better his French was than hers now. In the end Florence appeared behind him.

'*Salut*, Arty!' she said. She looked much better than she had in India. Much happier and more relaxed. Nicer.

'*Salut*, *Florence*,' said Arty, and she told her that, yes, she was in England now, living with her grandparents, and, yes, she was fine. They talked in the friendliest way they ever had, and then she said goodbye to Zeus and they agreed that they could speak once a week.

When she hung up Grandma wasn't around, so Arty went into the garden. She walked across the grass to the tree, and stood in front of it and looked up.

It was a different tree from the ones in the forest, but it was the same too. It was the origin of the clearing. This felt like a spiritual place to Arty, and she sat down on the grass, ignoring her wet bottom, and closed her eyes.

I can see my mother.

I can hear my mother's voice.

I can smell my mother's smell.

I can feel my mother's touch.

I can taste Dairy Milk.

She sat there for a long time. She tried to let it go, to let Venus go, but in a way that didn't involve Arty falling apart. She thought about Victoria and Matthew up this tree as children, pretending a world that was later going to be real. She pictured them, a little boy and a little girl, twins, pretending to be in the forest and her heart broke into pieces for the things that had happened to them. She tried not to be sad for her mother, because she had actually done it, and she had been strong and wonderful and happy, but now she was dead.

Though because Arty hadn't seen her mother's body, she was starting to think that she might not be dead. She could have got better before the medical people reached the clearing. She might have crept away and be living deep in the forest now, waiting.

It was no use. If Venus was alive, she would have found Arty. She would be here in Clevedon right now. She would not have abandoned her child in the outside world. Arty told herself that again and again. Venus was dead. She needed to accept that. That was why she needed to have a funeral.

'When you were on the computer-call thing before,' Grandma said. Her voice was very even. 'You had a bear you were showing to the little boy. Where did that come from?'

'It's the library bear,' Arty said. 'It's mine. I had it from when I was really small. I think Venus gave it to me. Vicky. I brought it with me because it's my special thing. It's been with me all my life.'

'Is that right?' said Grandma. 'Right. Well.'

Arty was back at the laptop, trying to sign into her email account again. 'Grandma,' she said, 'why don't they put the alphabet in the right order on computers?'

'Now I do know this,' said Grandma. Arty noticed that she was wearing a necklace that said MUM on it in curly writing, and she wondered whether Venus or Matthew had given it to her, or maybe both of them. 'It's to get the letters you use most in the places where they're easier to reach. See? You hardly ever use a "q", and there it is right in the corner.'

'Oh.' Arty looked at it. 'Yes, there's the "z" in the other corner.'

'You can learn touch typing. It's a way of training yourself to type without even looking at the keys. In my day girls were supposed to learn secretarial skills so they could find work typing up letters for bosses and so on, but these days I daresay everyone does their own. You girls want to be your own bosses, don't you? Not take dictation for some man.'

Arty didn't know what that meant, but she got the gist of it.

'That's quite right, Grandma,' she said. 'Let the man take his own dictation and I'll take mine. What you said sounds like a thing from the patriarchy and I don't like the patriarchy.'

'Oh my dear. You're your mother's daughter all right,' said Grandma.

They smiled at each other.

'Venus was a wonderful matriarch,' Arty said, and Grandma gave a little nod and looked away.

Arty typed 'Tania Roswell' into the Google screen. The only person it came up with who could possibly have been Persephone was a person who worked at a law firm in London. She wrote down the phone number for the company and went back to her emails.

She sent a quick apology email to Cherry and a chatty one to AMK, saying that she was here and that she was all right. She begged them to keep in touch with her, then shut the computer down because she could tell that Grandma wanted her to.

Grandma nodded. 'Come out for a walk,' she said.

They walked along by the sea, which was brown and rocky with a few people swimming in it. Arty could not even imagine how freezing those people must have been. She was huddled in an old coat of her mother's, shivering, but she liked the air in her face. It had the same smell of the sea that the air in Bandra and Colaba had.

She spoke to Grandma about Zeus. Talking to him had made her feel different. She loved it that they could still see each other on the screen. She loved it that they could chat and tell each other what they were doing. This showed her that Joe had been right when he said that not all internet things were horrible.

'Zeus is so adorable,' she said. 'I have to go to France and see him one day.'

'One day no doubt you will. You need to get settled here first before you go gallivanting away anywhere.'

'Just to see his little face,' said Arty.

She could tell that Grandma was preoccupied, and she thought perhaps she didn't like her talking about Zeus because he was from her old life.

'How about an ice cream?' Grandma said.

'Ice cream!' Arty was immediately on board. 'Really? I can have ice cream?'

'Of course.'

'I had lentil ice cream with AMK,' she said, and Grandma smiled a little smile.

'Only you, my dear,' she said. 'I must say, I'm intrigued by this AMK of yours. I'm going to look him up.'

'You should.'

When they got home Arty went to watch television because Grandma told her to. Grandma went upstairs on her own. As Arty put the TV on, she saw a man hiking through a forest, talking about how you could find water. It was interesting, but not as interesting as Tania Roswell, so she tiptoed across the hallway and into the kitchen to find the phone.

It was easy to call Tania Roswell's office. She just pressed the numbers in the right order and put the phone to her ear and there it was, making a ringing sound. Someone answered and said the name of the company.

'Can I speak to Tania Roswell, please?' said Arty.

'I'll put you through to her office,' said the person inside the phone, who might have been a deep-voiced woman or a high-voiced man. Arty couldn't tell. She waited and the phone rang again and someone else answered. Someone who was definitely a woman.

'Tania Roswell's office?' she said, and Arty took a deep breath and tried to make sense.

'Hello, Tania,' she said. 'My name's Arty. I come from India, from the clearing, and I need to meet you because my mum, Venus –'

She stopped when the voice interrupted her. 'I'm sorry, but I'm not Tania. I'm her secretary. Can I pass on a message?'

'Oh,' said Arty. 'Yes. Sorry. OK. Can you ask her to call me? If you tell her I'm Venus's daughter from the clearing, she'll know.' She left the number that was written on a white label attached to the phone, and then put it next to her and stared at it, waiting for it to ring.

It didn't.

After a while Arty went back to watching the television, while keeping the phone next to her all the time, staring at it often. She couldn't sit on the sofa without moving, so while the TV was playing she did stretches. She leaned over backwards and lowered her hands to the floor. It was weird doing this on carpet – it hurt her hands a bit – but it made her muscles feel good. She held the pose and counted to fifty in her head. Then she stood up, pulling herself upright with her stomach muscles, which made her realize that she hadn't done anything much with those muscles apart from eating for a long time. She sat on the floor and stretched her legs out, then put her head down on her knees. She held that, listening to the man on the television saying, 'But of course before we can do that we'll need to make fire.'

Arty knew how to make fire. She sat up again to see how he was going to do it. The stupid phone still hadn't rung.

Her grandfather came in. Arty wasn't sure what to say to him.

'Hello,' she said.

'Your grandmother says would you like a cup of tea?' he said, making a funny face. 'And have you seen the phone? Oh, yes. What's it doing there?'

He didn't seem to want an answer, so Arty didn't give him one. 'No thanks. I don't want a cup of tea, thank you.'

'Fine. Look, if you don't mind I'll need the television at five for the cricket.'

'Cricket?'

'It's a game. Don't worry about it.'

'I know it's a game! I *love* cricket!'

Arty sat up and edged on to the sofa. Grandad came and sat next to her.

'Do you? Real cricket? Not just messing around with a ball?'

'There's a place in Mumbai. Called the Oval Maidan. I watched it there. With wickets and runs and a wicket keeper and a fast bowler and . . .' Arty tried to remember all the words Joe had taught her. 'There was a man trying to do a doosra. It means *the other one* in Hindi. It was real cricket. It was men playing, and they wore matching clothes.'

'Ahh,' he said, and there was a spark of interest. 'The Oval? I suppose that would have been named for the London Oval. India is a good place for cricket, I'll grant it that.'

His pink shirt was bulging over his waistband.

'Who are the teams?' Arty said. 'Playing at five, I mean.'

'England and India, as it happens.' He looked at her face. 'And I for one shall be supporting England.' His voice was firm but there was a tiny sparkle of enjoyment in his eyes.

It wasn't five for ages. Arty watched to the end of the forest programme, even though it made her homesick. Then it was the news, which was horrible, and then Grandad came back in, holding a bottle of beer.

'Is that Kingfisher?' Arty said.

He barked a little laugh. 'Not in this house. It's Old Speckled Hen. Proper beer.'

He sounded amused and annoyed and Arty didn't know why. Still, he had happy eyes, probably because the cricket was about to start.

'Would . . . would you like one?' He changed his mind at once. 'No,' he said. 'No, of course you're too young.'

'I hate beer,' Arty said. 'So, no thank you.'

'Good,' he said. 'All the more for me.'

'I like wine, though,' she said, and he laughed again.

'Don't tell that to your grandmother.'

Arty watched him changing slightly before her eyes. They watched the cricket, and Arty was grateful to Joe, for this if nothing else. She thought she would write him an email and say so, but then she thought she wouldn't. She remembered him putting his hand on hers in that taxi. He was the first person she properly met, in the outside world.

Now, thanks to his meticulous explanations, she won her grandfather's approval. When she tentatively said, 'Right in the corridor!' he nodded and, although he didn't really look at her, she could tell he was pleased.

Mostly, though, she didn't say anything. She just switched her brain off and enjoyed looking at people playing cricket, because it took her back to India, to her home. They watched it until Grandma came in and told them it was dinner time. Then they watched it some more until Grandma sent Arty to bed at half past ten.

'You two,' Grandma said, and she looked pleased.

JUNE

I was lying on my back and there was a mask on my face. Whatever was coming through the mask was the thing I had to breathe, and I was trying to claw it off because I didn't want to breathe what someone else put there for me.

They held my arms down so I couldn't get it off. I had no choice, and the air that was coming through the mask didn't smell of smoke, and it did make me feel better, so I supposed that it was good. I didn't like it, though. I didn't like not being able to choose what I was breathing.

Someone was stroking my hair. 'It's OK,' she was saying. I tried to look at the person who was speaking. 'Just breathe it. Breathe. It's going to make you feel much better.' This person sounded kind.

'Can I go?' I said, but the mask was over all my face so she couldn't hear me.

Then we began moving. A siren started and I realized I was in an ambulance.

I hoped we were going to hospital, but I didn't know. We could have been going anywhere.

I was crying. Everything hurt. Even the nice air going down my throat hurt. I cried because I had been locked in the basement for four weeks. I cried because I knew why she had done it. I cried for everything. I cried because it was over.

'Where's my bear?' I said, but she didn't hear me. She took hold of my left hand, the one that didn't hurt.

'Hey,' she said. 'It's OK. It's OK. You're safe. You're alive. You're going to be all right.'

19

In the morning Arty put on the warmest of all the clothes, forcing her legs into jeans, which she was getting used to wearing. She tiptoed downstairs, anxious not to wake anyone. She made a cup of tea and went to the tree. It was the very early part of the day, the bit she liked the best. She put the tea on top of the back wall and looked up.

She touched the tree's trunk. She closed her eyes and felt the energy of the other hands that had touched this tree. This tree was the closest place to the clearing that she would find in this world.

She could see the way up to the top, and she climbed quickly, judging where to put each hand and each foot, pleased that she could still do this, even here. She stopped just before the branches got too thin and sat in a place where the trunk forked, and drew in a deep breath.

She thought of the two children who had been right here all those years ago.

She could see the sea from here, like they had.

Everything was better.

Arty concentrated on breathing, taking it in, holding it, and letting it slowly out. She said the words in her head. *We are all gods and goddesses. What happens to one happens to all.* She let the feeling of warm honey wash through her being. She was breathing the same air her mother had breathed, with the same sun coldly on her cheek, and that filled her with light. It was not joy, but it was light.

She focused on Zeus, and sent him all her peace and love, and she knew that in some way he would feel it. She couldn't imagine his life in France, any more than she would have been able to imagine this before she got here, but she could picture his face, and remember his heartbeat, and that was all she needed right now. She knew that she wasn't the only one out in the world.

I can see the sea.

I can hear birds, and leaves whispering around me.

I can smell bark and resin and old rain.

I can feel the tree beneath me and beside me and above me.

I can taste my tea.

'Artemis!'

If Arty turned round a little then she could see Grandma standing in the doorway, looking out into the garden.

'Up here!' she called, and she waved. She watched Grandma looking around, frowning, wearing a long nightdress and a pair of fluffy slippers. She saw her eyes moving up and up. Then she saw Arty and put her hand to her chest.

'Artemis!' she said. 'Artemis Jones, get down from there at once! At once! Oh gosh, you're going to fall. Don't fall, don't fall, don't fall.' She ran and stood under the tree, putting her arms out as if she might catch Arty, rather than Arty smashing her to the ground and breaking all her bones, were she to fall on top of her.

'What were you *thinking*?' she said when Arty was down. 'Up there like a monkey.'

'I was *thinking*,' she said, 'about how my mum and Matthew used to sit in this tree.'

'Oh, Artemis,' said Grandma. 'Yes, you're right. They were always up a tree. It wasn't this one, though. We used to have the old oak but we had to have it cut down. It got diseased. This one's been here fifteen years or so. It's a cherry tree.'

'Oh.' Arty looked at the tree. She tried to recalibrate her thoughts. 'Is it in the same place?'

'No. Look – that's where the other one was.'

She pointed to a stump that Arty hadn't noticed a little way away. She went and sat on that instead, but it was raining now and she didn't feel any connection at all. She decided to consider the cherry tree to be the real origin tree. She liked the fact that it had the same name as her friend.

Arty waited around the kitchen for ages, but Tania Roswell still didn't call her. Later in the morning, though, the doorbell rang. Arty wanted it to be Matthew (surely, she thought, he would come as soon as he knew she was here), or even somehow Tania, but it wasn't. It was a woman with long yellow hair and a smile that was so wide that it changed the whole shape of her face.

Grandma did a grand introduction. 'Artemis Jones,' she said, 'this is Lucy Allison. Lucy is a tutor who might be able to help get you up to speed for college. Lucy, this is my granddaughter, Artemis.'

'Call me Arty,' Arty said, shaking Lucy's hand, remembering the way she had shaken Cherry's.

'I certainly will!' said Lucy. 'Great to meet you, Arty. I'm really happy your grandma got in touch with me.'

Arty liked Lucy. Lucy was full of energy, and she was young. She wondered whether Lucy could become her friend.

'Me too,' she said.

'And wow. I mean, your story is incredible. I saw you online and I was rooting for you. So, if you're OK with this, we can just see where you're at and what we can do, with the idea of getting you ready for sixth form in September, like your gran says.'

Grandma had led them into the kitchen, and she flicked the kettle on to make tea. There was as much tea here as there had been in the clearing. She motioned to them to sit at the table.

Arty smiled. 'Going to school is quite a scary thing,' she said. 'I've read stories about school and I never expected to go to one.'

'It won't be *school* school,' said Lucy. 'It's sixth form. Different. It's not Hogwarts or Malory Towers or anything. You'll have much more freedom. It'll be fine.'

'OK.'

'Your gran says you're interested in English, plus history and economics. Is that right?'

'Yes.' Arty was trying to work out how old Lucy was. Younger than Venus. Probably not much older than Arty. Still, it was worth a try. 'Are you from Clevedon?' she said.

Lucy looked surprised. 'Yes. Yes, I am. I've always lived here actually. Went to uni in Bristol. I'm not as adventurous as you. I struggle with new things. Get a bit anxious.'

'Did you ever meet my mother?'

There was a pause, and then Lucy said, 'No. I'm afraid I never did.'

'Of course she never met her.' Grandma's voice was gentle. 'No one had seen Victoria for decades, Arty. Lucy's far too young.'

'Sorry. I just . . .'

'Anyway,' said Grandma, handing each of them a cup of tea. 'I'll leave you to it. Arty – try to focus.'

'I never met your mother,' Lucy said when Grandma had gone, 'but my boyfriend's mum remembers them as a family. And her brother. Mostly everyone round here had a story about her brother.'

'Because he was a drug addict?'

'Exactly. Your poor grandparents. He put them through hell. And her too. I think it was because of him that she went off to India.'

Lucy asked Arty all kinds of questions. Arty knew a bit of history, because they had covered that quite a lot at home. Lucy thought that some of it would be the wrong sort of history, but she said that didn't really matter. Arty

294

thought she could do the English all right, at least if it just involved talking about books, which it seemed it did. She thought she was perhaps more interested in economics than she was in anything else.

'Money's a strange thing,' Arty said. 'Isn't it? It doesn't exist. It's a token rather than a thing itself. I don't think capitalism is right.'

Lucy smiled. '*Now* you sound like a sixth-former. The bit about capitalism, I mean. To be honest, this isn't really my area at all. I'm much better with the English and the history. The good thing about economics A level, though, will be that pretty much no one will have done it before so you'll be starting from the same point as everyone else. And actually looking at economic theory from the point of view of someone who never handled money until the age of sixteen. I mean, you could write a blog about that.'

'Write a . . .?'

'Like a book. Or some articles? But online.'

'Online, like in people's phones? I could write something that goes into people's phones?'

'Of course you could.'

'I hate things on people's phones.'

'Well, write something good for them to read instead then. It would be fascinating.'

'In the clearing they said that money is the root of all evil. I'd like to decide whether it is or not. I thought it was when I'd never seen it. Now I don't like it, but I don't think it's all the evil in the universe.'

'I think,' Lucy said, 'that the quote is actually *the love of* money is the root of all evil. It's from the Bible. You could make a strong case for that. But anyway we'll have a look at what's going to be on the economics syllabus. English and history, we'll really grab them with both hands. So . . . are you at all familiar with Shakespeare? I mean, I know you've read some books, but do you know what a play is? I guess you've never been to the theatre?'

Arty laughed. 'Not a real theatre. I *have* been to a film. It was called *1921* and I saw it at the Regal Cinema in Mumbai, which is one of the finest cinemas in the world. I do know what a play is. I haven't read all of Shakespeare, but I've read *Macbeth*, *Hamlet*, *Othello*, *King Lear*, *A Midsummer Night's Dream*, *Romeo and Juliet*, and some of the history plays. Also, we used to put on plays sometimes in the clearing. We did a bit of *A Midsummer Night's Dream* not so long ago. Since we were in the forest already. Also, my friend AMK is a movie actor in Bollywood. He's the greatest actor of all time and he said he wants to make a movie about me.'

'Bloody hell, Arty. OK. You're better read than me. You'll have to tell me about your Bollywood friend. Have you ever written an essay?'

Arty thought about that. 'Essay means trying, doesn't it? I've tried to write down what I think about things before. It was something we did when we had lessons. I had my own lessons. I don't really know what . . .'

'You know, Arty? I think you're going to sail through this. How about we try to work out how what you've done compares with what the others will have done at school? Why don't you have a read of these pages of *Macbeth*.' She opened a book and handed it over. 'Because lots of your peers will be doing that for GCSE this summer. Then write down an analysis of it. Anything you want. The ideas, the language – anything. Try to organize your thoughts into paragraphs, so you talk about one aspect at a time. But really just write what you feel like writing, so I can get an idea.'

Arty smiled at her. 'OK. Shall I do it sitting here?'

'If you're happy like that?'

'Could I . . .' She looked at the kitchen door. Grandma had closed it. She was probably safe. 'Would it be all right if I sat on the floor? I work better on the floor than I do at tables. We never had a table. We always sat on the ground.'

Lucy grinned. 'Course you can. Write wherever you feel comfortable. Your grandmother would do anything for you, I can see that, but she's probably quite conventional. She's been through the mill, hasn't she? Poor thing.'

Arty rolled her eyes, and had a flash of the way she used to do that to Venus. She wanted to go back and unroll them, to unsay everything cross or mean she had ever said to her, to re-inhale every huff and suck back every sigh. It froze her for a moment, the regret.

'Are you OK?' said Lucy, and Arty nodded because she couldn't really say anything.

'Yes,' she said after a while, being careful to be fair. 'Grandma has been through it. She probably just wants to be normal, but she didn't have normal children, did she?'

'No she didn't,' Lucy agreed.

'And she hasn't got a normal grandchild.' Arty forced herself to focus. 'Anyway,' she said, 'I suppose I need some paper.' She noticed that she had said that in a bright and cheerful voice, and realized she knew this voice; at home the grown-ups had spoken to each other like this sometimes. She wondered now what they had hidden from her.

Lucy handed Arty some paper and a pen and she was surprised again at how easy it was to have new things here. At home they would use every single space on a piece of paper, and use pens until they ran out, then get new ink bits for the middles of them, and use them again. They hardly threw away anything. Here she knew the bin was filled with plastic. Arty had no idea where it all went. She hoped it ended up with people who needed it.

Now she had a new pad of lined paper and a choice of black or blue pens. It was an incredible luxury.

She read the passage from the play. It was Act One Scene Three, where Macbeth and Banquo meet the witches, who tell him he is going to be king, and Arty remembered it. She wrote quickly, not bothering to organize her thoughts into paragraphs, but just writing down everything that came into her head, about the rhythms and the words and the fact that those words to Macbeth set up the whole of the rest of the story. She enjoyed thinking about something that was in a time and a place apart from Clevedon and her grandparents and the utter weirdness of this world she had walked into. It was nice to be reading something she had last read in the clearing. She could pretend to herself that she was still there.

After a while she stopped writing, and when she looked up at Lucy, who had been doing something with her phone, she nodded and put it down.

Arty was stricken by the fact that Lucy could have taken a photo of her and put it on social media without her knowing.

'What were you doing on your phone?' she said, the words coming out fast.

Lucy looked surprised. 'I was playing a move on the Scrabble game I play with my cousin. Look.'

She held it out, and Arty saw a board of squares with some words criss-crossing it.

'I know Scrabble!' she said. 'We had that at home. Can you play it in a phone?'

'It's a bit addictive, actually,' said Lucy. 'Do you have a phone yet, Arty?'

'No.'

'Well, when you get one, install this app and we can have a game.'

'Yes,' said Arty. 'OK. Sorry. I was just scared you were taking my picture and telling people about me. Joe did that. He did it all the time.'

'Oh, you poor thing,' said Lucy. 'I never trusted that joeonthego account. I promise I'd never do that. What a twat he was. Let's have a look at your essay.'

Arty handed the pages over, then felt the air around her go green and purple with embarrassment as Lucy read what she had written. She had never felt like that when Diana was reading her writing. She would never have imagined any reason to feel worried or ashamed of something she had written down at all. And now she found that she was scared.

In this world people were judged on things like this and they were given a letter that said how well or badly they had done. There was a way to do things right and a way to do them wrong. In the clearing everyone just shared their thoughts and no one judged anyone on anything.

She sat and watched the clock, still trying to puzzle out exactly how it worked. The colour drained out of the room, and the red hand smoothed its way round the face again and again and again.

'Well,' said Lucy at last, and she looked up at Arty with a grin on her face, 'I don't think you're going to have much to worry about. Your handwriting is shocking, though. Maybe you could learn to touch type?'

'Grandma told me about that! She said it was so you could do patriarchal dictation.'

'It used to be. Now you just do it so you can write your own things. Matriarchally.'

'I did some emailing on Grandma's computer, but I only wrote short ones. I'm really bad at writing on the computer. I should definitely learn to touch type.'

'I bet you can learn online. I'll have a look. But the main thing is that everything you're saying here is sharp and interesting, and way beyond the GCSE standard your peers will be at. You're lucky to miss out the GCSEs; I think you'd have struggled with the prescriptive stuff you have to do. It was bad when I took them years ago but it's much worse now.'

Arty was glad she wasn't taking GCSEs too, even though she was only vaguely aware of what Lucy was on about. Whatever they were, they sounded like a good thing to miss.

'And we can talk about organizing your writing, with a plan and a rough copy before you write it up. But basically this is great, and you're going to be fine.'

As Lucy's words sank in, the colour seeped back into the world around Arty. It was great and she was going to be fine. That was the first time anyone had said anything along those lines to her for ages. She had felt bad and wrong and clumsy and stupid, and now she had done something good. She put Lucy on her list of friends, with AMK, Zeus, Cherry and Salman.

'Thank you, Lucy. I love you,' she said.

Lucy stopped talking and laughed again. 'Well,' she said. 'Thank you. That's very kind of you.'

'No one has said anything I've done has been good. Not here in England.'

'Seriously?'

'Yes.'

'Well, OK. I think everyone realizes you're remarkable. They certainly should.' She looked like she wanted to say something else, but she stopped herself.

'Do you think,' Arty said, her words coming out fast, 'that you could help me? I need to find someone called Tania Roswell. I know Grandma doesn't want me to, but I have to. She was a friend of my parents and she used to live in the clearing. I think I met her when I was a baby.'

'How intriguing!' said Lucy.

'I called her but she hasn't phoned back. I think I need to go and find her.'

Lucy sighed. 'And you have to find her? You sound like it's urgent?'

'Yes. It was the last thing that . . .' It was hard to say this part. 'That my mum told me to do. To find Tania. I've got it written down. I told the person who answered the phone exactly who I was, but she hasn't called me.'

'OK,' said Lucy. 'Let's email. We'll find her email address. Where does she work?'

They had just found it when Grandma came back into the room. She didn't notice that they suddenly went quiet.

'And how have you two got on?' she asked in a breezy voice, but with the air around her crackling with worry.

She really, really wanted Arty to be capable of being normal, Arty realized. Of course she did.

'We've got on great actually, Mrs Jones,' said Lucy. Her voice had gone super polite. Arty wasn't sure whether she changed her own voice when she was talking to different people. 'Arty wrote me an essay about *Macbeth* and it was brilliant. She'll have no trouble starting an English course. Next time we'll look at history, and we've agreed to work on the economics together, but really it's study skills that are the thing, and I think she'll be fine with those. She's an extremely bright, well-educated girl.'

'Well done, Artemis. I'm glad to hear that. Clever girl! So, you'll continue to come over, Lucy, as we agreed?'

'I'd love to.'

As Lucy and Grandma talked about details, Arty tuned out. She tried to imagine herself at school. In the book Grandma had shown her they weren't wearing uniform, but she still wondered if they might. She had seen children dressed in school uniforms in Mumbai. It was an exotic thing.

'Why don't you see Lucy out?' Grandma said.

Arty worked out that this meant walking to the door with her, but when she got there she decided she wanted to go out too.

'Can I walk with you a bit?' she said. 'I don't like being inside for too long.'

'Oh,' said Lucy. 'Yes. Sure. I was going to the shops actually. Do you want to walk to Hill Road with me? Maybe check with your grandmother first.'

Grandma said, 'Oh, go on then, but don't be long,' and Arty pulled on her new shoes, lacing them up carefully (it was still a strange new thing to be doing), and set off down the road with Lucy. The sun was shining in a very pale and weak way, and she longed for proper burning heat, for dust, to feel it on her skin. She loved being out of doors, but she longed for India with all her being.

'I've got that email address,' Lucy said as soon as the door had closed behind them. 'Why don't you dictate what you'd like to say into my phone, and I'll type it up and send it for you with an explanation?'

'Thank you! Thank you, thank you, Lucy.'

They sat on a wall and did it. Lucy promised she would send it right away, and Arty believed her.

JUNE

I was out. They made me lie on a bed in hospital and breathe lots of oxygen. They bandaged a couple of burns, but mainly they said I was very lucky.

The bear was next to me. The nurses sometimes smiled at it and asked who had given it to me.

'My mum,' I told them, and they said it was lovely.

The bear and I only spoke in the night, but during the day it stood there like a sentry and a protector. It felt like my only friend in all the world.

20

Dear Zeus,

I can't wait to talk to you this week. Here are some
photos of where I live now. These people are my
grandparents, Venus's mum and dad.

Florence, est-ce que tu peux m'envoyer des photos de
chez vous, s'il te plaît?

Arty xxxxxxxxxx

_____

Dear AMK,

Thank you for your messages. Thank you EVEN MORE
for the flowers that arrived the other day!!!! Even my
grandparents now think you are the greatest movie star
who ever lived, and they'd hardly even heard of
Bollywood. The house smells beautiful and the flowers

are so bright and perfect. They made me very happy.
Thank you, thank you.

I'm glad you went out and said hello to the people
outside your house!!!! I can only imagine how brilliant
that was for them. I wish you'd done that when I was
there. I gave all your photos to people I met on the way
here, apart from one that I have kept for myself. I have
it on my bedroom wall here now. Everyone was super
excited to get them.

You asked about life here in Britain. Well, first of all
it is COLD. It's cold and it's strange. I sleep in my
mother's old bedroom, which makes me sad. I miss
her every day, and it's like I'm living her life twenty
years after she left.

I'm having lessons with my friend Lucy, who is a tutor,
so I can go to school in September. Grandma wants me
to stay here forever, I think, but I can't. I just can't.

Remember I told you that I needed to find my uncle
Matthew and my parents' friend Persephone? Well,
Matthew is in Uganda, but he might come back in a few
weeks so I just have to wait for him. I've called Tania/
Persephone lots of times but she never calls back.
We've emailed her but she doesn't answer. I don't
know what to do. She's called Tania Roswell and she
works at a law company called Prince's. Maybe your

people in London know her? Please help me work out what to do.

Love from your friend,
Arty xxxx

———————

Dear Cherry,

I'm a bit better at typing now but it still takes me ages. I'm in Clevedon, which is a place by the sea, and you can see Wales from the end of the road. I'm still getting used to it.

I'm sorry that I pretended to be you to stay in the hotel. I know they found you to tell you that. I loved your messages from the train and I'd like to know what happened next.

So you said you've got lots to say to me. Go on then.

Love from your friend,
Arty xxxxx

———————

Dear Vikram and Gita,

I'm so sorry I ran away from your house. i really liked it there and you were so nice to me. I should have talked to you about it, but I knew no one would let me go and I just couldn't bear it when they took Zeus away.

I'm living in Great Britain now with my grandparents. We're in a town called Clevedon, which is beside the sea, and it's really cold but not snowing. I miss India. I miss the sun. I'm going to be studying in September, and one of the subjects I'm doing is economics. Do you remember you explained to me about how money works? I found that so interesting that I want to know lots more about it.

Also, I saw the Gateway of India like you said.

Thank you again for looking after me, and sorry again.

Your friend,
Arty xxx

———

~~Dear Joe,~~
~~How are you?~~
~~I kind of miss you.~~
~~I don't know.~~
~~I don't know if you're my friend. AMK says I shouldn't~~
~~trust you.~~

———

Dear Tania Roswell,
Please answer me.
Love from Arty xx

JUNE

I was lucky because the fire had hardly touched me.

I was lucky because I was out.

I was lucky because I was alive.

I listened to the machine beeping and thought about how lucky I was.

'You're not that lucky,' said the bear, 'but you're luckier than anyone else around you, aren't you?'

Yes.

21

'You are not going to London,' said Grandma. 'We've just got you here. I am not going to let you go.'

'But I need to find Tania,' said Arty. She wanted to say that she had a little note for her from Venus, but she stopped herself, as she always did, because she knew that Grandma would want to see it. She'd want to see something written by her dead daughter. Arty thought Grandma would be sad that Venus had written down Tania and Matthew's names and not Grandma's.

'You don't know who she is,' said Grandma. 'I mean, Tania Roswell? You have no idea if that's even the person you want. It's just someone you found on the blasted internet. If you find a friend of Victoria's, then by all means invite her down to Clevedon.'

'But I need to find her in real life,' said Arty. 'In London. I called and emailed her and she didn't reply. So I need to go to find her.'

'You do not,' said Grandma.

Grandad put his hand on Arty's shoulder. He was

wearing a pale-green shirt with short sleeves and Arty thought he looked like pistachio ice cream.

'One day you can go to London,' he said. 'Maybe when Matthew turns up, he'll take you. We wouldn't be able to go with you because we don't do London, do we?'

'Lucy doesn't either,' said Grandma. 'She says she hates it.'

'And you can't go alone, Artemis,' Grandad said. 'You must see that.'

She did not see it. She had been alone in Mumbai and there were a lot more people there than there were in London. Still, she understood that there was no point having the argument. She thought that Grandma wanted to keep her here with them forever, whatever it would take.

She wouldn't run away from them because it would be mean. And anyway she couldn't flee in the night because she had no idea where she'd go. She couldn't just buy a ticket and jump on a train because she didn't have the right sort of money, though she still had a lot of rupees (the wrong kind of money): it turned out that you couldn't change rupees into pounds anywhere in Clevedon as you weren't meant to take them out of India. Also, there wasn't a train station in Clevedon. She would need to get a bus somewhere to find a train.

So, for the moment, she stayed.

Every morning she had a shower and washed her hair. She studied. She practised typing. She sat in the tree, which she liked even though it was the wrong one, and stretched her legs out and did her best to vanish into a book if it wasn't raining. If it was raining, she sat in the tree wearing Victoria's old raincoat, and read her book under an umbrella that she propped up. She went out. She did all the things that she thought made her normal, and waited to feel all right.

At night, though, it exploded in her brain. She tried not to sleep because she knew that, when she did, her head would fill with those last few days in the clearing and she would wake up screaming. At night her whole being was ripped into pieces and she felt she had nothing, she was worthless, she had let everyone down, and she saw her mother, her sister, her friends, her family, and she watched them all die again and again and again.

She would grab her duvet and go out into the garden to feel the ground beneath her feet, the cold air on her skin. She would sit down on the earth wrapped in her duvet, and if it was clear she would stare up at the stars and remember and cry. She would often sit there until it started to get light, and then she found she could put it all away and get through the day.

When she did sleep she dreamed about the basement. Venus's words – *Don't go into the basement* – echoed through her sleeping mind, and dream-Arty opened that door to find unspeakable horror over and over and over again. Sometimes she would find it filled with writhing snakes, with mosquitoes, with Australian spiders that sank their venomous fangs into her skin. Other times her dream self would go through the door and find herself back in the middle of the worst of everything in the clearing. She found bodies down there. Men from Mumbai streets tried to grab her body. Tables were covered in goats' heads with wild cats licking up the blood underneath. Everything bad that she could possibly imagine lurked in the basement. She wished again and again and again that she had asked Venus why she shouldn't go there.

In the end she had to find out. She had asked to go down there a few times (Grandad went there often) but they always said no, so she had to take the opportunity when it arose. For a long time it didn't, and then the day came when it did. It was a Tuesday morning: Grandad was at 'the bowls', and Grandma had popped out to Tesco.

Arty had been to Tesco with her once, and it was not a thing she ever wanted to do again. It had freaked her out completely, and she understood now why everything was wrapped in plastic that had to go straight into the bin. It was because it had come from a place filled with stuff wrapped in plastic. It was so unlike real food, and there was so much of it that it scared her.

So she was there on her own, and as she walked past the locked door she thought it was time to find out what was down there, because whatever it was, it was going to be better than her dreams.

She was quite good at unlocking things now. From that starting point with the padlock at the edge of the forest, she had got used to putting keys into locks and turning them. She had opened hotel-room doors in India with a key at the Austen Hotel and with a card at the smart hotel, and now she had a set of keys to this very house, though she hardly ever used them because someone was always home.

This door, though, was a mystery. It was locked. It had a keyhole, but it didn't have a key, and so she wasn't sure what to do. She had seen Grandad going down there, but she had never seen what he did with his key afterwards. She tried all the keys that hung on the little hooks by the door, but none of them was even the right shape to go into the keyhole.

She looked in the drawers. All of them were so well organized that it made her head ache. Everything was in its own little section, and everything was labelled and sorted out. She looked through everything, and she looked further and further away from the kitchen, and then she decided to look in her grandparents' bedroom.

She had never opened the door before, let alone stepped inside, but she really wanted the key, and so she told herself they'd never told her *not* to go in there. The room had a very thick carpet that felt lovely under her feet, and there was a table on each side of the bed. One had a pink lamp with tassels, a magazine called *Good Housekeeping*, and some plastic sheets of pills. Some were called fluoxetine. Some were called diazepam. Arty didn't know what that meant, but she hoped it was all keeping Grandma well. The other side had a book called *It Doesn't Take a Hero* and a clock. It was not hard to work out who slept on which side.

She opened the drawers and had to sit down heavily on the bed.

Grandad's drawer of stuff was actually messy, and it was messy because it was filled with everything to do with Venus and Matthew. With Arty's mother and uncle. Victoria and Matthew. The twins. There were photos, in books and loose, and there were school reports and newspaper cuttings and photographs of them in school uniform, and all kinds of things.

Arty stared at it. She couldn't stop staring. She wanted to read every word of every bit of it, and she knew she would come back next time she was alone and do exactly that. For now, though, she just looked for the key.

She couldn't find it.

She touched her own neck. She had almost forgotten about them, but there were keys here. It didn't seem likely, but these were the only ones she hadn't tried. She pushed the drawer closed and tiptoed out of the room, hoping that she hadn't left footprints in the thick carpet.

One of her keys slotted straight in.

It went straight into the lock and turned easily. Inside the door there was a flight of stairs, and Arty went down feeling like Alice tumbling down the rabbit hole, not knowing what would be in here, but knowing that it would be something big. Whatever was down here, her mother had kept the key for twenty years, just in case.

At the bottom of the stairs there was another door. She knew her other key would work in that door, and it did.

It swung open.

Arty gasped and took a step forward.

And the door slammed shut behind her.

JUNE

She was at my bedside. I didn't want to look her in the face. I turned to the bear and picked it up instead.

'You need to talk to her,' it whispered to me. 'It's time. You need to say sorry.'

'I know,' I whispered.

She took my hand. I turned my head and looked at her eye, the one I had damaged. I hadn't stopped crying for days, but now I knew I had to be brave. I had to look at the thing that I had done.

But I couldn't. I wasn't strong enough. I looked away.

'Sorry,' I whispered. 'I'm so sorry.'

'You're alive,' she said. 'You're here.'

'I'm alive,' I managed to echo. 'I'm here.'

It was all crashing in on me. I knew the horror of it would stay with me forever.

'It's OK,' she said, her voice soft. 'It's OK, darling. I'm always going to be here. I did it because we love you. I was all out of ideas.'

'I want Vicky,' I whispered.

She looked away. 'I told you, Matthew,' she said. 'Vicky's gone.'

22

There was nothing in the basement at all.

'How the hell did you get in here?' said Grandad, who must have followed her down here, as he was somehow standing behind Arty, between her and the stairs.

'Venus told me not to come down here,' she said. 'When she was ill. It was one of the last things she said to me. *Don't go into the basement.* I've been so scared of it. I have nightmares about it all the time. But there's nothing.'

She looked again. The room was empty, except for a stepladder, a sheet on the floor, and a paintbrush and tray of paint. There was a radio plugged into the wall.

'Yes, but how? There's one key to each of those doors, and both of them are on my key ring at all times.'

She stepped back. This was not what she had expected, at all. It was a big room with a window high up in the wall. There was a light bulb hanging down from the ceiling, and a little room round the corner that had a shower and a loo in it.

Half the walls were black and dusty. The rest were bright white. The sheet on the floor was splattered with spots of white paint. Someone – Grandad – was painting the black away.

Arty held out her own keys, still on their chain. 'Venus gave me these,' she said. 'When she was ill. When I went to get help. She didn't say what they were for. The other one is for the gate out of the forest. I tried them, and they worked.'

'Good God.' He went and sat down on a step of the ladder. Arty sat on the floor and crossed her legs. It took Grandad a long time to start talking, but then he said more than Arty had ever heard him say before.

'Your mother and I used to use this basement,' he said. 'It was our project. It used to be a survival place. Vicky and I equipped it together. We were doing it just in case. In case there was a nuclear war – it sounds insane, doesn't it? But there was a very real possibility of it back in the nineteen eighties. Vicky used to say we would hide here from the zombies. She liked the idea of a sanctuary. I suppose that's what she was doing in India in a way. Making a different hideout.'

'Yes,' Arty said, 'I suppose it was. What happened?'

'And then. Well. You know about Matthew, don't you? You know about the drugs?' Arty nodded. 'But I don't think anyone who hasn't lived through it with someone close can understand it. He was obsessed. He was a monster. A real monster. Our perfect little boy tried some heroin and that was it. He would steal from us all the time as a matter of routine – anything that he thought might bring him a few pounds, as well as money. He stole your

318

grandmother's wedding ring when she'd taken it off to do the dishes. He sold the neighbour's cat. We had the police at the door an uncountable number of times. All he cared about was the next hit. It's horrible to relive it; I'd not wish it on my worst enemy. We'd send him to rehab and he'd come out and go straight to a dealer. We thought we'd lost him. Vicky thought she'd lost him too.'

Arty nodded. Her heart was beating very fast. This was the true Matthew story. She knew it.

'And this place,' he said, 'well, this was your grandmother's doing because I didn't have the strength for it, but she did. When I was ready to wash my hands of him for good, to kick him out on the street and disown him – basically to let him die – Jane said no. She said we had a secure room in the house. She said we should lock him up in it until he was clean because we and he had nothing more to lose. Just nothing. We were running on empty, all of us.' He sighed and looked at the ceiling.

'And she did it,' he said. 'I helped her take out all the tinned food and the gas canisters and all the bits and pieces your mother and I had assembled in here, and then she told him she'd left her purse down here and asked him to go and fetch it for her.

'That got him down the stairs. She locked both doors and that was it. She did it all herself. Went in twice a day with food. And some drugs. She had to get them illegally, but she did it. Methadone. He attacked her with something sharp he'd managed to make out of something. Pushed it in her eye. She nearly lost it – there's still a scar there if you look. She's an amazing woman, you know, Arty. Her strength was in your mother and it's in you too. You talk about matriarchs. Well, she's one. She kept him locked up, and it was meant to last until he had every bad thing out of his system, but it didn't. He managed to set the place on fire and get himself rescued.'

Arty heard herself gasp. 'He set the place on fire? He did this?'

'He did. Addicts are resourceful when they need to be. But before he did that Vicky had found it so distressing that she'd left. There was something he'd done to her that particularly upset her, though she never told me what it was. Oh God, we missed her. She and I used to sit upstairs hanging on to each other while Jane went down with his food. Jane was the only one who could do it. I couldn't bear to see him like that, and Vicky said that she couldn't go near him because she knew that she'd let him out the moment he asked, in spite of everything. And she couldn't handle it, and took off for India. I almost went with her.'

'Did you?'

'Not really. I couldn't have left your grandmother. And Vicky was very confused. She was hostile to us for doing something so cruel, but she knew why we had to.'

'Oh my God,' Arty said. She tried to think about it but she couldn't make it make sense. 'So what about the fire?'

Grandad shrugged. 'He did it. He did it well. He prepared for a while and stole one of those oven-lighting things that your grandmother uses out of her apron pocket. God knows how he even started a fire with it, but he did. By the time we realized, it was almost too late. Fire engines screeched up at the door, and they dashed down and pulled him out.'

Arty could hardly breathe. 'And then?'

All the tension seemed to go out of Grandad. 'That did it, it turned out. He was all right. The fire was his turning point. He did it. He stayed clean. He's been doing good works ever since to make some kind of amends for it all, but he's never come near us, really. I don't know if he doesn't trust us, or doesn't trust himself, but he comes to see us from time to time and then hurries away as soon as he can. He's a complicated man, your uncle.'

'And he never saw my mum again.'

'He went to India,' said Grandad. 'Years later. He said it was for work but we thought it was to look for her. But he never found her. We desperately hoped he would.'

Arty looked up at the blackened walls.

He saw her looking. 'It's been empty for a long time, Artemis,' he said, and he put his head in his hands. 'But now you're here,' he said to his knees. 'You're a breath of fresh air. I know I don't show it very well, but you've transformed my life. And Jane's. I couldn't bear to come down these stairs before. But now I can. I want to make this into a room for you, and for your friends when you start college. A happy place. Your uncle, I'm sure, will never set foot in here again, but you can. Your generation can do it all better.'

He blinked. He sniffed. Arty stood up and went over to him. She pulled him into a tight hug, whether he wanted one or not, and he sobbed into her shoulder.

JUNE

I stood in the hospital car park and looked around. My legs trembled so hard that I sat down quickly on the tarmac. Everything about being here felt miraculous. The sky was heavy with clouds. I was not used to the air, but I pulled it into my lungs and pushed it out. My body could do that. My heart could push my blood around my body. Physically I was intact.

I knew exactly where to go for the thing I was still craving, even after four weeks of hell. I could imagine the way it would feel, the relief of it. It called to me, the momentary salvation.

But then I would die. I knew I would. If I went back to it after everything my mother had done to keep me away from it, then it would kill me. I felt the first drops of rain falling on my face.

And I remembered the thing I had tried to do to Vicky, and I knew she had gone away to India, and I thought that the only chance I had of ever seeing my twin again was if I proved to her that I could be different.

I held on to the cuddly bear. In the light of day it couldn't walk or talk or fly. It was just a toy. Somehow, though, it meant the world to me.

There was no heroin in my system. There hadn't been for a long time. I could go to rehab and capitalize on this. I was nineteen years old and I could have a future. I took a deep breath, pushed every demon in the world aside, and chose life.

23

My dear Arty,

Well, that will teach me to be smug about giving up social media. You terrible girl! Oh, you poor thing. My heart broke for you. I cannot tell you. It's difficult to compose myself enough to write this, but here is what happened to me, and how it all became clear.

I set off on the train (blissfully unaware, might I add, of the fact that a certain young lady had never had any intention of going to ask the police for help, and was planning to check into hotels as Margaret Armitage – you are most welcome, by the way). But the strangest thing happened. I didn't want to go to Dharamsala. I was too besotted with everything you had said about your clearing, and it pulled me so strongly that when I was meant to change trains at Borivali I just got the next train back in the direction I'd come from and headed to Lonavala instead. I wanted to find your mother, and the rest of your people, and ask if I could hang out with them for a bit.

I got there easily enough. I spoke to a few people who talked about a plague that had been there, an Ebola-type of virus that had been contained before an outbreak really happened, but I didn't connect it to you. I got a rickshaw to take me to the radiation sign, which he didn't seem to think was that odd (and that should have been a clue). Then he asked if I wanted to go to the gate in the fence. I said that I did. I wasn't the only one.

I talked to people and started to piece it together. There was no chance of getting through that gate, but I still didn't quite get what had happened, so I walked around for a long time, and found a spot about two miles up the road where I could squeeze under the fence, so I did.

Can you even picture me lost in the forest? I could have done with your skills there, darling, I can tell you. Long story short – I ended up stumbling into your clearing a day and a night later, hungry and thirsty and so tired I thought I was hallucinating.

I'm so sorry, darling. I found it. I saw what had happened because of the tape round it and the things that were left and the silence.

It is a beautiful place you came from. I saw the pit, the treehouses, the shack – everything exactly as you had described it. The police were still around, and when they found me I was in Serious Trouble, but I followed your lead on that and just went with it until they let me go.

I wish you'd told me, darling. I would never have left you alone in Mumbai. I would have taken care of you so much more than I did. Tell me that you're safe. Tell me that you're happy.

Your friend,
Cherry xxx

––––––––––

Artemis Jones!

Tania Roswell of Prince's in London? Leave it with me.

Your devoted AMK

––––––––––

Dear Artemis,

Thank you for contacting us. We were very pleased to hear from you.

We were heartbroken when you left but don't worry. We have been foster parents for many years, and we have had far, far worse happen to us than Artemis Jones

coming and leaving. Both Gita and I are delighted
to know that you are safe and living with your
family.

We were, of course, terrified by your flight, but we are
now impressed with your resourcefulness. And you are
studying economics! How about that?

We very much enjoyed your brief stay with us. You and
Zeus will always be with us. Please, if you come back to
the area, come to say hello.

With our warmest wishes,
Vikram and Gita

———————

Dear Cherry,

Thank you for writing to me! I'm sorry about everything.
But I'm glad that you were the woman who got to the
clearing. I knew someone had and the fact that it was you
makes everything better. I'm glad you've seen where I
came from. That means a lot to me.

What are you going to do now? How is Barney? Come to
England to visit me!!!

It's a bit boring here. I miss India and I miss you.

I wish you could have met Venus. She would have loved you. I want you to be a matriarch somewhere. I want you to rule the world actually.

Love from Arty xxx

AUGUST

I lived, in some ways, the most straightforward of lives. I slept on a firm mattress on a single bed, sharing a room with Phil, who was much older than me and who had, most bizarrely, once been Mr Donnelly, my woodwork teacher. I remembered him leaving, but none of us had ever known why. He had only taught me for half a term six years ago, but I remembered him.

Now he had a hollowed-out face and the same desperation in his eyes that I knew he saw in mine. He wanted it to work as much as I did. We kept our room tidy. We went to meetings. We did housework together. We did not break the rules. I felt safe. With each day that passed, though, I struggled more and more with the remorse.

I went to meetings several times a day. It had taken me eleven days of this before I first told my story. Now I said it often, making sense of it as I went.

'My dad had a basement that he kept ready for a nuclear attack, or similar,' I said. 'It started as a joke but he actually meant it. He thinks there's going to be an apocalypse when the millennium changes.'

'Oh, the Y2K bug,' said someone, and there was a bit of a murmur around the room, which mainly seemed to be people either saying that they had, or that they hadn't, heard of that.

'So I made their lives hell. I can't even say the things I did now. The worst was a thing I did to my sister. I can't say it now. But I can say this: my mum saved my life. My sister wasn't talking to me, my dad had nothing left to give, and my mum locked me in the basement. She brought me food, and told me she loved me. She kept me there for weeks, and I don't blame her.'

There was a gasp around the room.

'Did she know how dangerous that was?'

'She didn't have any other options. Yes, I could have died, but, no, I didn't. And it worked. It kind of worked. I mean, I think I'd still be in there now if I hadn't set fire to the place.'

I looked around. No one was shocked by that last part.

I was doing all right so far. I had been clean and sober for fifty-two days, but more than half of them had been in the basement. I wanted to have more time outside than inside, and then I thought I would begin to believe that I could do it.

24

Arty was trying to work. She was sitting at her desk in the basement studying Marxist economic theory, but actually it was taking all her energy not to cry. She knew she had to do this: she had to do the work so she could go to school in September and meet people of her own age. She wanted to do the work, and she tentatively wanted to go to school too, although the idea of going into yet another new world of which she knew nothing, and somehow finding her way, was daunting.

And Grandad had been so pleased to give her the basement as a work room. He had finished the painting, and had put a desk and chair in there for her. There was a rug on the floor, and a little bookshelf. Her library bear was down here with her, but she kept it hidden when Grandma came in, as for some reason Grandma really, really hated it. She kept looking as if she wanted to say something when she saw it, but then she never quite did.

However, Arty could not work in this room in the way they wanted her to. She sat back in her chair and looked around. The walls were bright white and the room still had that paint smell that made her head hurt, but she knew too much about what had happened here. She didn't know any details about any of it but the bare facts were too much for her.

Matthew had been addicted to heroin.

He had done something so bad that his twin sister had gone away to India and never come back.

His mother had been in such despair that she had locked him down here until the drugs were out of his system.

He had been so desperate to get out that he had stabbed his mother in the eye and set fire to the house.

It was the place that had fractured lives and sent people spinning away from each other. The basement haunted her nightmares as it had before, but with different details.

I can't stay here, she whispered. *I can't do it*. She looked at the window high in the wall, and knew that the rectangle of grey sky had once been Matthew's view too. She sipped her black tea and told herself to be strong. Her grandparents had been through hell with both of their children, and they needed Arty. She was their redemption. They both said it to her in their different ways all the time.

But her grandmother had locked a human being into a basement and kept him prisoner until he had set fire to the place. She had a core of steel. Arty knew she had done it because she had to, but it scared her.

'What did we do,' Grandma had mused that morning, 'before we had you, Artemis? You've given us something to live for. We were just waiting to die now that I look back on it.' And Arty had smiled and tried to say the right things, but she felt differently now. She respected her because she had done an amazing thing, but she was worried too. She didn't want to be locked in the basement.

Grandad was more low-key but just as heartfelt. 'Good to have you brightening the place up,' he would mutter, and she knew exactly what he meant.

She pushed the economics notes aside and logged into her emails.

Then she jumped up and gasped. She sat down, and stood up again. She did some deep breathing, then sat down and read the message properly.

Dear Arty,

OK. You beat me.

A delegation of Bollywood dancers doing a flash mob in my office. A huge delivery of flowers, every hour for the whole day. A barrage of phone calls from a superstar in Mumbai. Every one of them with the message 'Speak to Arty Jones'? Yes, you win. Here I am. Please call it all off. I give in.

And, before I say anything else, I am so sorry and horrified about everything that's happened to you. It's unforgivable of me, I know, to have ignored you. I can't believe what happened out there.

The truth is I was very nervous for all kinds of reasons that I'd rather tell you in person than commit to paper. Please don't put any of this on social media, but, yes, I have a gap in my CV (I could explain what I mean by that when we meet, perhaps) where I say I was working as a nanny, but the only child I looked after was you. Yes, I did know you when you were a baby. In fact, I helped deliver you. (Kali did the professional part of that, as you can imagine.)

I'm sorry to have ignored your overtures. Yes, I'll see you, but please, please, please let's keep it quiet. And let's do it face to face. Can you come to London? And could you tell the persuasive Mr AMK that I've got in touch?

My mobile number is below. Call me on this, rather than at the office.

I am laughing at your persistence (not as much as my colleagues are), but also very nervous. Please can you make him stop?!

We are all gods and goddesses.

Tania xxx

Arty smiled, and then laughed. She laughed for a long time.

Dear AMK,

You are the best!! Thank you, thank you. Tania has
messaged me at last. I'm going to call her now. So you
can stop. Job done!

Arty xxxxxx

She called Tania's mobile number and it went straight to
voicemail, so she left a message. Then she called again,
and when she had called eleven times she decided to go out
for a walk.

She stood up. It was important to her to get out before
Grandma heard her because, in spite of everything she
knew, she was a bit scared of Grandma now.

There were footsteps on the stairs.

Arty shivered.

'There you are!' said Grandma.

Arty forced a smile. 'Here I am.'

'I never thought I'd come down here again.' Grandma
stood in the doorway, not quite coming into the room, and
Arty thought she looked much older today. 'Arty – could
you pop upstairs if you're not too busy with your studies?
We need to talk about a couple of things.'

Her manner was different. It was almost formal, and
that meant she was nervous.

'Of course,' said Arty, and she had taken a couple of
steps towards the door when Grandma said, 'Could you
bring that bear up with you?'

In the kitchen Grandma opened a packet of biscuits, the sort that were two chocolate ones stuck together with a creamy layer. Arty loved those. She took one and ate it slowly, performing how lovely it was to make Grandma smile, which worked a little bit.

'Two things,' Grandma said, taking a biscuit herself, which she never did. 'First of all – this isn't easy – I've had a call from the authorities with news from your old home. Well, not so much your home, but, well, the illness that so affected everything, that – that killed Victoria. They've established where it came from. Little Zeus told his aunt.'

'Zeus told his aunt what?'

'What happened. The two little boys, as I understand it.'

There was a long pause as Grandma tried to collect herself. Arty had no idea what was coming so she just waited.

'The two little boys,' Grandma said, 'were dressed as monkeys? Went into the trees to chase the monkeys away from your party? Well, it seems they went too close, urging each other on. They knew they were being naughty. That's why Zeus hasn't said anything before. Apparently he felt . . .' She stopped.

'He felt it was their fault?'

'His fault. He felt it was his fault. He said he and his brother were daring each other to go closer, to fight the monkeys. And one of them bit him.'

'Bit Zeus?'

'Bit Hercules. That was where it began. A monkey bite.'

*

336

Arty was back in the clearing. It was Kotta day. They had spent the entire day singing and dancing and having the last real day of their lives. It had been happy.

She remembered looking at Hercules and Zeus, little furry fake-monkeys in the moonlight. She had wanted to run over and give them both a hug. She had watched them going into the forest, daring each other to go further into the darkness, taunting the monkeys, laughing and laughing.

'A monkey bit him.' Arty said it slowly, picturing it in her head. It was probably Chandler. He was the one who went closest to the people. Hercules had taunted him, and he had attacked.

That was the missing thing. The bridge between Kotta day and everything else. The boys had been in the forest. They were messing around too much, getting too close to the monkeys, taunting them, and one had bitten Hercules. And then he got ill.

Her heart broke for Zeus all over again. All that time he had been by her side but he had never said it. He had retreated right inside himself. He had barely spoken. She revisited it all. Their walk out of the woods, and the time in hospital, and then Gita and Vikram's house. Through all that he must have been feeling the burden of his secret. She wished he had told her.

She was pleased he had told Florence. That was the surest sign she had had that he felt at home.

'Goodness knows,' said Grandma, 'how it was missed. The other little boy, I mean. The bite. Must have been quite something.'

'His dad buried him in the forest. No one saw his body. We didn't know there was a bite. Anyone who did see it died soon afterwards.'

Grandma put her hand on Arty's. 'You'll never know exactly what happened now,' she said, and Arty knew that that was true.

'What was the other thing?' she said a bit later.

'Oh,' said Grandma. 'Well. Shall we go for another walk?'

JANUARY

I sat at the counter of the shop and arranged the key rings that were in a basket, trying to tempt impulse buyers. They didn't need rearranging but it gave me something to do.

My name was Matthew Jones, the most unremarkable of names, and I had been clean for eight months and seventeen days. Today was my twentieth birthday and it was the first birthday I had ever spent without my twin sister. Vicky and I had done everything together. We had always had two cakes side by side, and blown the candles out for the camera.

I sabotaged it. I had driven her away.

Some student-type people were rifling through the clothes. I half watched them until Rhoda came and put a cup of tea in front of me.

'There you go,' she said. 'A nice cuppa.'

'Thanks, Rhoda,' I said. I hadn't told her it was my birthday because she would have done something kind and I didn't want it. I just knew she would have baked me a cake, and they would have lit candles and sung to me. The ladies here were so nice. They knew I had been 'troubled', and they were giving me a chance because they were good people. They never left me alone with the till for any amount of time at all, and I knew they were right not to. I knew I wouldn't steal from the charity shop, but they didn't.

I sipped the tea. I was a twin but the other half of me had gone.

I was in the process of learning to live without heroin, but it also meant living without my heroine (I almost smiled at the terrible pun). I took my pleasures carefully in safe places. I went to church sometimes, without believing in God but relieved to surrender myself to something bigger. Rituals, I found, were helpful. I went to meetings twice a day. They kept me sane.

I kept away from Clevedon. I couldn't go near my parents because the tide of remorse would have swept me away. I wasn't strong enough for it. I wrote them letters and sometimes I posted them but I couldn't bear to open their replies.

But my sister. My sister, the better half of me, had gone. She had always been the funny one, the clever one, the one who looked after me. She had always come first: we were always Victoria and Matthew. Vicky and Matt. No one ever said Matthew and Victoria. Vicky was better than me. She was a better person, frustrated with the world, always wanting to change it, make it better, do it differently.

And she was uncompromising. I had wronged her, and she had left. I wished her a happy birthday in my head, and hoped that she was happy wherever she was now.

Rhoda was talking to Sharon about Tony Blair. 'I like him, I must say,' she was saying. 'He seems like a nice boy.'

I tuned out. I didn't care about Tony Blair.

I forced myself to admit a few things.

I stole from Vicky over and over again.

I lied to her all the time.

I took her stuff when her back was turned and swore I hadn't. I pretended I was going to rehab so I could disappear for a while without her worrying about me. I lied about anything and everything.

But the big thing. The thing she would never forgive me for. I had actually done that to my beloved sister.

I couldn't face it.

'I think Tony Blair's good too,' I said, though I was only vaguely aware of who he was. The women turned and smiled, welcoming me to the conversation.

25

They walked down to the seafront again. Arty looked at the people they passed, knowing that she looked like everyone else except that she was half Indian. Most people were white, but not all of them, and she didn't feel she stood out particularly. She was wearing her jeans and jumper, like a normal Clevedon girl. The social media thing had stopped as far as she could see. She was unremarkable.

They passed a girl a bit younger than Arty, a tall girl with red hair. Arty glanced at her in passing and then looked again. She thought she must be imagining it. She stopped, and Grandma stopped next to her.

'What is it?' Grandma said.

'Did you see that girl's T-shirt?' said Arty. 'I might have to run after her and check.'

'What was wrong with it?'

'It said . . .' Arty could hardly believe it. She *must* have imagined it, because of Hercules. The words had hit her right in the stomach. 'I thought it said Chandler and Phoebe and Monica and Rachel and Joey and Ross. It can't have done. It can't.'

'Why ever not?' Grandma smiled. 'Lots of people like *Friends*.'

'But those aren't friends. They're enemies. How do people know about them?'

'What do you mean?'

That was how she discovered that the monkeys had been named after characters from a television programme called *Friends*. 'Your mother loved it, just before she went away,' Grandma said. Arty decided she must never watch it.

They walked on, but seeing those names, particularly Chandler's and Monica's, had made her jittery. She didn't feel quite safe. Hercules had been bitten by a monkey and that changed everything. She didn't know quite why, but it did. People had that monkey's name on T-shirts.

'Let's get an ice cream,' said Grandma, because she knew Arty would love that. There was a queue at the ice-cream shop, and Arty could see how wobbly Grandma was.

'You sit down out here,' Arty said, 'and I'll go and get them.' Grandma gave her the money and sat down in the pale sunshine at a plastic table.

Arty queued up behind a woman with three small children who Arty thought must have been her grandchildren. One of them held the woman's hand. Another jumped up and down trying to look at the ice cream in its freezer, and the third, who was very small indeed but extremely fast, kept running away. It was a child who might have been a boy or might have been a girl, and every time the grandmother turned her attention away it ran for the door. Arty noticed how difficult this was for the grown-up, and the next time the child ran, Arty went after it.

She caught up with the child on the pavement and scooped it up from behind. The child laughed, and when she (Arty thought) turned round and saw that Arty was a stranger, she laughed even more. She had straggly brown hair and a face that was full of laughter and joy.

'You are such a cheeky monster,' Arty said, and she giggled too.

She pulled the child on to her hip and took her back into the shop, passing Grandma who gave her a sad smile and said, 'Oh, Artemis.'

The other grandma put a hand to her chest and mimed being relieved. She had short grey hair, like real Grandma, and bright pink lips.

'Thank you so much, my love!' she said. 'Oh, you are a minx, Lily. Come back to Nana. What am I meant to do!' She looked at Arty. 'This little lady is more trouble than her brother and sister put together. All she wants is to run away. She doesn't know where she's going! She just wants to go, don't you, darling?'

'I know how she feels,' said Arty. 'We're two of a kind. Why don't I look after her while you buy their ice creams? I'll take her outside to wait. My grandma is out there. Then I'll get the ice creams for me and Grandma afterwards.'

'Don't be silly!' said Nana. 'What would you like, dear? Both of you. I'll gladly buy you a hundred ice creams if you'll keep this one out of mischief.' She looked at the two other children. 'Poor Nana can't keep up with Lily, can she?'

'No,' said the one who was trying to see the ice cream. 'Mummy can't either. Daddy says Lily is a little bugger.'

'Well,' said Nana, 'far be it from me to endorse that, but I see where he's coming from.' She looked at Arty. 'So, what's it to be?'

'Please could I have a strawberry ice cream?' Arty said. 'And my grandma too. Thank you very much.'

'See how polite the lady is?' she said to all the children. 'Of course you can.'

Arty went outside and sat down with Grandma, the wayward child on her lap.

'This is Lily,' she said to Grandma. 'Lily, this is my grandma.'

'Hello, Lily.' Grandma sounded sad, even though Arty knew she liked little children normally.

Lily seemed quite happy to stay still now she was with Arty. She twisted round and patted Arty on the face. Arty could smell her sweet breath, see the pen marks on her squishy hands.

'Nose,' said Lily, and she touched her own nose.

'That is your nose,' Arty said. 'And this is mine.'

'Mowf,' said Lily. She touched her own mouth, and then Arty's.

'Yes,' said Arty. 'Mouth.'

She sat outside, talking about ears and hands and teef, and looked across the road to the sea. The sun was shining and everyone but her was clearly finding it extremely warm. People looked happy. Everyone but Grandma looked happy at least.

She looked back to Lily.

'Do you like this bear?' she said, and she took the library bear out of her bag and held it out. 'Hello, Lily,' she made it say. 'I'm the library bear. I like books.'

'Not the bear,' said Grandma. Her voice was so firm that Arty handed it to her, and Lily didn't complain. Grandma held it on her lap and twisted it round and round.

Lily played with Arty's hair, twiddling a strand of it, and she put the thumb of her other hand in her mouth and leaned her head on Arty's chest. Arty held her tight, and longed for Zeus with every fibre of her being.

'Well, look at you!' Nana was there, her hands full of ice-cream cones. 'The magic touch! Oh, Jane! Hello! This is your granddaughter – of course! It all falls into place. She's a wonderful girl. Here, we got you both a strawberry ice cream. Now, the kids and I will be off. Thank you so much for running after Lily, my dear. If you ever want any babysitting work, I'm sure they'd love to have you.'

When they had gone Grandma put the bear on the table.

'Artemis,' she said. 'I need to know everything about how you came to have this bear. Did you really bring it from India with you?'

'Yes. I had it all my life. Venus gave it to me. I told you.'

'But that's not possible,' said Grandma. 'Vicky went to India without the bear. This was Matthew's bear. I got it for him when he was a baby. Just a silly thing, but he loved it. It was in the basement with him, Arty. It was the only thing he saved from the fire.'

FIVE YEARS LATER

I was clean and sober when I arrived in Mumbai, and I knew exactly where I was going to go. I'd been trying to track Vicky down for years and years, and finally I had a clue.

It was more than a clue, in fact. In no sense had I managed to find my sister. She had sent someone to find me. As ever, she was the capable one.

It had started with a phone call. An unfamiliar number on my mobile-phone screen.

'Is that . . . Matthew?'

It was a woman, one I was sure I didn't know.

'Yes.' Should I even have said that? Yes, it turned out. I should have.

'Hi. Matthew. Found you at last. I got your number from your dad, but I had to pretend to be a friend from work, even though I didn't know what work you do, because I was strictly not allowed to say who I really am.'

I felt scared at that point. 'Who are you really?'

There was a pause. 'My name's Tania Roswell,' she said. 'And I'm a friend of your sister's. Until recently I was living in her community, in India.'

It moved fast after that. I went to London to meet Tania Roswell, who was small and Irish. She had long curly hair and all the answers. For years I had agonized over what had become of Vicky every single day. And now I was with someone who had known all along.

'I met her in a backpackers' hostel,' she said. 'In Mumbai. Years ago. She took me to meet a friend of hers at a meditation retreat. They were planning to set up something new. He had the land – a huge section of forest he'd inherited. So they were going to build a new community there. It was very, very hardcore. It was going to be a matriarchy and contact with the outside world would be minimal. They'd advertised for people through the internet, which was a kind of new thing then. And they were pulling together a bunch of people.

'I decided to join. It was exciting. I had a shit home life. I'd not long come out of an abusive relationship. I was ready to cut myself off from all that. Long story short, we did it. We planned and worked it out. Vicky came up with a list of rules. We were all going to be gods and goddesses. We all took new names, god and goddess names. I decided to be Persephone, because I'd always loved the sound of that word. It all sounds so simple to say it now, but it wasn't. Still, we got there.'

She told me everything. Where the community was, how they had tried to give it a name they'd carefully chosen by committee but ended up calling it 'the clearing' instead. The way they had started living in tents and gradually built treehouses.

'So why,' I asked, sipping my mineral water, 'are you here? And why isn't Vicky?'

'I couldn't do it any more,' she said. 'It was amazing for a while. Liberating. An experiment that worked. It genuinely worked. I'm sure it will carry on working. But it wasn't for me. It was for a bit, but not for the rest of my life. And why am I here now, talking to you? Because your sister wanted me to give you this note. You are the only person I'm meant to talk to about it. They don't want to become a tourist attraction. No one knows where they are and they're very, very keen to keep it that way.'

I was walking on what seemed to be the right road out of Lonavala, but I stopped in the shade for a sip of water, and unfolded the note again.

Matthew, it said in what was unquestionably my sister's writing. *I hope you made it through. I think you did, but maybe I just want to think that. If Persephone finds you, then I just want to say that I forgive you. It hasn't been easy but I genuinely do. I live differently now. Don't try to find me. I send you blessings and love. I want nothing to do with my old life, but I need to send you forgiveness and light and hope. You can beat it, my twin. You can, and if you are holding this in your hand, you will have beaten it. Love xxx*

I pushed my hair back off my face and kept walking. I was covered in sweat and really feeling very unsuited to walking up a hill in India with only the smallest idea of where I was going. I wasn't sure this was the right road, and I hadn't been able to ask anyone because I was going to a place that nobody knew.

My legs wobbled, but I was stronger these days, and I kept going. I rarely felt a craving any more, but I monitored myself all the time. During the two days I'd spent in Mumbai, acclimatizing, I had been to three Narcotics Anonymous meetings. I had sat in a church in Bandra and found my people, and they had given me the strength.

I kept walking. The sun was strong on my head. Tania Roswell could have been hallucinating it all, but the letter from Vicky was real. I walked, believing that I was walking towards her.

The DANGER RADIATION sign was there. I felt a surge of triumph. That showed me I was on the right road. I sped up, and there was the gate in the fence, and I could reach through and open it from the other side just like Tania had said.

I opened the gate. It squeaked as I pushed it inwards. I stepped into the forest.

I followed the path straight ahead as far as I could, mainly travelling downhill. Sometimes I would have to choose a direction, and once or twice the path I took petered out and I had to go back and take the other one. I circled round and found myself back where I had started. I pulled out my sleeping bag when it got dark, and spent a night awake in the forest.

In the morning I found them.

I looked between the trees and saw it. A clearing deep in the forest, with hills on every side. There was a shack, and an area of packed-down earth, and a fire and everything that Tania had said there would be.

I stood and stared, my heart pumping fast. I was entirely uninvited. Tania had told me not to come here. Vicky had specified that I mustn't look for her. I had told my parents I was here for work and they believed me because of course they did.

I stood and watched for a while. A man and a woman were digging a hole in the ground. I remembered the people Tania had described, and decided that these people were now known as Inari and Hella. I watched for a while, and then I must have moved slightly, because Hella stood up and said, 'What was that?'

She looked right at me.

I stepped forward.

She walked towards me, looking furious.

'And who the fuck are you?' She turned and shouted to the rest of the clearing, 'Anyone know why there's a white guy standing in the trees spying on us?'

It all happened at once. They pulled me into the centre of the clearing and demanded to know what I was doing. Before I could answer, though, someone came running out from between the trees, and she was my sister.

And she was holding a baby.

26

Grandma and Arty tried to piece it together. They walked along the seafront, the wind cold in Arty's face.

'Could it be another bear the same?' Arty said. 'One that Venus got me in India or something?'

'I really doubt it.'

'Me too.'

'Matthew went to India,' said Grandma. 'He must have found your mother after all. He must have done. He never said.'

Whatever scenario they tried, they always came back to that.

There was a tree that had been blown so hard by the wind that it had grown in a wind-blasted shape. They turned up a road to walk to the town and straight away it was less windy.

'That Lily was a sweet girl,' said Grandma. 'I hadn't seen Tessa with her grandchildren before. She had her hands full! She lives just down the road. Tessa Bourne. We've known each other years.'

'She was nice.'

'She used to be hard work. She's mellowed a little.'

'She looked like a lovely grandma. Not as nice as you, though.'

'Oh, Arty.' Grandma put her hand on her shoulder and gave her a tiny hug. Arty stopped, turned round, and hugged her grandmother properly, enveloping her in her arms.

They went to the library because Grandma needed to give her books back.

'I daresay your bear will like it here,' she said with a little smile. She handed her books back (Grandma liked books about orphans with drawings of sad children on the cover) and went to choose some more of the same.

Arty loved the library. It made her think of her clearing job, when she had been the librarian, but it didn't make her sad. In the clearing the library had been her window on to everything else, and here in Clevedon it was still exactly that. You could find all the wider worlds you could imagine, and many more, inside the pages of the books here. She loved the smell of the place. She could calm herself in here. She did it now. She felt confused by the news about the bite, and the puzzle of the bear, and the email from Tania, which she hadn't told Grandma about because she thought she might get too worried that Arty would leave.

She stood in the middle of the room and took some deep breaths.

I can see shelves of books.

I can hear the librarians talking and it's a comforting sound.

I can smell books.

I can feel the warm air on my skin and the ground beneath my shoes.

I can still taste the ice cream if I think about it.

I am here.

I am in the library with Grandma nearby.

I am present.

She sat on a chair with a random book from the shelf. It was a thriller about a missing girl and a birthday party, and she turned page after page, throwing herself into the book world.

She felt that this place was a bigger version of the library she had looked after at home, and she adored that. The people in this one were kind and always said cheery hellos to her. They never looked annoyed at the sight of her.

She sat there reading, and then Grandma came and said, 'I'm off now, Artemis, but there's no need for you to come. I'll see you at home. I want to make a start on tea. Just be back by three for Lucy.'

Arty checked from her face whether she really meant that, and she did.

'I won't be long,' she said, and then she read for ages more, losing track of time altogether until the librarian came over. She was a tiny woman, and she looked as if she could have been Indian too, though Arty didn't ask.

'Excuse me,' she said. 'I'm so sorry to interrupt your reading. But we've had your grandmother on the phone,

Arty, and she sounded a bit worried about you. I said, "Don't worry, Jane. She's right here where you left her, lost in the selfsame book." But she wanted me to tell you that Lucy's waiting. If that makes sense?'

'Oh!' Arty closed the book. 'I forgot. Oh, sorry.'

'Don't be sorry to me, Arty. I'd love to see you curled up reading here all day long. But you'd better be off.'

When she got to the house Grandma was standing on the pavement waiting for her.

'Sorry, Grandma.' She had run all the way back, and it had made her feel better. She could feel her heart working, the blood in her cheeks.

'Honestly, Arty,' said Grandma, but she didn't seem cross. She was wearing a bright green jumper that Arty had said she should buy when they were shopping last week. She looked much nicer in proper colours than she had when Arty had first met her, when everything was grey.

'Is Lucy still here?'

'Well,' said Grandma, and she was excited about something, Arty could tell. 'She is. Yes. But we're going to skip today's lesson. Come on, Arty. Come in! Come on, darling. Something amazing . . . an absolutely wonderful thing has happened.'

She led Arty into the house, past the door to the basement and into the kitchen. There, sitting at the table, was Lucy, and next to Lucy was a man.

Arty had to stare at him for quite a long time before she was sure, because it was impossible. She thought that perhaps she was in the basement, hallucinating, the way Uncle Matthew had done. Perhaps she was asleep in the library, dreaming. Maybe she was dead, and now she would meet her family one by one.

His hair and his beard were shorter. He was thinner. There were bags under his eyes and he looked exhausted. But it was him. He was sitting right there at her grandparents' table with a cup of tea in his hands, and he was smiling at her with the kindest eyes in the world.

Arty put her bag down and ran as fast as she could into his arms.

'Oh, Vishnu!' she said. 'Oh, Dad. Oh, my dad.' And she cried and cried and cried.

JANUARY

Vicky saw me and she froze. I saw her pulling the baby tightly into her, resting its little face on her shoulder. She stared at me. I stared back. She had wanted me to find her, but she couldn't tell any of the rest of them that. I could read that in her face, because we were twins, because we had known each other since we were cells.

But a part of her still hated me.

'Matthew,' she said. She said it so quietly that I couldn't hear the words at all. I had to lip-read them.

'Vicky,' I whispered back. 'I'm sorry.'

Everyone, even the cross woman, Hella, was silent. They watched as Vicky walked towards me, and I stepped towards her. When we were in front of each other I reached out to touch the baby, but she took a step back.

'No,' she said.

'You had a baby?'

She smiled at that. 'Looks like it,' she said. 'And you found us. You look well.'

'I am well. Vicky, I'm so sorry. I know that counts for nothing, but I am. I'm sorry. I was a monster. I'm clean

357

now. I'm good. I'm all right. What Mum did. It worked in the end.'

'You sat in the basement and got better? I don't believe you.'

'Well, no. I set fire to the basement and then got out of there and got better.'

She nodded. 'Yes. That's more likely.'

I nodded to the baby. 'Who's this?' I asked, but again she stepped back and shielded it from me.

One of the men stepped forward. He was tall and thin and not at all pleased to see me.

'I'm Vishnu,' he said. That seemed to pull Vicky back to herself. She handed Vishnu the baby and turned round, beckoning everyone forward like a teacher.

'This is my brother, Matthew,' she said. 'I imagine his appearance has something to do with Persephone.'

'Who have you told about us?' said the man who had been digging, stepping forward. 'Persephone swore. She promised she'd tell no one. This is very bad.'

'I've told no one,' I said, and I hadn't. 'I swear. No one knows I'm here. I just said I was coming to India for work, and our parents believed me. My friends believed me. My work takes me all over the place. Vicky's been gone so long that no one even asked if I was coming to look for her. Not now.'

'But Persephone clearly told you exactly where we were,' he said.

'There's nothing we can do about that now,' said Hella, but she looked furious. 'We're never going to see her again.

But if she's going round telling everyone how to find us. Shit.'

'Sending junkies through the forest to us. Thanks a lot. Jesus fucking Christ.'

'Inari,' said Vicky, and her voice had a strange authority to it.

'Sorry to swear, but this is the fucking worst-case scenario come true. This was not meant to happen! I knew we should never have let her go.'

'Of course we had to let her go,' said Vicky. 'She's a free agent. We're not a prison. What would you do – kill her to keep her quiet?'

While they argued about it I watched my sister. Her hair was long and tied back at the nape of her neck. Her clothes were loose and faded. Her face was clear and, despite this setback, I could see that she was, above all else, happy. She lived in this weirdest of places, but she was utterly in her element. She had made something new.

And she had a baby. I tried to look at it as Vishnu cradled it in his arms, but all I could see was a shock of black hair and some pumping fists. He wouldn't let me get close either.

'I'm sorry,' I said in the end. 'Tania called me because she had a message from Vicky. I wanted to tell Vicky that I was alive. That I was well. That if she ever did come back everything would be different. I pieced together where you were from the things Tania said. She didn't tell me. In fact, she very much told me not to come here, as did Vicky.'

Hella turned to my sister. 'You sent a note out with Persephone?'

Vicky looked back at her. 'Yes I did. He's my twin and last time I saw him he was about to die. I thought I was writing a note to a ghost. I might as well have written it and burned it on the fire.'

'You bloody well should have.'

The other people were staying silent. I looked between them, matching them up with Tania's descriptions. The young white woman with tangled curls was Delphine, now known as Kali, who had been to medical school in France, then left when her boyfriend attacked her. The black man with the afro was Odin, who was from Senegal and had escaped addiction in much the same way I had. I hoped I would get to talk to him. The Indian woman was Diana, a fearsome intellect who had refused a good marriage.

'Look,' said Vicky finally. 'Forget everything else. We should be welcoming to strangers. I don't want us to be the sort of people who consider all outsiders to be intruders, and who turn them away before they've said a word. Is that us? Is that in keeping with what we do?'

Vishnu put a hand on her shoulder. 'I agree with Venus. Let's get the man a cup of tea and a bowl of rice, at least.'

'Oh yes,' said Inari. 'The white man is among us. Everyone drop everything and attend to his needs.'

Odin burst out laughing at that, and even though it was at my expense I joined in. Someone gave me a cup and I sipped the drink, which was strong minty tea and the best thing I had ever had.

I sat on the ground with them and stared at Vicky.

'Go on then,' she said. 'Tell me everything.'

They softened towards me as I slowly convinced them that I wasn't going to sell the story of 'my sister and the tribe of dropouts' to the papers in exchange for drug money. I sat by the fire and ate the rice and vegetables that Vishnu gave me, and I told them my story, right up to the moment I had walked into the clearing. I knew I wasn't allowed to meet the baby until I had in some way proved myself, so I talked and talked until I had nothing more to say.

But it turned out there was more I had to say. I finished my story in the middle of the afternoon, and everyone went off to do the things they did. There was a buzz of industry as wood was chopped, washing was taken to the stream, and people went off to where I could see cultivated land behind the clearing itself. Vishnu showed me a treehouse and told me to go up there and rest. There was a mattress on the floor with an embroidered throw over it and very little else, and as soon as I lay down I was asleep.

It was dark and Vicky was shaking my shoulder. I was confused for a second, because Vicky had woken me by shaking my shoulder countless times, for midnight feasts, or for school, or, later, when I was in a drugged or alcoholic coma and she thought I might be dead.

'Matthew,' she said. 'It's the evening. Come down. Come to the fire.'

She still hadn't mentioned the baby. It wasn't with her now. She disappeared down the tree and I stretched, pulled myself together, and went too.

'Right, everyone.' Vicky was focused. 'As you know, my brother, Matthew, is here. I thought he'd be dead, but he's not. I'm sorry I asked Persephone to find out for me, even though I never thought I would know the answer. I wanted her to know. I wanted one of us to know that fact. But he's here and I'm afraid I'm glad he is because he's my twin.'

There was a bit of muttering about it, but she shushed it quickly.

'However,' she said. 'I do have a test for him. Matthew. You've come to a place you've been specifically told not to visit. I need to know how much you've changed, because that behaviour belongs to the old Matt. I need you to own a few things.'

I realized what she was going to make me do. I swallowed hard.

'Go on,' I said.

'Please will you tell everyone the things you did that affected me directly. Everyone, bear in mind that he did just as many things that were directed at our mother, our father, our neighbours, our wider family, everyone at our school, everyone in our town, strangers on the street, and so on. Odin, you can step in any time you like because you've been there too. Everyone else, please just listen.'

I took a deep breath. This was worse than any therapy I had ever been to, because I realized I wanted to stay here, and I knew that Vicky was testing me to see whether or not I could be allowed.

'Vicky,' I said.

'Venus,' said Hella and Inari together.

'Venus,' I said. 'Sorry. Venus, I wronged you in so many ways. I started stealing from you when we were fifteen. I stole your birthday money because I'd spent mine on drugs. I stole your savings. I stole things from your room and sold them for pennies. I lied to you. I looked you in the eye and swore on both our lives that I was just popping out to the shop and that I had no intention of doing anything other than buying a can of Coke, but then I would get a gram of coke instead. I took every type of drug. I went from being your best friend and partner in everything to being your worst enemy.'

'What about the cat?'

'The cat belonged to the neighbour, Mrs Bourne, but it used to come and visit us in our tree when we were small. It was a Siamese, very beautiful and particular.'

'She was called Gizmo.'

'Yes. Gizmo. Vick– Venus, you loved Gizmo. You'd take her up into your bedroom and talk to her and cuddle her and take comfort from her. I'd hear you talking to her through the wall. I was so jealous. I hated myself, and I hated that cat.'

'Oh, man,' said Odin. 'I'm not sure I want to hear it.'

'Go on, Matt,' said Vicky.

'I overheard my mum and Mrs Bourne talking. Mum didn't even know I was in the house, but the fact was I'd crept in and was looking for her purse. They were talking about Vicky and how she was doing, and how awful it was for all of them, having to cope with me and what a nightmarish person I'd become. And Mrs Bourne said, "Vicky's welcome to look after Gizmo all she likes. She's a gorgeous cat. Worth the money!" And my mum said something like, "How much did you pay for her anyway?" and Mrs Bourne said, "Five hundred pounds, and it's the best money I've ever spent." '

'And all you heard was *five hundred pounds*, right?' said Odin.

'Yes. Next opportunity I got, I took that cat and sold her to my dealer. I told him she was worth five hundred. I bartered her for heroin. No idea what happened to her after that.'

'And was that the worst thing you did?'

This was it. I stared into the flames.

'No,' I said. 'That wasn't the worst thing I did.'

No one said anything for a long time. They were all waiting. I knew that they would sit here in silence waiting for me to speak indefinitely. Nothing else would happen until I told this part of my story.

I closed my eyes and forced the words out.

'The worst thing I did . . .' I said. I paused, opened my eyes and looked back at the fire. '. . . was when my dealer said I could have free smack for a week if I let his friend have sex with my sister.' I stopped, but no one spoke so I continued. 'I thought I could make her do it for me. But I knew she wouldn't if I just asked, so I tricked her. I made her think she was going with me to an NA meeting. Narcotics Anonymous. And the dealer and his mate met us on the corner.' I stopped again. Carried on again. 'They grabbed her. She fought them off. I didn't help. I didn't help her or them. I just stood there. She kicked them in the balls and got a passer-by to call the police. We all ran away. She didn't speak to me again until today.'

I had said it. The birds and insects, I noticed, made a huge noise, but the people said nothing. The fire crackled. Insects screamed.

'You tried to prostitute your own sister for heroin?' said Hella eventually.

'I did. Yes.'

'Hence, ladies and gentlemen, why we are here,' Vicky said. 'I told my mum. She, to give her her dues, stepped up. She said she had had enough of him and that he was never going to do that again to me or to any other human being, and that she was going to keep him in the basement until he was different. She said she wasn't going to tell our dad what Matthew had done, because it would destroy him and he was almost destroyed already. And she kept her word. She tricked Matthew into the basement by saying her purse was there, and she locked him in.

'I couldn't stay for long after that. I packed a bag and took all my savings, which was the money I'd earned from my job in the ice-cream shop, hidden away where you couldn't find it, Matt, and I told my parents I was off forever. I wanted to set up a world in which women weren't seen as property to be traded between men and used as currency. I had absolutely had it. I would have killed you if I'd stayed.

'Our parents begged me not to go. I thought you'd die in the basement, and I left. I didn't go back. Perhaps I never will. Maybe I should have stayed in touch with them, but I couldn't. I'm glad Mum did it. She's the strongest person I've ever met.'

'He needs to leave.' It was Diana, speaking quietly but with total certainty. 'I don't care if he's sorry. He needs to go. There is no place for this person in our world.'

Vishnu leaned forward and put another piece of wood on to the fire.

'What did you plan to do, coming here?' he said, sitting back and looking me in the eye.

'Nothing,' I said. 'I wanted to get here. That's all. I'm sorry, Vicky. I don't know how to live with myself really. I wanted to say sorry to Vicky.'

She shuffled over and sat down in front of me. She took my hands. I looked around, suddenly realizing that the baby wasn't there, but then saw that Kali was holding it.

'Thank you, Matthew,' she said. She breathed deeply a few times. 'I forgive you,' she said. 'I truly forgive you because you came here to make amends. I believe you are sorry. In this world we have no addiction. No crime. No violence. No war. No misogyny. We have none of that. This is our world away from all the bad things. You spurred me on to make it real. I forgive you.'

I looked into her eyes and I could see that she really did forgive me. I clung on to that. It would stay with me forever. I watched my sister turn and reach out for her baby. Kali gave it to her, then Vicky held it out to me.

'I think it's time for you to meet your niece,' she said. 'This is Artemis, but we all seem to call her Arty.'

I reached out and took the baby as gently as I could. I looked into her eyes, and she looked back at me with a gaze older than her tiny age.

'Hello, Arty,' I said.

She stared back at me, right into my soul.

27

Vishnu was alive. He had been alive all along. Of course he had, because that was how life worked. To be alive, you had to have been alive for all your life.

Arty didn't want to know exactly what had happened. Not yet. She just wanted to be as close to him as she could possibly be, and she wanted to look at him, and she wanted to grab hold of his arm and feel his warmth.

She had been an orphan and now she was not.

'Arty,' he said. 'I'm sorry. Such a shock. I should have written or something. But I just wanted to come and find you. I don't know how to do these computer things yet. They weren't around before. Not in the same way.'

She made an effort. She wiped her eyes on her sleeve. She bit her lip to stop it trembling. She focused on the here and now.

'But how?' she said.

A moment ago she hadn't wanted to know, and now she did.

'Oh, Arty.' He took a deep breath. 'You and Zeus went. I know that now. If I'd had the tiniest of ideas then. Finding you were alive, that you were on the internet as the girl who came out of the woods and that everyone knew you, was as astonishing to me as this is to you. When you left I must have been completely out of it.

'I don't know how long it was afterwards, but it can't have been that long because I didn't die of dehydration, I woke up. I realized I had been ill and now I was getting better. I was pleased for a fraction of a second but then I looked around for you and you weren't there. I looked for Venus. And she was.

'It was the worst thing. You know, Arty, I can't talk about it, but I could see that only half of us were there. You, Zeus, Odin, Diana, Hercules. You had gone. But I had a half-memory that Odin was taking the bodies to the forest and burying them, so I thought that had happened. I could see that I was the only one.'

'What did you do?'

'I waited, but no one came. I walked around and looked, but no one was there. I walked into the woods. You walked out of them, and I walked in. I wasn't thinking, darling. I don't even know what I did. I knew I had to get away from the clearing. I gathered some food and water and I set off. Away from any place where I might meet anyone. Because it was my land, you know? I don't think you ever did know that because we weren't about that kind of thing, but that forest belonged to me. I had inherited it years before. I wandered off, slept in the woods. I knew how to survive, and so I did. I lived in the forest, gradually healing – physically at least – until I was strong enough for the world. A few months, I guess. It's hard to piece it all together.

'I didn't want to see people when all the people I cared about were gone. The last thing I wanted to do was to walk to Lonavala, go to Pune, Mumbai, whatever. I lived by myself. I was mad with grief. I kept waiting to wake up, but it was real, and so my universe shrank. There was just me, getting water from a stream, eating the forest food, staying alive because I didn't even have the energy to bother to die. I got better and I got worse, and better and worse. I'd lost everything.'

They looked into each other's eyes. Arty wanted to say something but she couldn't, and so she just rubbed his arm and told him with her eyes to carry on.

'Time passed. You know. The same time was passing for you, my Arty. I didn't know where I was, but I started to work it out, to get a sense of myself in conjunction with the rest of the world. You never knew, but I have family living a couple of hills away, and once I started to think I could see another human again and that that might be a good thing I walked to their place and gave them the fright of their lives.'

'I bet you did.' Lucy was rapt. 'They thought you were dead.' Arty had forgotten Lucy was there.

'They knew I was living there all along as a hermit. They didn't know anything else about it until everything happened. So, yes, they'd very much thought I was dead. And then I got up to speed on it all, but they kept talking about a forest girl and I had no idea what they were saying until I realized – I realized that my daughter was alive. And not only was she alive, but she was also the bravest person in the world.'

Arty pulled her chair even closer to his.

He took her face in his hands and stared at her. 'And here you are,' he said. 'Living in Venus's old house. Going to the library. Studying economics. Oh my God. Just. Oh. My. God.'

'Oh my God,' she said, and she leaned into him and never, ever wanted to be anywhere else.

JANUARY

I longed to stay there. Vicky and I had imagined this world, and she had, through her formidable willpower, and spurred on by the fact that her twin went wholeheartedly to the dark side, made it happen. We used to sit in that tree and pretend we lived in a forest, in a treehouse, with monkeys. In our world the person in charge was Vicky. I always felt safer knowing that she made the rules.

Now that world was real, and not only was Vicky in charge but she had a baby, and she had a boyfriend who actually deserved her, and she had made it from nothing.

They found me a place to sleep that night, in the shack with books and games, and in the morning I cradled my niece and sat by the fire and waited for someone to ask me to leave.

The baby looked at me, and I looked at her. We just stared at each other for ages. I wanted to look after her forever, but more than that I wanted to stay away from her. I fucked up everything I did. I had destroyed my parents and my sister, and I needed to stay away.

I had my bear with me. It was a talisman that went with me everywhere. I took it out of my bag and held it out to Arty.

'This is for you,' I told her. 'It's a protective bear. It will always look after you. And I do love you loads and I always will.' She smiled at it.

No one spoke to me apart from Vishnu, who was handsome and warm. I was glad he was Vicky's boyfriend. I stared at the contours of his face, knowing that he could have been a model or something. He made me feel intensely mundane.

He called me over to him while he chopped some vegetables, and I shifted over to where he was, being careful of his daughter (I presumed) in a way I had never cared for anything before.

'Thanks for talking to Venus last night,' he said. 'I don't think she'd told anyone except me that story before. It must have taken a lot to say it. To strangers, in a strange place.'

'It did,' I said. 'But I'll never stop feeling shit. You know what, Vishnu. I don't think I can live with myself. It's a considered position. As soon as you stop, sober up and realize the horror, well, the fucking horror, it swamps you.'

He smiled. 'Your sister doesn't let us swear round here, man.'

'Sorry. Well, everything I just said apart from the swear then.'

'That's OK. Hey – you should stay here with us. Though – well, we do grow weed. It grows well. We sell it.

It's how we fund our life. So capitalism isn't so far distant after all. And, you know, drugs.'

'That's OK. I never cared for that anyway. I mean, don't worry about me running off with it or anything.'

'We don't touch it ourselves. It's strictly forbidden. It's just our currency. An economic decision. The best money we can get from a crop.'

'Do you drink?'

'Once a year we get a crate of Kingfisher and a few bars of chocolate, and we indulge ourselves. To celebrate the birthday of our community. That's it. When you take out all the extraneous stuff you find you live right here in nature. It's hard to describe the transcendence of it, but it's something we all need for our different reasons.'

'Why did Tania stop needing it?'

'Persephone? She just did. Her family was pulling her away. That's OK.' He smiled. 'Or it was, until you turned up.'

I sat in silence, rocking the baby. I didn't think I had ever held a baby before and I very much wanted to treasure her. I knew that handing her to me had been Vicky's way of letting me know I was forgiven. I had done my best to sell my sister. She would have been perfectly sensible not to trust me with her child.

I desperately wanted to stay but I knew I couldn't. I told myself that I wouldn't even if they asked me to, because I could never trust myself around the most precious people in the world: Vicky and baby Artemis. However, I hoped they would ask me. I hoped they'd persuade me.

When Arty started to fuss and root around for some milk I called for Vicky, though I remembered to call her Venus. She appeared at once, dropping down from a tree and landing lightly.

'Thanks, Matt. Hello, babykins! Hello, chikoo! Hello, my darling. Are you a thirsty girl? Are you hungry? I'd say you are.'

As she fed the baby, she said, 'You know I'd like it if you stayed. Vishnu would be fine with it too. But the rest of them wouldn't. We can hold a formal meeting and put it to a vote if you like, but we won't win. I can tell you that now. And it's not something I'd overrule them on. The balance of personalities is too important. I can't disturb it.'

I looked at my sister, the one who ruled her own world and did it properly.

'I understand,' I said. 'I would stay. I'd do anything. But I'm going to go. Thank you, Vicky. Can I tell Mum and Dad about Arty?'

I watched her thinking about it.

'No,' she said in the end. 'They'd send the police. You know they would, and it would be the end of everything. I'm sorry, but I'm not risking it. This is my life now. We might come out one day and if we do I'll go to see them, but for now – no.'

I nodded. 'I promise I'll never tell them,' I said, and I never did.

28

Much later in the evening, when they were all sitting round the table with an Indian takeaway (unprecedented in this house, as far as Arty could tell), Vishnu said, choosing his words carefully, 'Could I ask about . . . Matthew?'

'Matthew?' Grandma said. 'Did Victoria talk about him?'

'She did,' said Vishnu. 'She did, yes. She spoke about him often.' He looked as if he wanted to say something else, but he didn't.

'Well,' Grandad said, 'Matthew is Victoria's twin brother. We had a terrible time with him. I suppose none of us ever got over it. That's the evil of drugs. It breaks your heart.' Grandad had never seemed like someone who said things like this until recently.

'Yes,' said Vishnu. 'Is he . . .?'

Arty could see what he was asking. 'He's still alive and he doesn't take drugs any more,' she said. 'He's living in Uganda, working in a refugee camp. He's going to come back and visit us, but he only calls once in a blue moon.'

Vishnu smiled. 'That's good,' he said. 'That's extremely good. That he's well, I mean. Not that he doesn't call.'

'He visited you,' Grandma said. 'Didn't he?'

Vishnu nodded. 'I didn't know whether to say. He told you then?'

'No,' said Grandma. 'Artemis and I have pieced it together.'

'It was the bear,' said Arty, and she put it on the table.

'Oh, the bear!' Vishnu picked it up. 'Hello, library bear! Yes, he gave this to you, Arty. When you were a baby.'

'He gave it to me when I was a baby?'

'He did. He came to us once when you were maybe six months old. Persephone had told him where we were. Some of the community were horrified. But, yes, he just turned up. He spent a night. He was utterly besotted with his niece. He apologized to Venus very sincerely. Then he left. That was his last official visit.'

Arty was so tired. She wanted to go to bed, because she thought that tonight at last she might be able to sleep properly. Before she went, though, she had to ask her father one more question.

'Vishnu,' she said. 'Did you see her body? Did you definitely see her with your own eyes? Venus?'

He pulled her close. 'I did, my chikoo. I'm sorry. I did. I closed her eyes. I covered her over. I did see her. She was ill, and then she died.'

Arty cuddled in close to him and then she cried all the tears in the world. She cried for her mother and her brother and sister and all the rest of her family. She cried with relief because she was not alone any more. Snot ran out of her nose and on to Vishnu's clothes. Grandma put a tissue in her hand but she couldn't say thank you. Vishnu held her, and then she felt, from his breathing, that he was crying too.

Eventually there were no more tears, and Arty hiccupped and then yawned. Her face was red and swollen, and her throat hurt, but she felt, in some way, that she was healing. For the first time she believed that her mother was dead.

'Better?' said Grandma, who was blowing her own nose. Arty nodded.

She slept for longer than she had for a very long time, and when she woke up she was certain she had dreamed Vishnu's return. When she remembered it was real she tore down the stairs.

He was there. Her dad was there, in this house. He was holding a cup of coffee and talking to Grandad about cricket.

'Of course,' he was saying. 'I grew up in India! We had cricket on every street corner.'

'Are you . . .' Grandad started to say.

Arty thought Grandad wasn't quite sure how to say it and she smiled as he tried to get it right.

'Are you one hundred per cent Indian?'

'I am not,' Vishnu said. 'Indian father, international mother. I have, of course, reintroduced myself to my father's family rather dramatically, so next up is a visit to my mother's side of things. How about it, Arty? Shall we go and seek out the rest of the family?'

'Yes,' said Arty. 'I want to do everything.'

It was raining outside, but she still took Vishnu into the back garden to show him the tree.

'It's not even the right tree,' she said, pulling herself up into it, knowing that he would follow. 'The real one died. That's its stump over there. But this one has the same spirit. It's the clearing tree in its second incarnation.'

He sat there with her and they looked at each other.

'Just look at you,' he said. 'I'm sorry. I'm going to look at you forever.'

'Good,' she said. The rain was plastering her hair to her face.

'When we feel a bit more settled we need to make a plan. Your grandparents are trying not to say it at the moment, but they're terrified that I'm going to whisk you away. I can see it. They just got you, and they've spent hours telling me how you've transformed their lives, and now they think I'm going to take you back to India. What would you like to do, Arty?'

She sighed. 'Being here made me feel so bad. Like I couldn't breathe. Like I had to be everything to them all the time. And then I felt a bit better. But I do love them. I don't want to leave them because they've lost everyone.'

He squeezed her hand.

'Well,' he said. 'Maybe you could go to the college thing here? Your grandmother could not be more proud of your studying, and Lucy thinks you're amazing. Get two years of education. If you want? I'll live wherever you live. They've said that I can stay here in the house too. And after that we'll go wherever you want. And you can do whatever you want. We can travel the world. We'll find Matthew, and my family in Australia, and anyone else you fancy.'

'Zeus, Cherry and AMK,' Arty said at once.

'Cherry and AMK,' he agreed. 'Zeus – well, we need to go and see him right away. Get the three survivors together. Tell him that the monkey bite wasn't his fault. You must tell me all about Mr Bollywood. We can check in with Persephone. We can do all that, and then you should go to university wherever you like. London? Mumbai? Anything you want.'

'I'd love to see snow,' she said.

'Then we'll find you some snow.'

MATTHEW

I was twenty-four, and it was the beginning of the rest of my life. I wobbled when I got back to Mumbai. I knew it would be easy to find any drug I wanted here, because I knew how to do it. That was the way in any big city. I pictured myself living on the streets, hollow and desperate, until I died. For a few days it felt like the most appealing option I had.

Then I remembered what Vicky had said: 'We might come out one day.' The baby might come out into this world one day. Of course she would. It's one thing looking after a tiny baby away from the rest of the big bad world, but no one could grow up there. Vicky and Vishnu and Arty would appear in my life at some point, and I needed to be ready for them.

I decided to do all the good that I could. I started working with homeless people in Bristol and, sixteen years later, I was living in Uganda working with refugees from Sudan. This was my life now. I never had time or inclination to think of anything else. I worked hard, drank soft drinks when my colleagues went for a beer, and slept well because

I was exhausted. The people I saw every day had lost everything, and my shame spread to cover the fact that I had had a comfortable home, a family who loved me, and I had never been hungry, yet I had still messed it up irredeemably.

I moved from place to place. Charities make you take time out in between placements to avoid burnout, and I would go back to Europe when I had to, but I rarely went back home.

Whenever I had the chance I spent my free time in India. I flew to Mumbai and took the train to Lonavala. I walked to the radiation sign and into the forest and I walked up to the clearing.

The first time I did it, I thought I would somehow lurk in the trees and secretly glimpse my sister and my niece. Of course it didn't work like that, but, luckily for me, the person who spotted me was Vishnu. He signalled to me to wait further away, back in the forest, and twenty minutes later he and Artemis appeared.

I went back three more times, and each time I spent time with her. We talked to each other and she treated me, unquestioningly, as her friend who was only occasionally there.

As soon as I knew she was old enough to tell other people about me, Vishnu and I agreed that I should stop going. After that I would just watch from far away, on the hillside, just to check there was movement and the community was still going. It broke my heart to know that she had no memories of me at all, that we had no relationship, but I knew it was payback for what I'd done to Vicky, and I had to live with it.

Our last conversation was when she was about three. She toddled into the woods with Vishnu at a distance behind her. I jumped down from a tree and said, 'Hello!'

She pointed at me and said, 'Lorax.'

I rarely looked at the news. My colleagues were online as often as they could be, but I wasn't interested in anything beyond the world I could see around me every day.

I missed the flurry about the forest girl completely. No one mentioned her to me and, even if they had, I probably wouldn't have made the connection. Not unless I'd heard the name Arty.

I had missed calls from my parents and I intended to call them back. I didn't have voicemail because no one uses it, really.

I was busy, and talking to my parents always left me feeling bad, because I knew that to complete my atonement I needed to go back and spend some proper time with them. I had never felt quite ready for it.

Eventually, though, I did call them back. Then my world changed again.

29

Arty was sitting in the clearing. It was a different clearing, but there were trees round it, and insects shouting, and birds calling to each other and perhaps, far away, the distant sound of monkeys. The afternoon heat had faded and the shadows were long.

There was no pit here, not yet, but they were sitting on the ground cross-legged. She looked around. Everyone had come, except one, who she thought would never turn up anywhere.

She gazed at Zeus. She would never stop gazing at him. He was all right. He was with his family in France, and was settling into his new home, and he was going to be OK. He was bigger than he had been before, and he spoke French much better than any other language, but when he saw Arty he had run into her arms and for a few moments it was as if they had never been apart.

'It's not your fault,' she had said to him again and again and again.

He knew that now. She could see it in his eyes. His real self was back again, and a lot of the time he was a normal five-year-old boy.

Florence was here with him, and she was much more friendly to Arty this time. Arty thought that perhaps that first time she had been more scared and sad than mean, though Arty hadn't been able to see it.

Vishnu caught her eye across the circle and smiled. She grinned back at him. He was sitting with Persephone. She could see exactly why Persephone had been Venus's friend.

Persephone had been so scared to talk to Arty, because she had never told anyone about her time in the clearing. It was because of the herbs, it turned out. She was a lawyer, and lawyers couldn't have anything to do with drugs. She had pretended that she'd worked as a nanny for those years, and if anyone knew she had lied she thought she would lose her job.

Now, though, she was their best friend. Arty adored her, and she also loved Luke, who was sitting on Persephone's other side.

Luke was also from the clearing in a way, because Persephone had found out after she left that she was pregnant. Luke's father was Odin and that made him a clearing baby too. He was the lost clearing child.

Arty turned to the woman sitting next to her. 'You're really going to do this?' she said.

'Are you kidding me? Of course I am, sweetie. It's my dream come true. You know that. From the moment you first told me about it I wanted this. I wish – of course I wish it could have been different.'

'I know,' said Arty. 'Me too. But thank you. This is exactly what Venus would have wanted. Exactly. It's what

385

Vishnu wants, and Tania, and me and Zeus and Luke, and we are the clearing people.'

Cherry put an arm round her and hugged her. 'It's going to have to be a very different set-up. But we'll stick to her principles, I promise.'

This new clearing was in the Maharashtra hills, but it was nowhere near Lonavala. AMK had bought this piece of land, saying it was so he could make his film in peace, and had given it to Arty as a present. She had refused it as a gift and eventually he accepted a thousand of her leftover rupees and put it in both their names. Now, except when the filming was happening, Cherry was going to run it as a retreat. Anyone who needed to shelter from the outside, for any reason, could apply to stay here, and people would spend months at a time living away from the modern world. There were no phones allowed, no screens, and Cherry was to be the matriarch, just as she had always wanted.

AMK was pacing around, but now he came over to join the circle. His people had melted away somewhere, even though Arty had invited them all to stay.

'Goodness me,' he said. 'Why must we do this? Help me down, Artemis.'

She helped him to sit. He huffed and puffed and called himself too old, but when he was actually sitting cross-legged he looked considerably more comfortable than Arty had expected, and she wondered how much the huffing had been for show. AMK had presented her with a script a couple of days earlier. She hadn't read it yet.

'Tell me about it!' said Grandad from across the circle. 'Deckchairs for the old folks next time please, Artemis!'

Grandma had stayed at home. India, she said, was too much for her, and anyway she always wanted to be at home just in case Matthew came back. Arty had seen at once that no part of her was willing to be persuaded, so she had promised to look after Grandad, and set off with him and Vishnu with the primary aim of watching some cricket at the Oval Maidan before they did anything else.

Arty had watched her grandfather shedding his bluster. At first he had been shocked by Mumbai; as she watched him it seemed to Arty that the huge hot city with its car horns and extremes of everything was as far removed from his life experience as it had been from her own when she had first arrived there. As the days passed, though, he had started to acclimatize. They had sat in the shade at the Oval and watched people playing cricket. Arty had missed Joe just for a few minutes, but then she remembered all the people chasing her with their phones, and she had stopped missing him.

'There's no balance any more,' said Grandad. 'It's all about the batsman. There's no contest. Who'd be a bowler?'

'Maybe the batsmen are just getting better,' said Vishnu, who had adjusted quite a lot to the outside world now.

Arty tuned out of that. She looked round this circle. Soon, she knew, she needed to get up and talk. She would wait just a few more minutes just in case. He still might make it.

No one came through the trees. That was all right. She looked at Cherry, at AMK and Grandad, at Zeus and

Florence, Persephone and Luke, and at Vishnu, and she drew strength from all of them. She looked at the crate of beer and the box of chocolate bars that were waiting in the shade. In the end, the rest of her leftover rupees had gone on Dairy Milk.

She stood up. 'Welcome to the twenty-first Kotta day,' she said, and her voice broke with the emotion of it. 'We are here to honour the memory of everyone who lived in the clearing from the moment it was set up until the moment it ended on the twentieth Kotta.'

There was a rustling in the trees. A cracking of twigs.

If it was a monkey, Arty thought, she would want to kill it herself. If it was a monkey, it might bite them. She saw Zeus thinking the same and leaning into his aunt.

Then she saw a figure emerging from between the trees. He was wearing cotton trousers and a T-shirt and he looked like her mother, his twin sister.

Everyone turned to stare.

'Hello again, Arty,' he said. 'Sorry it's taken so long. Mum said I'd find you somewhere round here. I seem to spend my life trekking through Indian forests trying to track you down in clearings.'

She stared at him. He was a man with the same face as her mother. But he was a man. He was not her mother.

It was Uncle Matthew. And she already knew him. He was the Lorax of her dreams.

'Sorry I'm late, everyone,' he said.

EPILOGUE

This was snow.

Arty was walking down a white street, looking at the white that covered the houses, the trees, the cars and everything else. It was falling from the sky. Snow – freezing, beautiful snow – was falling all around them like feathers.

'This is the most amazing thing I've ever seen,' she said.

It was. Vishnu had asked them where in the world they would most like to go for a family holiday, and Arty had asked for snow and the Northern Lights.

'It might be mine too, actually,' said Luke.

Luke was her best friend. He was a bit more than that. He might be. They hadn't talked about it. He was younger than she was, but taller, and he was the most astonishingly handsome boy she could imagine. His skin was dark like Odin's, and he had freckles like Tania. He made her laugh. She loved to laugh with him.

They were walking behind the adults, slowing them down because they kept stopping to throw themselves into snowdrifts or to make snowballs and chuck them at each other. It was nearly dark, even though it was three in the afternoon, and there was a green tinge to the edges of the mountains on the horizon.

Tania and Vishnu were walking ahead, turning round every now and then to wait for them.

'Come on, guys!' called Tania now. 'Some of us are freezing here. There's a beer with my name on it just over there.'

Arty took a deep breath of frozen air. She was wearing the warmest clothes in the world, but she was still shivering a bit. That was all right. She quite liked it.

'We could do it here maybe,' said Luke, pointing to a pristine patch of snow under a lamp post. 'Before it's too dark.'

Arty agreed. She pulled the library bear out of her pocket. Luke pulled some snow around until he had made a throne for it to sit on, and they sat it down. Arty got out her new phone and took the bear's photo with it. They took lots until they had one in which its quizzical face looked just right.

Her fingers were freezing, turning red and trying to stop working, but she managed to write the message.

> Hello, Matthew. I am having a
> lovely if cold time in Tromsø with
> my family. We all wish you were
> here. Love you loads x from Bear

She sent it and smiled. Uncle Matthew would love that.

'Coming,' she called, and they walked fast, their arms touching through all their layers of clothing, to meet their parents in the pub. The sky above them started to dance with light.

ACKNOWLEDGEMENTS

From the moment my editor Ruth said, 'Actually can you do the one about the girl coming out of the woods?' this book has been a joy. Thank you to Ruth Knowles and Tig Wallace, whose editorial notes were incisive and inspiring at every stage; and to Wendy Shakespeare, Jennie Roman, Marcus Fletcher and Libby Volke for copy-editing, proof-reading and generally picking up mistakes.

Thank you, Emily Smyth, for designing this beautiful cover.

Huge thanks to Stephanie Thwaites at Curtis Brown for everything she's done on this book and so much more, with the help of Izzy Gahan. Thanks to Jasmine Joynson at Penguin Random House for all her help with absolutely everything.

To research the Indian section of the book, I went to Mumbai where an incredible taxi driver saved us from the fact that we went to the wrong station and got us to the right one incredibly fast, where we improbably caught the train that took us to the forest, telling us his life story all the way.

Thank you to all the staff at the Machan resort, outside Lonavala, including Deepak and David (who took us for a night-time walk through the forest where we met a very poisonous snake, to his delight). It's far more luxurious than the clearing, but the descriptions of the clearing are very much grounded in that place. And thank you to the many people in Mumbai and its environs who helped me in all kinds of ways.

Finally, Craig Green has read this at every stage, and supported me in every way while I wrote it, so I owe him everything. Thank you to the gorgeous Gabe, Seb, Charlie, Lottie and Alfie for all kinds of distractions and worries and laughter.

Also by Emily Barr:

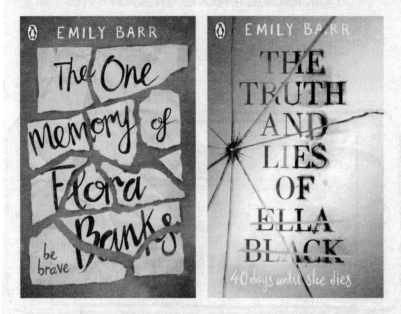

Praise for *The One Memory of Flora Banks*

'An icily atmospheric story with a captivating hook . . .
A pacy page-turner that packs a significant
emotional punch'
Guardian

'An extraordinarily moving and original novel,
a story of secrecy and lies, love and loss that manages
to be both heart-breaking and life-affirming . . .
This is Barr's first novel for teenagers and it is
as brave as Flora herself'
Daily Mail

For loads more about the things you love, make sure you follow Penguin Platform.

@penguinplatform

youtube.com/penguinplatform

@penguinplatform

tumblr. penguin-platform.tumblr.com

SHARE, CREATE, DISCOVER AND DEBATE.